# THE LONG JOURNEY HOME

---

## A PRIDE & PREJUDICE VARIATION

## J DAWN KING

Published by Quiet Mountain Press LLC

Follow J Dawn King on Twitter: @jdawnking

Like her on Facebook: www.facebook.com/JDawnKing

Or connect by email: jdawnking@gmail.com

Please join my mailing list at http://jdawnking.com for news about latest releases.

# ACKNOWLEDGMENTS

I have been dreaming of this story for the last seven years. It took a tremendous amount of research to write and a fantastic team to proofread. A great big thank you goes to Debbie Fortin, Beatrice Neary, Betty Madden, Melanie Crosgrove, and Anji Dale for picking this to pieces and helping me put it back together again.

Thank you to Jane Dixon-Smith of JD Smith Designs for the gorgeous cover.

To my mother Marie Jones, Nicole Clarkston, and Jennifer Joy, you three are brat children with massive sticks you skillfully used to prod me along.

To Jane Austen – you are a **ROCKSTAR!!!**

**WARNING:** Because the nautical terms I used are American English, I used the same throughout the book. If you are anticipating a complete novel composed entirely of Regency British, you will be disappointed.

# 1

---

Elizabeth Bennet woke to utter darkness. Her immediate surroundings dipped and rose in an irregular rhythm unlike anything she had experienced in her nearly twenty-one years. Holding her breath, she listened carefully for clues to her circumstances since her vision was completely ineffective.

Distant sounds of men yelling indistinct commands, what sounded like bed sheets flapping in a strong wind, and the creak of wood paneling being pulled taut, then let go, warred with a quiet trickle of air flowing in and out above where she lay on her side. Her mouth tasted and felt like it had been filled with threads of dusty cotton. She swallowed the nonexistent saliva at the back of her throat, desperate for a hint of moisture. Her shoulders screamed in agony. Flexing her fingers, Elizabeth attempted to move to a more comfortable position, only to discover she had been bound tightly at the wrists with her palms together, her hands behind her back. Another quick movement verified her ankles were tied as well. Her nose and chin were pressed up against a stone wall that smelled of salty air and ... sandalwood?

While those scents were inoffensive, unpleasant odors insulted her sensibilities as they wafted into her nostrils from the surface upon which she lay: that of unwashed bodies and the dampness of mildew.

*Where was she? What in the world had happened to her? Who had done this to her?* Panic at the unknown flooded her body. She quivered from head to toe.

"No! Dear God, no." Tears threatened.

Swallowing them back, she shook her head quickly to dispel the remnants of thick fog swirling in her skull. Elizabeth immediately became aware of three facts. First, she had to have been drugged. She had read enough from her father's library to understand the effects. Second, the sounds, smells, and movement indicated she was no longer in her home shire of Hertford. Where she was exactly, she could not determine. Third, after rubbing the end of her nose against the "stone wall" that felt remarkably like intricately woven fabric, Elizabeth's head cleared of most of her confusion. A man, not a wall. It was his breathing she had heard amidst the other noises.

Her inclination was to scream at the top of her lungs in hopes that someone would come to her salvation. Fear at waking the beast next to her kept her silent. Horror filled her; terror nipped at its heels.

In vain she attempted to roll away.

"Trapped," she gasped, registering a solid surface behind her and that rigid man in front.

Her pulse pounded as her breath quickened. Never had she been in such close proximity to a grown male who was not her father.

Had she been violated?

Her breath caught in her throat.

Had this man tied her up to restrain her from fighting his

forced attentions? The pressure in her skull grew until she worried her brain would explode with the intensity of her anger.

No, she was far beyond angry. The bitter brew of ire blended with unrestrained fear threatened to consume her.

Slowing her breath to better tame the pounding of her heart, Elizabeth frantically considered her options.

"Escape. I need out—now!"

Scrambling into a different position with the goal of freedom, Elizabeth pulled and contorted until she sat upright. Sweeping her eyes from side to side, she surveyed her surroundings. Nothing! Not one hint of light appeared in her line of vision. She and the unknown man pressed against her side were in a world entirely encased in black.

Pulling her knees towards her, she felt them with her chin. Lace slid over the cotton below. Relief coursed through her at the discovery of being modestly covered. The man, too. was still clothed, she realized, or it would have been his skin or the soft cloth of a nightshirt against her nose when she woke, not the silken garment she had felt.

Who was this man? He had not moved. The only evidence he lived was the slight rise and fall of his chest as he inhaled and exhaled. Whatever had been given her to render her senseless had to have been given him as well.

Powerful emotions surged through her, pounding out the necessity for a frantic bid for freedom. Ignoring the pain and the cold filtering through the thinness of her gown, she dug her heels into the lumpy mattress upon which she lay, using the slickness of the cloth under the overskirt of lace to propel herself backwards until she was practically sitting upon her fists. Thinking she could slide her form in reverse through the loop between her distended elbows, Elizabeth wiggled and squirmed until she was made to stop from the misery— clamping her lips together to keep from crying out. The strain against the muscles holding her arms in their joints forced an unnatural arch to her back. Panting, she gulped in a huge breath then expelled it from her lungs. Hunching into a tight ball while pulling her knees up to her chest, she lowered her shoulders as far as humanly possible and pushed the heels of her feet with all of her might.

The instant her posterior landed on top of her fists; Elizabeth pushed harder. Grunting from effort and agony, she gripped a handful of wisp-thin embroidered netting and the heavier printed fabric of the gown bunched beneath her. Beads of moisture dampened her temples; her stomach churned from the misery. Swallowing the bile threatening the back of her throat, Elizabeth bent to the task, pushing and sliding until the fabric ripped to shreds under her slippers. Finally, her bottom bounced down off her fists where they currently rested under her thighs. Tears streamed down her cheeks as she wiggled her tortured hands out from underneath of her.

She stretched her arms in front of her as far as the ropes at her wrist allowed. Blessed relief made her sigh when the tendons and muscles surrounding her shoulders and neck relaxed. Despite wiggling her fingers in front of her face and not seeing them, Elizabeth wanted to crow her victory. Instead, she breathed in and out until the nausea passed and the galloping of her heart calmed.

In an attitude suspiciously mirroring something her mother and two silliest sisters would have done; she mourned the ruin of her gown. It was the finest garment she had ever worn. Hours upon hours had been spent forming the Van Dyke points at the hem of her skirt, sleeves, and bodice. In an oddity of mind, Elizabeth mourned the waste of days of intense labor more than her present situation. Briefly.

Shaking off the thought, and uncaring whether her unknown companion witnessed her unladylike actions, she lifted her shredded hem until she could reach the knots binding her ankles. Her tied hands and the movement of their mode of transport increased the difficulty of the task. As she tugged and twisted the hemp rope, several factors settled in her mind. There were no bumps typical of a ride in a carriage which indicated the rocking back and forth meant they were on a boat of some sort. She had no pelisse. Cautiously touching the fine heavily woven silk of the garment worn by the man alongside her, she discovered he wore no greatcoat as well. She had on her dancing slippers not her walking boots. Her stockings were intricately woven, unlike the knitted wool she typically wore at the approach of December. The only gown she owned with an overlay was newly made and worn once, at the ball their new neighbor, Mr. Charles Bingley, had given at his estate, Netherfield Park.

*Oh, good Lord!* As the events of that night clarified, Elizabeth recalled where she had last worn that gown *and* smelled sandalwood. Mr. Darcy! She was sharing what she concluded was a ship's bunk with Mr. Fitzwilliam Darcy of Pemberley in Derbyshire. Aghast, Elizabeth intensified her efforts to free her lower limbs. A million unanswerable questions flooded her brain, all beginning with how, who, what, where, when, and why.

Her family had been at the Netherfield ball. Elizabeth and her sisters had looked forward to attending for two whole weeks since Mr. Bingley and his supercilious sisters had personally traveled the three miles between their estates to hand-deliver the invitation. New gowns had been procured, along with matching ribbons and shoe roses for all five Bennet daughters. Their mother had even convinced her spouse of the necessity of a new garment. Thus, it was a polished group who had ascended the steps under the front portico of the grand edifice on the twenty-sixth day of November in the year of our Lord, 1811—a Tuesday.

Elizabeth had arrived at Netherfield Park half excited and half in dread. Her ungainly cousin, Mr. William Collins, had earlier requested her company for the first set. She suspected his uncoordinated movements on the dance floor would mirror his uneven gait. Before the first notes of the chorus began, she was proven correct as her toes sorely testified.

Her only hope for salvaging her evening rested on the broad shoulders of Mr. George Wickham. A charming man with a handsome presence, he had sought out her company at every gathering they had attended in the month since the militia's arrival in Hertfordshire. She knew he would be in attendance; he had promised her the supper dance the day prior to the ball. Smiling his beatific smile and moving with skill and finesse at the small gatherings they had already attended, Elizabeth dreamed of how they would glide across the floor of a splendidly decorated ballroom. Thus, she had given special attention to her looks in hopes of capturing and holding Mr. Wickham's notice for the entire evening. Perhaps they would dance more than once. She sighed.

*Such a disappointment!* Stuffy, antagonistic Mr. Darcy's being at Netherfield Park made it too difficult for his sworn enemy, Mr. Wickham, to attend.

Worse yet, was Mr. Darcy's request; Elizabeth was unable to escape dancing with him for a full thirty minutes. He was a terrible man, a veritable monster dressed in fine clothing. Where he was bereft of pleasant personality traits, he possessed an abundance of wealth and status—an unequal exchange in her opinion. Despite being the most attractive man of her acquaintance on a purely physical level, his assets failed to appeal or impress Elizabeth at all. She loathed him—despised him with a vigor she had never felt towards another human being. In truth, he was the last man on earth with whom she wanted to stand up. Nonetheless, the rules of propriety and common manners were clear. To refuse him would have kept her from enjoying the rest of the evening. How much she resented Mr. Darcy!

Everything about their dance was uncomfortable. Oh, surprisingly, he performed the steps with fluidity. However, their conversation was heated until bitter words were exchanged that would never be forgotten. His unfair treatment of poor Mr. Wickham made Mr. Darcy lower than low in her eyes. Her challenge and the officious man's rebuttal satisfied neither of them, only serving to stir their ire.

Abandoning the gathering once the final notes of the second song ended, Elizabeth sought the seclusion of a small balcony with a stairway running down to a private walled garden. Breathing deeply, she gazed at the heavens in supplication for help to overcome her loathing of another human being. For yes, she hated Mr. Fitzwilliam Darcy with a passion she had never felt towards another person. Not even young Johnny Lucas, who deliberately spattered mud on her first grown-up gown six years prior, had earned her anger to the extent she felt that night.

Dreadful man!

Gasping when the ship took an unnatural roll, Elizabeth bumped into what she concluded was the man's waist. How unfortunate! Instead of walking away from him at the ball, she was now stuck with him it seemed.

Elizabeth snorted as she continued with her task.

Thinking back, she was unsettled by her sudden mental clarity.

Reviewing the night, she shockingly recalled that Mr. Darcy had followed her to the balcony. Why had he done something so foolish? Surely, he would have known it was improper to be isolated with her even for a few moments. Yet, it had appeared he was not finished with their argument. In truth, neither was she.

They were each so caught up in pressing their point that they failed to note the approach of several men from the garden below. As quickly as she was overpowered, so was Mr. Darcy. The ruffian who jabbed a pistol to her throat jerked her back to his chest, holding her in an iron grip. This immediately halted Mr. Darcy's actions to defend her. When another man approached him from behind, covering his mouth with a thick cloth, it was a matter of moments before the gentleman crumpled to the ground.

Just before the kidnapper moved the same sickeningly sweet-smelling cloth to her mouth, Elizabeth heard the rogue whisper, "Good thing we know they's brother an' sister cause they fight like they was married."

*Bah!* Being tied by birth or vows to Mr. Darcy would be a penalty no sensible female would desire—fortune or no fortune.

Turning her full attention to freedom, Elizabeth again pulled at the hemp.

Married or brother and sister? *Harrumph!* Not with Mr. Darcy. No, never!

Wait! Why ever would the man believe them to be siblings? There was absolutely no familial connection between the Bennets and the Darcys. Snobby Mr. Darcy would never allow it to be so.

Oh, her poor father. And Jane. They would be sick with worry over her being missing. With Mr. Darcy having disappeared at the same time, the rumors and speculation would be rife. How would dear Papa and Jane cope? They were both tender of heart.

This last thought refocused her thoughts on her most pressing need. Freedom.

"Come on, Elizabeth," she muttered to herself. "You can do this."

When the threads of the rope binding her ankles started to loosen, she celebrated far more aggressively than had been her intention. Flinging her bound hands into the air, Elizabeth wiggled her hips then again bent to her task, giving little thought to the bump she had inflicted on the man. It was not until there was a shift on the bunk and she felt cool air on the outside of her thigh that she realized she might have tilted their universe off its natural course rather abruptly. However, it was the heavy thump and moan as the man hit the floor that jolted her into feeling a figment of sympathy at his plight.

"Mr. Darcy," she hissed. "Mr. Darcy, are you well?"

The sound of pounding footsteps approaching outside their room stole her attention away from the groans of the man lying on the floor. Without his body as a barrier, she was openly exposed to whomever was approaching. Hurriedly arranging her skirt to cover her ankles, she lay back down, hoping beyond hope that the person would not notice that her hands were in front of her instead of behind.

With a brief scrape of a key in a lock, the door to their quarters was thrust open, allowing ambient sunlight to provide Elizabeth with her first glimpse of their surroundings. Blinking rapidly to filter the shards shining in her eyeballs, what she saw was hardly reassuring. There was their one bunk, a small shelf holding a pitcher and bowl with a chamber pot underneath. No candle. No lantern. No luggage. Only a man on the floor and one at the door.

The sailor had bare feet and pants that were torn off below his knees, revealing tanned skin covered with a coating of coarse dark hairs. His once white linen shirt was open at the throat and tied at his waistband. Over that he wore a dark navy wool coat thin enough that it barely covered his muscled arms. The butt of a pistol sticking out of his waistband and the fierceness of his expression brought Elizabeth's efforts to cover her ankles to a halt.

"What's goin' on here? Ye tryin' ta escape, Miss Bingley?" The oaf glanced at Mr. Darcy, immediately disregarding the man as a potential threat. "Ye an yer brother ain't goin' nowheres. Cap'n Bartolomew wants ye right where ye are 'til we reach port."

"Miss Bingley?" Elizabeth was confused and appalled. Miss Caroline Bingley, their hostess for the ball, was equally as arrogant and boorish as Mr. Darcy. Elizabeth wanted to snort, knowing the lady would be thrilled at being elevated to the equal of the man she longed to wed, even if it was due to an unpleasant personality trait.

"Yes, ma'am. Yer to be our 'guests' til we reach port, weather permittin', so I suggest ye not be makin' a fuss. Cap'n Bartholomew allows fer no trouble on his ship."

With a final sneer, the man slammed the door shut, turning a key in the lock.

At his departure, the only sounds in the room were the creaking vessel being slapped against the waves, the sails flapping in the breeze, and moans coming from the man on the floor.

THE COOLNESS of the hard surface against his cheek and temple felt good on Darcy's battered face. At least, he assumed it was battered. The slightest movement of any of his facial muscles caused discomfort and pain. *Who or what was responsible? He would have their head for this!*

Awareness of present circumstances assaulted him in stages. Surprisingly, it was the smell that first penetrated his skull with a modicum of accuracy. Blood! Lifting his head slightly, a sticky dampness dripped from the corner of his mouth down to his jaw. *Lord in heaven!* He was lying in a puddle of his own blood. He twitched his nose, immediately sensing a drip trickle from his right nostril. Reaching for his linen handkerchief was ... his attempt failed as his hands were apparently tightly bound behind him. He tugged to no effect. *What was happening?*

Immediately following smell was sound. A rustling of fabrics, a female voice exclaiming in whatever victory she was celebrating, and pounding footsteps assaulted his senses. *Where in the world was he? And who was the lady inhabiting the same small space?* At least he hoped she was a lady.

Sight immediately followed when the door not two feet in front of his face was thrust open. His eyes snapped shut against the light. When the intruder spoke, matters began to make sense.

The movement and the claim from his captor indicated they

were on a ship bound for an unknown port. *Where was he, and who was that rude man who had no clue how to open and close a door properly?*

He groaned as the intruder's words filtered into his fuzzy brain.

Caroline Bingley? He was trapped with her? *Good Lord!* He wanted to vomit.

She was a grasping, social-climbing shrew with close roots in trade who did everything within her power to attract his attention. Her single-minded goal was to become Mrs. Darcy, mistress of Pemberley. She cared not how she achieved her purpose. Yet, Darcy had to admit, if only to himself, that having him kidnapped and forced to spend possibly weeks in her close company was more than he had assumed she had the wisdom to arrange. While she was not entirely unattractive on a physical level, her mental comprehension would fill little more than her maid's thimble.

As fast as the speed of light, Darcy realized he would be forced by his own honor to offer her his hand, no matter how unwilling the groom.

He growled. For all of his almost twenty-eight years, he had acted in a manner that allowed only his parents and then himself to determine his course. That someone else had taken the reins served to increase his anger and frustration until it loomed in front of him like a living breathing monster.

"Mr. Darcy," came a harsh whisper from behind and above him. "Mr. Darcy, wake, I beg you."

He had had enough!

"Miss Bingley," he hissed through sore lips, his words not sounding as clear as he had intended. "I refuse to play into your schemes. I will not marry you, despite flagrantly flaunting propriety. Your brother knows my feelings on the matter."

He heard her harsh inhalation.

"You oaf!"

He felt a thump at his shoulder.

Spinning as quickly as he could, he sat up in time to receive another slight blow to the side of his head. Leaning quickly against what he assumed was a bunk, he trapped Miss Bingley's arm against the wood.

Except it was not an arm. It was ... he lowered the side of his face until he felt the texture of lace at his chin along with the firmness of ...

*Oh, Good Lord!* It was her thigh. He inhaled sharply, wanting to erase the image of Caroline Bingley's form from his mind's eye. Horrified, he scrambled back as quickly as he was able.

Their tight quarters kept him from moving far.

Had she kicked him with her foot? Surely, it was not accidental. Why ever would a woman who yearned to be bound to him cause him to suffer deliberate physical abuse at her...

Without warning, she jumped up only to trip over his outstretched legs. With his bound hands he could do nothing to help her.

An exclamation, a loud thump against the inside of the door, and an "ugh!" at the contact had him wondering at the mental stability of Miss Bingley. For someone who wanted to marry him as she did, her attempts at escape were quite unexpected.

Except ... when the goon who had threatened them earlier reopened the door, it was not Miss Caroline Bingley who stared back at him with lightning bolts shooting from her eyes.

No, the lady facing him was none other than Miss Elizabeth, the second daughter of Bingley's closest neighbor, Mr. Bennet of Longbourn in Meryton, Hertfordshire. Within a quick glance he discerned that she, too, was bound, she was still in her ballgown, her limbs were draped inelegantly over his with the hem of her skirt resting about mid-calf (her ankles were trim, her feet were small, and he was, in truth, both mortified and pleased he had caught sight of her appendages), and she was madder than a stirred-up hornet.

# 2

"What be goin' on here?" Upon seeing Mr. Darcy was awake, the sailor jerked his pistol from its resting place, pointing the barrel directly between the gentleman's eyes.

Not taking a chance Mr. Darcy would offend the sailor as quickly as he had offended everyone who had met him since his arrival to the farming community of Meryton, Elizabeth replied.

"I beg your pardon, sir. I thank you for your speedy return. In truth, I was hoping to gain your attention to inquire about the possibility of receiving something to quench my thirst in addition to having our bonds released. We are, after all, captive in this room. We have no weapons. We have no compatriots amongst your crew. The lock on the door would prevent our escape. The ocean surrounding us renders us completely at your mercy." Boldly, she inquired, "You are merciful, are you not?"

Without taking his eyes off Mr. Darcy, he said, "I have no orders to show mercy, Miss Bingley. Nor am I inclined to do so." His gaze swept over her slowly before glaring back at Mr. Darcy. "Ye be captives at the benevolence of the cap'n, al'right. Now, settle ye'selves down. T'will go better for ye if ye be silent and ask for nothin'."

As soon as the last word was out of his mouth, he shoved the pistol down his waistband, flung the door closed, and locked it behind him.

Frustrated and seething, Elizabeth ground her teeth. What an odd man. His manner of speech was first polished and then barely comprehensive, changing with each sentence. However, it was his pistol that spoke the loudest. Against that weapon they had no power.

"Miss Elizabeth, are you well?" Mr. Darcy's voice was muffled, as if it were the icy cold of winter and he was wearing a thick scarf to cover his face.

She had only a quick glance at him after the sailor appeared in the doorway. Like her, his wrists and his ankles were bound. Mr. Darcy's dark wavy hair was mussed, a bump and bruise had formed over his right eyebrow, his cheekbone was a brilliant purple hue, his face was shadowed with whiskers that had appeared sometime during the night, his upper lip was swollen, and his nose and chin were bloodied. Compared to him, she was in perfect health.

Again, they were in complete darkness.

"I find I am far better off than you are, sir." She leaned precariously against the wall next to the door where she had landed after tripping over his big feet. "Might you roll back towards the bunk? I am desperate to see if there is water in the pitcher. I have no desire to fall for the second time in minutes, bruising you or myself on the way."

Once she heard his clothing slide over the wood, Elizabeth maneuvered to her knees. Using her fists, she pushed against the floor until she stood, the restless sea slinging her back against the wall. Immediately, she hopped four steps forward, then leaned against the paneling. Cautiously reaching in front of herself, she felt the coolness of the upper rim of the porcelain vessel against her palm. Running her hands down to its base, she wrapped her fingertips around the narrow railing holding the pot in place. Tugging to make certain it was firmly fastened into the studs behind the panels, Elizabeth rested her hip against the wooden surface to stabilize herself. Gripping the pitcher at its mouth, she lifted it slightly to weigh the vessel in her hands. When the movement of the boat caused the contents to slosh against the inside, Elizabeth wanted to sob in relief. Water!

Carefully, she timed her drink with the rise and fall of the sea. The first few sips lead to a large gulp. Blessed relief!

Turning, she considered how best to provide the same service for Mr. Darcy. His mouth had to be as dry as hers had been.

"Sir, are you alert enough that you might shift closer to me? I am afraid that if I attempt to move closer to you, I will spill or drop the water before you can take a drink."

She heard his efforts, resulting in a muffled curse or two. As hard as she found movement to be with her feet still bound together, at least she had her hands in front of her despite them being tied at the wrist. He was completely restrained.

Once Mr. Darcy's foot brushed her ankle, she judged his position to be nearly in front of her.

"Are you seated upright, sir?"

"I am."

"Then I will lower myself to the floor when the next wave throws me back against the wall opposite you." She had to count to five before the boat leveled then tilted to her expectation. Elizabeth did exactly as she suggested, hesitating only slightly when the back of her gown snagged and tore on the rough wood behind her.

"Do not harm yourself, I pray you. My thirst can wait."

She was slightly confused at his comment. Was he looking out for her behalf, putting her care ahead of his own needs and wants?

How odd! The man had been rude to the extreme on every single occasion she had been in his company. Never would he consider the comfort of a gentleman farmer's daughter ahead of himself. She knew him better than that. Whatever was he about?

*Harrumph!* If there had been a river or a stream nearby with potable water to replenish their supply and if she had the means and the space to jump back out of the way, she would gladly have dumped the pitcher's contents over his head. Despite his kind words, she knew who and what he was. Despicable man!

"Hah!" Elizabeth grumbled to herself. *His thirst could wait, indeed!*

Sliding her feet forward, her knees were barely bent before her toes bumped the bunk. Tilting slightly to her right, her elbow brushed what had to be the side of Mr. Darcy's knee. With her back against the wall and her feet pushing the wood in front of her, she was better able to clasp the jug. At that discovery, she still needed to determine exactly where the man's face was in relation to where she sat. As much as she despised him, she had no desire to accidentally shove the porcelain's edge into his already battered lip or chip one of his front teeth.

Wedging the pitcher between her knees, Elizabeth leaned forward, cautiously searching for him. Once her hands lit on something solid, she rested the side of her fists on what turned out to be his cravat. Despite not wanting to touch him, *ever*, she ran her fingers up until her palms cupped his face.

She swallowed hard as unexpected tingles started under her nails and ran across her hands, streaked a path from her wrist to her elbow, then raced up her arms. *What was happening?* Her body shivered at the intimacy of her touch. The roughness of the shadow covering his face had not caused the sensation. When she was a little girl, Elizabeth would greet her father each morning with a kiss on one cheek and a rub of her palm on the other. She did the same before retiring to the nursery. She marveled at the difference between Thomas Bennet being shaved in the morning and bristly at night. Thus, it was not the man's whiskers that were responsible.

Shaking off her confusion, Elizabeth made the decision to take an elevated path of kindness and consideration.

"Sir, there is an element of danger involved in seeing to your comfort."

He replied without hesitation, "I am at your service."

Keeping the inside of her arms against the pitcher, she slowly guided his face towards her. When he was close, she warned him, "You are a scant distance away. If you were to put your lips on the rim and not lose contact with the jug, I will lift it when the boat tilts my way, giving me the most control."

What followed was measured amounts of the beverage spilling into his mouth. After they climbed up and sailed down three waves, she pulled the pitcher back.

"I thank you, Miss Elizabeth." He inhaled deeply, then said. "I am grateful your hands were tied in front of you, or we would have had life-giving water close with no ability to drink."

She snorted. "Far be it for me to correct you, sir, but my hands were bound behind me."

"Then, how?"

Should she share with him her unladylike actions to change her situation? A brief consideration brought enlightenment. His constant disdain while he was in Hertfordshire at the Bingley residence gave her confidence that she could not possibly lower herself further than his already set-in-stone opinions. Therefore, she said, "Sir, I used the advantage of my ball gown having two layers of slippery fabric resting between myself and a well-worn mattress. In all honesty, getting my ... uh, my ... well, my ... Mr. Darcy, I simply cannot repeat the process as it was, without a doubt, the most unladylike move I have ever performed in front of a man."

"An unconscious man," he quipped.

She smiled. "This is true. Without thinking, she added, "With the width of your shoulders being much broader than your hips, you should not have so difficult a time."

*Oh, good heavens!* Why had she said that aloud? Now he knew she had studied his form until she could ... *Oh, good grief!* Could a person possibly be any more mortified than she was at that second in time?

He chuckled under his breath. "I shall take your advice under consideration."

Holding the water container to her chest, she rested the back of her head against the wall.

*Insufferable man!*

"Miss Elizabeth, my brain appears to be working in slow motion. Whether this is from whatever was given me at our capture or the beating I sustained, I am uncertain. When last I saw you before our current capture, a man was holding you roughly with a pistol pointed at your throat. If I live to be a million years of age, I do not believe I will ever forget the look of terror on your face. Again, I will ask you, are you well?"

"Again, I will tell you that I am in perfect health. What is not perfect are our circumstances."

"I agree," he grunted. "Do not worry. I am sure this is something that a large sum of money will fix. We will be returned to our families and our homes before long."

"You are sure of this?"

"Miss Elizabeth, in my tenure as master of Pemberley, there has never been an occasion or circumstance where money was not the solution. Not once."

"A very jaded prospect, sir."

"Indeed." Darcy added, "We cannot be far from London or whatever port from which we sailed. When the captain appears, which I suspect will happen at a given time, the negotiations will begin. Once his offer is agreed upon, he will turn this vessel back to port."

"You will agree to his terms, then?"

"I have no other choice, do I?"

She certainly hoped the solution was that easy. Elizabeth pondered her own situation. For a certainty, her father would be able to provide little towards a ransom. Longbourn barely paid for the expenses of a frivolous wife and five unwed daughters.

Elizabeth felt and heard him struggle to arrange himself to a better situation, his frustration evident by his swift movements and growls.

She asked, "You have been on a ship before?"

"I have several times."

"I see."

"My father inherited an estate in Ireland shortly after the loss of my mother. He refused to leave his children behind when he traveled each year to review the property. Since his death, I have traveled alone since my sister did not want to miss any of her schooling."

"Then, you are familiar with the movements of a ship?"

"Only as a passenger, I assure you. Of the operations and piloting, I am entirely unaware."

Everything she had experienced since waking was unfamiliar. Unlike him, she had never been on a ship or a boat. Rarely had she left her shire, wandering fewer than three miles in any direction from her home. An occasional journey to London to visit her mother's family was the only opportunity to break the monotony that had become her life. The same faces appeared at all the social gatherings. The same topics were discussed. Until Mr. Bingley brought his party from London to Netherfield Park, Elizabeth had never noticed how easily her life had slid into a rather boring sameness.

Now, she was paired with the worst man in the universe, the

man who had declared, in public no less on the evening they had been introduced, that she was not handsome enough to tempt him to dance. Merely tolerable, he had said. Of course, she probably was not supposed to overhear, yet she was seated close enough to him that she could not help but be affected by the rude insult.

*Shame on him!* That was not how a true gentleman spoke of a lady. He was, by and large, a...

"Miss Elizabeth, I appear to have failed in my task." The disappointment in his voice was clear to her. "I cannot ... seem ... to ... ah, let me attempt the feat again."

Instead of being absorbed in her own musings, this time Elizabeth attempted to follow his actions by the movement beside her and the noises he made. After a few minutes of intense struggle, he again confided his inability to slide his hands underneath him.

"Mr. Darcy might we help each other with the knots binding our wrists?" She waited for his response. And waited. After what seemed like forever, he mumbled his agreement.

"Pray if you would turn your back to me, I shall seat myself behind you." Elizabeth followed her words with actions, first standing to replace the empty water pitcher in its holder. Pausing until the inertia of the waves pressed her against the wall, she slid to a seated position, reaching blindly to determine where he had situated himself. Her hand jolted back the second her fingertips touched his shoulder. She was shocked there was no smoke from the flames.

*Good heavens!* What in the world was happening to her? Had she lost her mind in the attack? This was Mr. Darcy!

Without complaint he had done as she had asked. Pushing herself to her knees, she reached forward until she felt the fabric of his tailcoat. Running her hands down his spine, her fingers found his joined wrists. She traced the knot, finding the two loose ends.

Elizabeth was shocked by her own temerity. Her fingers

burned where they brushed against the hard surface of his back, almost losing feeling completely when they touched his fisted hands. *Hmmm!* No padding or soft flaccid muscles for Mr. Darcy. She immediately dismissed the discovery.

As she worked, Elizabeth contemplated what she knew of their circumstances.

"Mr. Darcy, are you cognizant enough to discuss our situation?" She tugged the hemp only to have him jerk against the knots. "Sir! Pray do not pull against the rope as it makes the binding tighter. I understand your discomfort. If I can loosen the..."

He adjusted his wrists to allow her slightly better access. Within moments, pushing one end back through a loop then pulling at the other, the knot began to give way. Instinctively, Mr. Darcy yanked against his restraints.

"Mr. Darcy! Cease and desist immediately." Elizabeth barked, then chuckled.

"Would you be willing to share your humor? I would appreciate the opportunity for anything to lighten the dreadful thoughts plaguing my mind."

"I will." Again, she followed the knots with her fingers to see where she needed to pry or pull. "At the grand age of ten years, I regularly played highwayman with Johnny Lucas, Sir William's second son. Despite longing to be the rogue outlaw, I was forever the damsel in distress. For a decade, the opportunity to be the Dread Highwayman Lizzy had not presented itself, until now. You must think I am quite the hoyden."

"I do not. It was a role I also was denied since my two cousins were both older than me."

"You were the hero then." She accidentally tugged the wrong rope.

"I wish!" He grumbled. "My eldest cousin, Viscount Stanton deemed it impossible that any other could ever be a hero. Richard, my other cousin who was long destined for the army, loved nothing more than to oppose the restrictions of the law. Thus, I was forever the hapless victim. I took to carrying small snakes and frogs in my pockets to have my share of the fun. Richard is the bravest man I know but he is immediately felled by a serpent of any length, whether poison or not."

She laughed. "Perhaps you might do the same at a ball, sir. Even those ladies lacking a partner would avoid trying to gain your attention. You would be left alone to your silent contemplation of the evening."

He snickered. "I will gladly take your advice should we gain our freedom without destruction to our reputations. Otherwise, I would have captured a snake to no purpose as no invitations would come my way."

Mr. Darcy hunched his shoulders and back, allowing him to relax his arms and wrists as much as possible. She could have appreciated his current pose in the light of day. Never had she witnessed the man in any attitude other than rigid restraint and composure.

As she continued to work on his fastenings, she pondered the moments since Mr. Darcy became conscious. Prior occasions when she had been in his company, he remained silent for the most part, conversing rarely. His sharing his past was unusual. Their typical conversations tended toward animosity and contention.

If only he had remained mute at the Netherfield ball. She would have walked away from him in hopes of quickly gaining another partner—a pleasant one. Mr. Darcy would have returned to his post by the wall, sneering at all in attendance. Instead, they had argued, flinging hateful words at each other with vigor.

If only.

She had sought the cool evening air merely to relax and enjoy the strains of music with nothing or no one to disrupt her.

Oh, no! That would never do. For she would have been alone on the balcony, more vulnerable than ever with ruffians lurking about.

She was grateful for his presence. *Grateful for Mr. Darcy?* How was it possible? As she pondered what could have happened to her had he not joined her on the balcony, he kept silent.

"Miss Elizabeth," he whispered. "In my attempts to make myself clearly understood when I thought you to be Miss Bingley, my lip started bleeding. I apologize for my silence, but it has again begun to drip. I am attempting to stop the flow by keeping my mouth tightly shut."

She nodded then shook her head, despite knowing he could not see. Had she known it would have kept him quiet, she would seriously have considered a quick jab to his lip before he had asked her to stand up with him at the ball.

A chortle threatened. Clearing her throat, instead she said, "You are indeed a mess."

"I suppose I am. How are you faring?" Mr. Darcy insisted.

She sighed. "Sir, I am in better circumstances than you are." Elizabeth grimaced as another fingernail frayed under the strain of pulling against the rough twine. "I will confess for your ears alone, that you ... improve upon acquaintance the longer you are silent. At the same time, I admit that your opinion as to the events that led us here would be appreciated."

Bent forward to allow her own bound hands better access to his, she was rudely bashed in the forehead when he threw his head back, for what purpose she had no clue.

"Mr. Darcy!" she hissed as he quickly begged her pardon. "Be still, I pray you!"

"I beg you to accept my sincerest apology, Miss Elizabeth. I cannot believe that harm was caused to you by my own hands."

"No, sir. I believe it was the granite surface of your head that did the damage." She could not help herself, she chuckled. Had she truly called him a hard head? She had.

"Miss Elizabeth, the unnatural position I find myself in and my frustration demanded relief. I am sorry it came at a high cost to you."

Rubbing the rising bump at her hairline with her forearm, she again bent to the task, being aware of his every movement.

*Who was this man?*

Minutes passed slowly as she pried and twisted. Eventually, she met with success. With one final pull, Mr. Darcy's left hand was freed. Immediately, he moved his hands to his front to stretch his tortured muscles to work on the final knot.

Sitting back on her heels, she buried her battered fingertips in the soft fabric of her gown.

Elizabeth realized what was missing. Their gloves. Aloud, she said, "Sir, our gloves are gone."

The rustle of cloth being patted down told her he was doing his own inspection of his person.

"My watch and fob, my cufflinks, my stickpin, and my signet ring are missing." He grunted as he finally released the last of his bindings. She heard the rope hit the wall next to the door as he tossed it away from him. "My shoes have been taken."

Selfish man! Attempting to free his feet before returning the favor to her. *Oaf!* She cleared her throat to draw his attention. "Will you not help me with my wrists?"

"But of course." He spun to face her, blindly reaching for her hands as she offered them to him. "I was hoping my dancing shoes were present. They are for the most part useless, but the leather of the heel is hard enough to be an adequate weapon."

"Against a pistol?" She was incredulous. "Our captors are fully armed."

"This I know, Miss Elizabeth." The rope rubbed abrasively against her skin as he tugged and twisted the hemp. It hurt. And, she had done the same to him, adding to the injuries he had sustained on the balcony. A pettiness she did not know she possessed kept her from acknowledging any increase to his suffering she had caused. *No, she could not be like that, despite her negative opinion of the man.*

"I apologize for hurting you," she admitted, immediately feeling better about herself. "The rope ..."

Instantly, he dropped the ends of the braiding binding her wrists, taking her hands gently in his. "I beg your pardon, Miss Elizabeth. Again, I have harmed you, something I never wanted, ever."

*Harrumph!* "You have given thought to not causing me pain? When was that, I might ask? And why would you not be aware of the pain your words and actions have already wrought? What an odd man you are!"

"Miss Elizabeth, I ..." he paused. She felt his fingers encircling her wrists.

She gulped at his touch, feeling foolish for continuing to bear a grudge when his efforts were for her immediate benefit.

She felt each tiny cell vibrate with the movements of his fingers. Where was her ire? Where was her disgust with the man? She inhaled deeply to regain her sense of self as he continued to pull at the ropes with far less vigor than he had before.

"Ah, I am familiar with this configuration." He sounded exultant. "You have a bowline knot in a bight, looped around both wrists then pulled tight. My cousin, who is now a colonel in the army, used to practice navy knots on his brother and me during our youth. I should have you out of ... in a moment ... I only need to draw the rope, or as he called it, the line back through ... and ..."

The relief to her arms was immediate. As soon as the pressure from her bindings relaxed, Elizabeth rubbed furiously at her wrists, restoring feeling and removing the tingles.

"I thank you, sir, I ...oh!" Elizabeth was beyond surprised when

Mr. Darcy lifted her hem to pull at the hemp surrounding her ankles. Sucking in a breath, she was eternally grateful for the dark. She felt the heat as her cheeks flamed. *How dare he?* No, the freedom his efforts would provide was worth snapping the rules of propriety in two.

A thought occurred to her.

"I have a million questions begging for answers." Elizabeth mused, trying to give some order to the thoughts plaguing her.

"For example?"

She could tell his teeth were gritted as he tugged and pulled on the ropes, jerking her feet from left to right.

While the darkness shrouded them in black, it allowed her a measure of boldness she would not have had in the light of day.

"Have you read Macbeth, Mr. Darcy?" she asked.

"Shakespeare? Of all the matters you could ponder with our present conditions, I had not guessed you might be thinking of him. However, whatever your motive, I am familiar with the text," he replied. Giving a sharp tug to her bindings, he grunted when the knot held despite her efforts to loosen it earlier.

She asked, "What do you believe Shakespeare meant when he wrote, "Stars, hide your fires; Let not light see my black and deep desires?"

"A philosophical question? I am unsurprised," he whispered under his breath only inches from her. "Um ... I believe his point was that darkness provides a safe haven to do or say things we would not do or say in the light of day."

With a final twist and pull, Elizabeth felt the bindings drop to the floor. Rubbing the skin at her ankles, she pulled her heels close to her then wrapped her arms around her knees, smoothing her tattered gown over her legs when she heard the man attempting to loosen the knots on his own ankles. "Mr. Darcy, perhaps it is my belief that the lack of light intensifies my thoughts or hides my inhibitions, but whatever the cause, I feel I must share my observations and concerns with you for your opinions."

Surprisingly, he chuckled. "I am at your service."

Elizabeth easily imagined him bowing at the waist despite his position on the floor.

"Then, pray prepare yourself." She grinned, unexpectedly desiring to disconcert him. "Here would be my first example. Why are our gloves missing?"

"The sailors are suffering from chaffed hands?" he teased.

"Mr. Darcy, you, sir, have a flare for exaggeration." Containing a smile, she asked, "Then, where do you think your dancing shoes are hiding?"

"I suspect Captain Bartholomew will present himself as the best shod ship's captain at the next soiree he attends once we reach port, Miss Elizabeth."

"A captain dressed as a gentleman?" She smirked. "I see."

"Miss Elizabeth, the matters weighing heaviest on my own mind are why the man who has presented himself at our door twice speaks with polished refinement for a few phrases amidst his sailor slang, why he believes we are the Bingleys, how we will escape without being forced to wed, and how we can care for our physical needs with no privacy."

She was grateful he had put into words her own concerns. "These are my questions as well," she agreed.

"Like you, I find the darkness makes it easier to address my worries aloud." He sighed once he pulled the ropes from his own ankles. "I do not fear speaking thus, for it is many weeks since I have considered you as one of the most intelligent women of my acquaintance."

"What?" Elizabeth had no intention of making such a loud exclamation. However, his words left her completely flummoxed.

Turning on the floor to place their backs against the bunk, he continued, "We can easily forgive a child who is afraid of the dark; the real tragedy of life is when men are afraid of the light."

"Plato," she offered.

"Yes." He huffed. "Despite the fact that I find our current location to be intolerable, in all honesty, matters would have been much, much worse had you been Miss Bingley."

For some unexplained reason, that idea pleased Elizabeth far more than it should have.

A dmittedly, the water had temporarily quenched Darcy's thirst. However, the first touch of Elizabeth's fingers on his skin set him afire until he burned from the top of his head to his toes, drying his mouth, his throat, and emptying his brain of all thought. *What was he to do?* Who knew how long they would be in enforced confinement together? *Good Lord in heaven!* There were two of them and only one bunk.

In the nearly two months since they had first been in company, Darcy's opinion of Miss Elizabeth Bennet had gone from disdain to intrigue, from completely shunning her to having her captivate his mind at all hours of the day and night.

It should not have been. The comparison between his host's sister and Miss Elizabeth Bennet should have weighed far heavier in Miss Bingley's favor. While Miss Caroline Bingley was the daughter of a tradesman, she had been educated to higher society when an influx of wealth resulted from her father's hard work and good business acumen. She knew what to wear, how to act, and could perform with skill on the pianoforte when pressed to do so. Miss Elizabeth had not the benefit of exposure to that sort of training. She was the daughter of landed gentry, albeit a man of far less property and wealth than most gentlemen of Darcy's acquaintance. The impression he had of Mr. Bennet was that he despised London society. From frequently riding the pathways between Bingley's estate and the farming town of Meryton, it was easy to observe the lack of initiative to make the Bennet estate prosper. Being a responsible landowner appeared to be entirely absent from his character. Thus, he had absolutely nothing in common with Darcy. Neither should Miss Elizabeth. In fact, she should not have attracted his attention at all.

Since puberty had hit him full force during his fourteenth or fifteenth year, his eye tended to follow petite ladies with blue eyes, pale skin, and flaxen hair like Miss Jane Bennet, Elizabeth's eldest sister. Elizabeth Bennet was about as tall as his own sister, had dark brown hair bordering on a walnut hue with even darker eyes that sparkled in both pleasure and anger—for he had been witness to both emotions several times in their acquaintance. No, he was incorrect. It had been many times she had displayed her ire with him.

He felt her move away from him. Being free of restraints, she must have risen to sit on the bunk.

Although needing to rein in his thoughts and finish loosening the ropes binding his feet, he instead inquired, "Have you any other subject you would like to address, Miss Elizabeth, for I am quite at my leisure."

Her soft chuckle was a delight to his ears.

Clearing her throat, she began. "Sir, I cannot help but wonder what troubles Mr. Bingley and his sister have got themselves into that would lead to forced kidnap, violence against you, and the removal of brother and sister to an unknown place. Is Mr. Bingley in debt to unscrupulous money lenders? Has he broken the law in a way that has angered someone in authority?"

Darcy shook his head and then recalled that she could not see him. Pulling at the final knot, he mused, "I will admit to being perplexed myself. When it comes to business, Bingley is as constant as the sunrise. More than that, he is cautious with his money, appreciating his father's hard work. This led to him leasing Netherfield Park rather than taking on a large purchase before having the experience needed to run an estate. My only complaint is his rather cavalier attitude toward his correspondence, hardly a fault worthy of note unless I await his reply to an urgent question. He is genuinely kind."

"For Jane's sake, I am pleased to hear it." Elizabeth sighed. "I would hate for her to give her heart to an undeserving man."

"Her heart?" He asked in disbelief as the binding finally let go. *Freedom!*

He had no idea those two words would provoke a violent outburst from the lady.

"What are you implying, Mr. Darcy?" Her tone was as brittle as thin glass.

Despite the darkness, he fully comprehended that he had upset her. He considered how best to answer before replying. However, he had no clue as to exactly why she was angered. Darcy had noticed no preference on the part of her eldest sister for his friend.

He pushed himself up from the floor, determined to present himself in a more favorable attitude. In his haste and the lack of light, he was unaware how low the ceiling was in their quarters until the top of his head bounced off the hard surface. *Ouch!* Rubbing the pain away, he dropped down beside her—far too close to her—practically on top of her, in fact. Embarrassed, he slid away from Elizabeth to the far end of the bunk.

Fortunately, he was saved from stirring her ire any further by a tap on the door and the scraping of a key attempting to fit itself into the lock.

Habit had him blurting, "enter" before he considered his current position. He was not master of Pemberley here.

A young boy of perhaps ten years entered carrying a plate holding two slices of bread with a small piece of unidentifiable meat plopped in the center. How in the world were they supposed to have eaten the meager offering with their hands tied behind their backs? Like dogs tearing at their prey with their teeth?

Darcy's stomach rumbled at the sight. In his other hand the young lad held a key. Quickly the boy slid it into his pants pocket.

He was long and skinny. His hair, a mottled mixture of yellow and brown, was poorly groomed. Bright green eyes shown under a fringe of bangs. His face was far dirtier than it was clean. He carried no weapon. Darcy's confidence in his ability to gain their freedom against the lad soared.

"My name be Jonah Hackett, ship's boy on the *Peregrine*. Cap'n Bartholomew tol' me not ta say a thing so don't ye be askin' me nothin' cause I ain't 'pos ta talk."

"Say there!" Darcy looked past the lad into the light available from the open doorway to see if anyone older and larger loomed behind him. No one appeared to be there. "I demand ..."

Elizabeth rested her hand on his arm, stopping him from continuing.

"Master Hackett," she smiled. "Pray do not be concerned. We would never want to do anything to cause you to disobey a direct order from your captain. Are those provisions for us?"

"They sure is." He slapped his free hand over his mouth. "I weren't 'posed ..."

"Do not worry for the neither of us would ever say a word." Elizabeth waited until he nodded and placed the plate on the bunk. "Sir, if you would not mind, I would appreciate the opportunity to ask a simple question, only suggesting a nod yes or no as a reply. Would that be permissible?"

Jonah dipped his head slightly before nodding. Darcy could

tell the young fellow was pleased to be addressed as "sir" by a woman of Elizabeth's beauty.

"Master Hackett, I would like to know more than anything else if you like sailing under Captain Bartholomew. Pray just nod or shake your head."

He nodded.

"Would you not like to sail with a friendlier crew?"

His head moved vigorously from side to side.

"I see," she paused, her index finger resting on her chin. "Then, I can only wonder if you have been on this vessel for a long time."

He nodded.

"How long?"

"Two years or more," he answered without thought.

"You must be a very important part of the crew to be entrusted by the captain with the task of seeing to our care," Elizabeth smiled again. "Therefore, we, the both of us, offer to you our sincerest thanks."

"Welcome, ma'am." He looked beyond him to the wall behind where they sat. "Say, why don't ye take down the black canvas covering the port light? It must be awful dark in here when the door is closed."

Darcy's eyes shot to where the lad's gaze had gone. Sure enough, there was a square of thick fabric about two feet above the surface of the bunk. Reaching back, he ripped it down.

Darcy turned back to the boy, hoping he would reveal more that could help them. Before he had the opportunity to voice his many questions, Elizabeth spoke.

"Just one more question, then you can return to Captain Bartholomew to let him know your job was well done."

"Sure!" he said instead of nodding.

Darcy watched as Elizabeth's gaze started at the boy's bare feet and went to the thatch of hair at the top of his head. He had no idea what was going through her mind.

"Jonah Hackett, are you not cold?"

The question took both males by surprise. Until that time, Darcy had not noticed the chill. Immediately, the cold air surrounding them hit him in the face. *For goodness sakes!* Elizabeth, in her thin ball gown, must be freezing!

"Nah, miss. I have too much ta do runnin' up and down the riggin' both day and night to feel the chill except when the cap'n sets the course t'wards the north star. Then it be cold enough ta freeze the balls off a brass monkey." He shivered.

"Mr. Hackett!" Darcy was appalled at the lad's language.

"Oh, I mean no offense ta the lady, sir. Ye see, the brass monkey be the ring holdin' the cannon balls in a stack on deck, so they don't roll around. Once, when we were above the Arctic Circle haulin' supplies to whalers, it was so cold the brass blowed up like a harpooned humpback where the iron balls stayed the same size. Once those balls got free of the ring, I chased 'em around the deck and stacked 'em until the cap'n finally told me to grab a crate from down below to put 'em in." He looked to Darcy before he continued. "Don't ye be worryin', mister, me ma taught me some manners b'fore I went to sea. I'd not speak disrespectful-like ta a lady."

Before he could reply, Elizabeth asked, "Do you miss your Mum?"

Her tenderness seemed to hit the lad squarely between the eyes for he backed out of the doorway without a word. With one final glance at Elizabeth, Jonah Hackett closed the door and locked them inside.

Darcy's second glimpse of Elizabeth hit him in the chest so hard he feared his body would crumple. The lace of her gown was in shreds. Her hair was matted close to her skin on the right side. The left side had come loose from her hair pins until it drooped over her ear. The curls that had bounced joyously during their dance were touching her shoulders. Her forehead sported a red lump that was turning a purple hue. However, it was her eyes that stopped his breath. They were as warm as he had ever seen them, brimming with compassion and care. For him?

Clarity served to provide another blow. No, not to him. For the ship's boy, Jonah Hackett.

Disappointment shot through him, rendering his tone harsher than he had wanted.

"Miss Elizabeth, why would you waste the opportunity of gaining needed information by asking about his mother?" Darcy challenged, as he searched their quarters for who knew what. He was irritated. He was irrational. He was unable to stop himself. "Why not ask what we most need to know? Where are we headed? How long until we reach port? These are matters that even a lad would comprehend. Yet, you asked about his parentage. What were you thinking?"

Instead of being intimidated, she rose to her full height, the top of her head brushing the ceiling.

"Why, you ask?" Her chin thrust out as the fire in her eyes transformed into icy coldness. "Because, Mr. Know-Everything Darcy, we need a friend, a compatriot on this vessel—someone who will look out for our interest as well as his own. Had you demanded answers which would have been in direct defiance of the captain's command should young Jonah have provided you satisfaction, we would have lost any hope of aid."

She turned away from him, then immediately spun back.

"You are not the one in charge here. Not one person on this ship, including myself, needs to submit to your whims, sir."

"Whims?" His frustration simmered below the surface, bubbling up, threatening to consume him. He had been kidnapped, assaulted, shanghaied onto a ship leading to an unknown destination with a lady who had turned his world upside down. He wanted her concern. He needed her to want even a fraction as much of him as he needed of her. Her defiance lit the fire of his temper.

"You appear to be under the impression that I am unable to act in a manner that would see to our interests. You could not be more wrong, Miss Bennet."

"Wrong?" Her head tipped back. Her eyes narrowed as she peered down at him. "Had it been Mr. Bingley here instead of you I would have stepped back and allowed him to approach young Hackett, knowing his kindness would have moved the lad to speak freely. But you? Oh, no, Mr. Darcy. Your arrogance and selfish disdain for the feelings of others would have come at a cost far too dear for either of us to bear."

He felt her insult to his core. "Arrogance? Selfish disdain? What are you saying? You prefer Bingley to me? I admire my friend greatly but recognize that confrontation is not something he handles well. He would step back and allow you to take the lead." Shaking his head, he sat at the end of the bunk, turning away from her. Was this what she wanted? Was she a female who balked at a male exercising his God-given authority? Did she somehow see herself as their savior? "I will have you know that not one day has passed since my father's death that I have not had to untangle problems with unsavory businessmen, troublesome tenants, and disputes between family and friends."

"You? Are you certain it is not you at the root of these problems?"

"Certainly not!" Did she not know who he was? He sought to enlighten her. "Everything I am today is a result of trying to become the man my father taught me to be." Gritting his teeth, he leaned towards her.

Her shoulders pressed back. Fiery red covered her cheeks. "He taught you to be rude?"

"He taught me to know my place in society, my value as a Darcy and the master of Pemberley." He barely kept from yelling.

"I see."

"Do you? For it appears to me that you seek to diminish my standing until I equal yours. What did you learn from your father? Complacency, disregard, idleness? What of your mother? Avariciousness, meddling, and self-aggrandizement?"

Her expression was fearsome. He knew without a doubt that had she been a man, she would have struck him. Regrets pooled at the pit of his stomach, but he could not bring himself to apologize.

"How dare you!" Her arms were stiff at her side, her hands fisted. "You are nothing to me!"

He felt the pain of her words in each pore. Did she truly feel that way about him? He was nothing to her?

Glancing at her, nothing about her stance relaxed. In the two months they had been acquainted, he had never known her to be less than honest. Why would she be different now? She would not. He sighed.

Silence filled the room with the leaden weight of a thousand mountains, settling upon his shoulders until Darcy considered how his words would have wounded her. It was as if his conscience had doused him with icy water. Instantly, he was ashamed. Each expression, each syllable had been flung at her like an arrow aimed at her heart. She was correct. He had not acted the gentleman. Rather than being proud of him, his father would have been heartily ashamed of his only son.

"I beg your pardon, Miss Elizabeth." He would not look at her. Instead, he spoke to the wall. "These circumstances do not show either of us to our best advantage, I fear. I see now that your approach with Hackett was the best."

She shivered.

Removing his jacket, he offered it to her. "Pray do not allow my foolish, wild talk to dissuade you from accepting the warmth of this garment. It is not its fault that its owner is an idiot."

"We finally agree on something," she whispered, appearing to be stunned at his admitting a fault. Elizabeth exhaled, her eyes closing before reaching for his coat. Settling it around herself, she pulled the lapels up under her chin. Removing herself to the other end of the bunk, she sat, leaning her temple against the wall.

The plate of untouched food rested between them. Despite the rumble in his gut, he would forego eating so she could have it all. It was the least he could do.

He felt like kicking himself. When he glanced at her again and saw a tear trail down her lovely cheek it hurt his heart. While she was the stubbornest, most hard-headed woman of his ... he stopped himself from placing all the blame for the tension between them on her.

He swore under his breath. How was he ever going to get himself out of the chaos caused by their kidnapping and the mess he alone had created between the two of them?

# 4

There were few things Elizabeth hated more than having someone see her cry. That it was Fitzwilliam Darcy, her self-proclaimed enemy, made it more galling.

He was correct in much of what he said. He did move in a sphere far above her own. From what Caroline Bingley had repeatedly mentioned, he was firmly ensconced in the upper ten thousand with one of the largest estates in all of England. He was the grandson of an earl. He was insanely wealthy. His power was almost unlimited. He answered to no man other than the king.

She knew her roots. Her family was firmly planted in the rich Hertfordshire soil. Her father was a humble man who was contented to remain in his position as a gentleman farmer. Her mother's closest relatives were in trade. Elizabeth loved them dearly, but they were humble by comparison. She had no doubt Mr. Darcy would ignore them should he ever be in their company.

She knew what he thought of her. He had not been shy in his opinions. On each occasion where they had been in company, he had stared at her, examining her as if she were a bug under a microscope.

She saw his disgust as he looked at her torn dress, which was so much worse in the light than she had imagined it to be in the darkness. Her hair was a mess and now she was bawling like a toddler denied a favorite toy. She was not in pain, nor was she sad. No, she was reeling from all that the morning had tossed at her.

Inhaling deeply, she swiped the moisture from her face with the back of her hand. Her internal lecture reminded her that her courage rose with any attempt to intimidate her. Lifting her chin, staring directly at him, just as he was doing to her, she resolved then and there to cower no longer. She could do absolutely nothing to change his attitude or actions. She could, on the other hand, have full control over herself. She would begin anew.

"I sue for peace, Mr. Darcy." Elizabeth extended her hand as she had witnessed her father do after signing a document completing a transaction with his man of business.

Mr. Darcy hesitated before his fingers touched hers. Finally, he gripped her palm against his own. It was not a tentative touch or the barely-there meeting between an unattached male and female with the barrier of gloves between them. No, he met her with respect for her plea.

"I accept. Do you have terms that accompany our treaty?"

There was no humor in his tone nor smirking on his face. She was grateful.

"Yes, I do." Pulling her hand from his, she rubbed her palm against her leg, surprised at the tingles where his skin had met hers. He was a horrid man. How dare her body respond in a pleasing way to someone so... so terrible? Clearing her throat to regain her thinking, she said, "As you mentioned, we have no idea how long we will be held captive on this vessel. Therefore, I desire that polite conversation should rule the day."

"What? You are suggesting that we should only canvas the weather and the condition of the roads?" He swung his arm toward her with his palm up. "Examine closely our situation, Miss

Elizabeth. We have weighty concerns. I simply cannot believe, knowing your character, that you do not want to thoroughly review each and every one of them."

She stared him in the eye. "You are entirely in the right, Mr. Darcy. Like my father, I enjoy discussing world conditions, exploring new opinions and ideas, and heated debates over matters that touch my heart. However, I am tired of you arrogantly promoting your belief that you know best about ... everything." She huffed. "Condescension is unattractive to me in all of its forms."

"Hah!" he exclaimed. "There is nothing wrong with condescension where there is a genuine reason for pride. Where there is a real superiority of mind, pride will always be under good regulation."

It was her turn to exclaim. "Again, I disagree. Vehemently! You see, my aunt is unparalleled when painting landscapes. Her efforts are no less than the great masters found in museums. Yet, when her young daughter shows her mother the pictures crafted under the tutelage of her governess, my aunt's appreciation is genuine. She, who has every reason for pride in her own artwork, would never condescend to believe others are somehow less than herself."

"You misunderstand, as per your usual attitude." He ran his hand through his hair, wincing at the bump at the top of his skull. Speaking slowly as if he considered her to be a half-wit, he said, "Providing critique in an attempt to help someone better their circumstances is a kindness, Miss Elizabeth, not condescension. How you could possibly see that as disdain completely escapes me." Before she could reply, he continued. "Bingley is a good example. His wisdom in being cautious comes from his inherent knowledge of his own character. Because of this, when he chose to take a giant step toward becoming a landowner, he asked for guidance. I responded to his request, not as an act of arrogance in believing myself more knowledgeable to him in every way. My experience in caring for my estates made me superior to his lack in that area alone. He is by far more remarkable when it comes to amiability."

What? The great man admitted a human flaw? How was that possible?

"Then, by what right do you seek to enforce your opinions and practices upon him in other more personal areas, Mr. Darcy?"

"Of what are you speaking?" Darcy's voice was getting louder with each word.

Breathing deeply to control the steam rising inside of her, Elizabeth decided to set him on his tail. "You, sir, have used your authority, your position, to manipulate the lives of others. You look down from your superior height as if the rest of the world could never measure up. You are wanting an example? Fine! Why do we not return to the source of our disagreement at the ball. Mr. Wickham. In one fell swoop, one single choice you made to disregard your father's will, you robbed him of his hopes for a better future. Tell me, I pray you, in what manner do you find that an act of kindness? Rather, was it not the pinnacle of haughty egotism in deeming your opinions far more important than his?"

"Wickham!" The muscle at the side of Darcy's mouth bulged as he inhaled deeply. "How dare you bring him up when we were speaking of Bingley, two men so disparate as to be black to white."

In her ire she failed to regulate her voice.

"You are evading the very issue that ignited our argument last evening, which tells me you cannot adequately defend your conduct."

Before he could offer a defense, a key turned in the lock and the door was thrust open. Standing at the entrance was the third member of the crew they would meet that morning. He was approximately the same age as Mr. Darcy with hair bordering on white. His clothing was the image of the first sailor although of much finer quality. His countenance was that of a man in charge.

"I am Captain Lucien Bartholomew, master of the *Peregrine*. This means the two of you and everyone else are here at my mercy." His icy blue eyes went from Darcy to Elizabeth and back. "My ship. My rules. First and foremost is no fighting. The penalty, without care to your sex, is to let my cat out of the bag."

With each word, the fear creeping up Elizabeth's insides made her stomach churn. Confronted with absolute authority, she lowered her eyes to the deck at the man's feet as her mind absorbed each word with terror.

The captain continued, "As per my agreement with my client, I will transport you both to the Carolinas. However, know this ... he only needs you, Mr. Bingley. Any more noise like I just heard from these quarters and she will be swimming back to England after a sound thrashing. Do you have any questions?"

Chills shook her very foundation. "I ...," Elizabeth began when Mr. Darcy stopped her by clasping her hand in his own.

"We have nothing to say, Captain." Mr. Darcy tipped his head towards the man.

*What?* She had much to say! She had just been threatened with being thrown to the sharks hovering below. And what did the captain mean that of the two of them, it was she alone who was of no value? How dare Mr. Darcy speak for her! She was more than capable of speaking for herself. Fear and frustration all but overpowered her.

"You are a wise man, Mr. Bingley. Should the two of you comply over the next hour, I will send Hackett down with fresh water, extra blankets, and more to eat. Should you not obey, only one of you will be sleeping in the bunk tonight."

At that, the captain turned away from them to make his way back up to the deck. Jonah Hackett stuck his head inside the door.

"Ye best listen to the Cap'n. He don't lose his temper often, but when he does ... well, I'd rather rope and ride a hurricane than face 'im." At that, the lad stepped back and locked the door.

Silence followed their departure. Dead silence.

Elizabeth felt that to take in a breath was a possible violation of the captain's orders. Her insides were quivering at the man's threats.

Mr. Darcy dropped her hand, then slid back on the mattress to rest his back on the wall next to the porthole. Breathing in and out seemed to take every fragment of strength from him.

"Miss Elizabeth, his threat ... well, I could see where it could discompose you."

"You said he would ask for a ransom. He did not," she challenged, her fear unloosening her lips. "We were *not* kidnapped for money. In fact, the captain said I was not an intended victim. Why am I here? What will happen to me?"

"I do not know."

In truth, she wanted to appear unaffected. Nonetheless, the captain had not wavered once during his pronouncement. She gulped. "Additionally, why would I be afraid to meet his cat? Would he have a fierce tiger on board to devour recalcitrant passengers?"

"No, there is no tiger." Mr. Darcy rubbed his eyes with his fingers. "He refers to an instrument of punishment and torture used against crewmen and boys who steal, lie to a superior, or rebel. It is a whip of nine braided strands with knots tied down the length of each cord. Some vengeful masters weave iron balls and bone chips into the braids to do unimaginable damage to the guilty party's person. It is either referred to as a cat o' nine tails or the captain's daughter."

She shuddered. "I see."

"*Blast!* A ransom would be so much easier than this." He growled. "The Carolinas, of all places." Darcy scoffed. "His comments reminded me we are the Bingleys as far as he and the crew are concerned. Therefore, I ask you not to call me anything other than Charles, Bingley, or brother. I do not know if they are aware of Miss Bingley's first name, but I do not think we should take the chance. If we slip up, we can always claim Darcy is my middle name and Elizabeth is yours. As my "sister", I would not call you "Miss". Thus, from this moment on I shall speak to you as if you are my sister. Is this reasonable, do you think?"

"Yes, Charles." Grudgingly, she added, "And I thank you for asking."

"Sister, our condition is one of delicacy. If you would agree not to attack me about Wickham, I will say nothing about the conduct of your family. In this I believe we should agree to disagree, so we have the peace you offered earlier. Nevertheless, rather than tell you what I feel the two of us should do, how we should comport ourselves with one another and those outside these walls, I will instead endeavor to ask your opinion on the matter."

She peered at him closely for a fragment of mockery. She found none.

"Very well, Brother. I will behave if you will."

He settled his back into the corner.

After a lengthy silence to calm her body and clear her mind, she noted, "I know very little about the Carolinas, only what I have read in my father's journals from the last century when the thirteen Crown colonies declared their independence from England. The Carolinas are to the south and are reputed to be beautiful and of a much more temperate climate than places such as Boston and New York. Much of the indigo imported to England for clothing came from there."

"Hmm, yes. I know little more than that, as well, to be honest," he muttered. "Elizabeth ...,"

"Caroline," she reminded him.

He frowned, his brow furrowing. "I simply cannot call you by that name. It conjures up images of a petulant female with a sharp tongue and claws instead of fingers. The association of Caroline to you is something I cannot do."

She nodded. Referring to him by his jovial friend's name felt equally unnatural to her.

"As I was saying," he continued. "One of the things I do recall reading in the circulating papers is that some plantations in the Carolinas have refused to obey the law restricting the importation of slaves. It is a disgusting practice promulgated by intense greed. Bingley told me of a man, a distant cousin of his father, who refused partnership in the family business at an early age. Instead, he sold his portion to his brother and moved to the Carolinas after purchasing a large tract of land. I do not recall if I was ever told whether it was one of these plantations."

Elizabeth was intrigued. "Might not this be the reason the 'Bingleys' were kidnapped? Was there something underhanded about the agreement between the brothers where the one who left might feel he had the right to inherit rather than your friend?"

He started to rub his hand over his mouth but stopped. "I simply do not know. What we do know is that something requires Bingley's presence in the Americas, something to justify the use of force."

She nodded, her mind spinning. "Then why bring me along? Why did they not leave me behind once they had you?" Elizabeth knew her friends and family would have watched her walk away from Mr. Darcy. Blatant curiosity about the source of their disagreement on the ballroom floor would have had them following her without too many minutes passing. The hue and cry would have gone out rather quickly.

He stared at the wall opposite them rather than look at her.

"I do not know," he whispered.

"I wonder, sir," she bit her lip, vacillating at the wisdom of voicing her concerns aloud. "Are you certain you have a thorough knowledge of Mr. Bingley's business practices and character? For

Jane's sake, as well as ours, I do hope he is a man of honor rather than a scoundrel who has participated in underhanded activities, forcing someone to take drastic measures to achieve justice."

Resting his head against the wall, he closed his eyes.

"Before the events of this day I would have unequivocally supported a man I have claimed as one of my closest friends for the past four years. As of this moment, I simply do not know."

## 5

L ater, Jonah Hackett arrived with an armload of the promised items and a quick reminder that he was not to talk to them. Captain's orders!

Darcy, who appreciated his attempts at obedience, stood to remove the pile from the lad, forgetting the lowness of the ceiling. The blow dropped him back onto the bunk.

After a quick glance at Darcy, with not a hint of sympathy in her expression, Elizabeth gave her full attention to the boy.

"Master Hackett, would you mind if I were to ask another question where the answer would be a shake or nod of your head?" she inquired.

At the rapid bouncing of his head, she said, "You mentioned that you are pleased to work under Captain Bartholomew. Would you consider him to be an honorable man?"

The boy's head bobbed up and down.

"That is very good to hear. Is the *Peregrine* a battleship?"

Darcy wondered where she was going with her question. There had been no evidence of uniforms or the precision of the military in the bearing of any of the crew they had observed up to that point.

Hackett shook his head to the negative.

"A passenger ship, then?"

Again, his head went from left to right.

"A merchant's vessel?"

There was a slight hesitation this time before he shook his head 'no'.

Elizabeth put her finger to her chin. Tilting her head slightly to the side, she said, "I am afraid I have reached the limit of my knowledge of ocean-going ships, young sir. I cannot quite understand what sort of boat we are aboard, Mr. Hackett."

He stood to his full height; shoulders pressed back in pride. "Pardon me, Miss, but this be a ship. You see, ye can carry a boat on a ship, but ye can't carry a ship on a boat. The *Peregrine* be a privateer with a commissioned letter of marque signed by President James Madison his self. Cap'n Bartholomew ain't one ta skirt the laws like some others I knowed. He be a fair man."

"Are there many crew aboard? Do you have friends here?"

"We have nearly seventy on board, Miss Bingley. Me best friend is Quartermaster Boone. He's a good matey w' a savvy head who don't take no guff off o' nobody. T'was he who helped me sign me articles so's I could come ta work on the *Peregrine*."

"We are happy to hear this, Jonah Hackett. Now, one more question before you return to your duties. How soon will it be before you see your family again?"

Immediately, the boy's eyes dropped to the floor. He shuffled his bare feet against the boards before answering.

Elizabeth slid forward on the bunk until she could stand. Approaching the lad, she gently brushed the fringe of stringy hair from his brow.

Darcy longed to pull her back to safety. Although the lad was in his tender years, he had associated with ruffians, no doubt learning the violent tricks of their trade.

Before he could reach her, the ship's boy looked up.

Hackett's gaze at Elizabeth was a mesmerizing mixture of disquietude and admiration.

She softened her voice, empathy dripping from her tongue. "Do not worry yourself to answer, Jonah Hackett. Instead, I will ask you where on this good earth you were born and raised before you began your sailing career?"

"I be pretty sure I was born in me ma's bed somewheres close ta Charleston cause that be where the Cap'n found me lookin' fer work."

"Master Hackett!" Elizabeth exclaimed. "You must have been only seven or eight years old at the time, far too young to be searching for work."

The boy again stood to his full height.

"I don't know much, Miss, but I know how ta work hard an I'm pleased to do so for the Cap'n." He gave a cursory glance around their quarters. "Miss Bingley, the Cap'n 'requests the honor of your presence' at four bells on the dog watch. It be his dinner time. Ye can eat with 'im." He bowed.

"No!" Darcy exclaimed, scampering forward to sit on the edge of the bunk. Fearful dread overpowered him at the damage a rogue captain and crew could do to an unprotected female. "Miss Elizabeth will ... my sister will remain under my protection as long as we are on board this ship."

Hackett scuffed his feet before addressing him.

"Mr. Bingley, ye have nothin' ta fear. I've been charged by the cap'n to care for the lady. I'll protect her should the need arise." His skinny chest puffed with confidence.

Elizabeth curtsied as Darcy sat there dumbfounded. A boy of ten against a crew of seventy grown men. He had to give the lad credit for his brashness.

Her eyes sparked as she said, "Young man, I thank you for your interest in my care as I also thank the captain for making sure I have few worries while I am here. Before the captain mentioned letting a cat out of the bag. My brother explained its meaning. Now, you say there is a dog watch. Since there are no apparent animals on board, I have no idea of what you are referencing."

After glancing at Darcy to see if he was going to provide the information, pure delight covered Hackett's face at being able to share his expertise.

"Each day be broke into six pieces o' four hours each. Each time the officer o' the deck turns the hourglass, which be every thirty minutes, the bell is rung. They ring that bell eight times each watch. The count starts at thirty minutes after midnight with the middle watch. After comes the morning, forenoon, afternoon, dog, then first watches that brings us back ta midnight. Each and every single day the cap'n shoots the sun an' the horizon fer noon with 'is sextant so a man knows when ta work an' when ta rest. Cap'n sits down to eat at the same time every day when at sea."

"Then, six o'clock would be four bells on the dog watch if I have calculated correctly."

Hackett's pride in Elizabeth's acuity swelled the lad's chest and put pink in his tanned cheeks.

"You be a right smart lady, Miss Bingley. I will come to get ya a few minutes before the ringin' o' the bell." Bowing, he excused himself, then locked the door firmly behind him.

"I do not like this," Darcy muttered, before launching himself at the door. His fierce pounding brought a rapid response.

The ship's boy unlocked the door.

"Hackett, I see you have brought clothing. Might I join you outside so my sister can dress in private?"

Without hesitation, the lad moved back, allowing Darcy to step through the doorway. Blessed relief at being able to straighten his back and neck almost brought him to tears.

"I do hope she be quick about it, sir. I have me duties to see to. Cap'n Bartholomew is a fair master, but he expects each man ta see ta his assigned task."

"Yes, well, while I have a moment of your time without my sister or any of the crew around, I wonder, have you attended school?"

"What makes ye think I already don't know how ta cipher and add?" The sunlight caught the boy's eye as he tipped his head back.

"Do you?"

The lad shrugged. "I do alright. I be pretty good with me numbers. You a teacher? I ain't goin' back to Charleston to no schoolroom. I'm a workin' man now."

Darcy's inclination was to chuckle, but he would do nothing to damage the lad's pride, something Darcy understood all too well.

"I am a teacher of sorts," Darcy admitted. "When my sister was little, I would help her with her letters and numbers until they were clear in her mind. She seemed to learn easier from me than from her governess."

"Ye musta been little yerself for yer sister tisn't much younger than you be, right? Did your pa teach ye?"

Darcy realized his mistake. Georgiana was twelve years his junior. Elizabeth was only six or seven at the most.

"My father began teaching me when I was still in the nursery."

"I don't know me pa."

"I am deeply sorry to hear this, Jonah Hackett. Do you have any sisters?"

"Nope! No girls in our house!" He poked his thumb at his chest. "Me an me ma were a team. Then she got sick an then I needed to find work to get medicine fer her. Cap'n Bartholomew advanced me wages but by the time I got back to our room, she was ..."

Darcy ruffled his hair like Elizabeth had done.

"I understand." Kneeling, he looked the boy in the eye. "I, too, lost my good mother when I was young. It was a blow from which I believe I will never recover."

Hackett nodded, his right foot shuffling on the deck.

"Master Hackett, I will offer you a gentleman's agreement. If you will be diligent in caring for my sister, I will gratefully offer my services to improve your education while we are at sea."

The boy took the time to consider his offer before extending his hand.

Darcy gripped his slim fingers then asked, "Might there be a slate on board or some paper we might use? If there was a book of any sort, that too would be helpful."

"I will see what I can do." He looked back to the door. "You need ta go back inside, sir." Without knocking, he flung the door open, startling Elizabeth.

Elizabeth had been right. They needed a friend and Darcy desperately needed something to take his mind off his worries and the attraction of his enforced cabin mate.

He turned his back as, at first glance, Elizabeth appeared not quite ready to receive visitors. She was so lovely, he ... sighed. His fear for her was a living thing, threatening to strangle every morsel of air from his lungs.

They knew nothing of Captain Bartholomew. What appeared as honor to a seasoned lad of ten summers could be quite the opposite of reality when presented with an unprotected female of Elizabeth's caliber.

"Sir, ye need ta go back inside." Hackett insisted.

Keeping his eyes averted, Darcy dipped his head, mindful of the lumps that had already formed on his skull. He entered the quarters to seat himself with his face to the wall. He would give her as much privacy as possible.

Her deep sigh sent chills down his spine. Unable to restrain himself, he glanced back at her. What he found left him speech-less. In fact, he might have drooled—slightly.

She was dressed in a simple gown a housemaid might wear. The dull green of the skirt and the cream blouse served to enhance her loveliness. The hem barely covered her ankles, the waistband was loose around her middle, and the bodice strained to ... *oh good heavens!* The seams were stretched taut across her ... he gulped. Obviously, the garment was intended for a female far less blessed than Elizabeth.

When she pulled the last pin from her hair he was captivated. Heavy strands dropped to her waist. Tendrils bounced and curled as they finally came to rest upon the curve of her hip. The first pull of the brush through those silky strands had him metaphorically swallowing his tongue.

How had he ever thought her too plain in appearance to tempt him? He was a fool! A flaming idiot! A bonehead, at the least.

Quickly, she braided her hair then wound it into some sort of knot at the back of her head, pinning it into place. Her economy of movement told him more than words that she cared for her own grooming. In a household of six females, there must not have been enough helping hands to go around.

Would Caroline Bingley ever fashion her own hair? Darcy could not imagine she would. Rather, she would sit in state while her lady's maid tucked and prodded her tresses into place.

Not since his sister was little had he watched a female ready herself for departure from her rooms. When Georgiana was in her fourth year, she balked each time her maid attempted to brush her hair. She would come running to find him when he was home from Eton so he would fix the situation. At the time, he had been at the important age of sixteen where the tears of a little girl should not have impacted him like they had. Nonetheless, with no mother to oversee her grooming, Darcy had patiently combed her golden hair and plaited it just as Elizabeth had done. By the time he had moved to university, his sister had convinced her governess to perform the task. Mrs. Morton had been kind, firm, and skilled with a brush.

"Is something wrong?" Elizabeth smoothed the coarse fabric down her sides.

"No ... nothing is wrong." Darcy did not mean to be evasive. But how did you admit to a lady you never would have offered for under normal circumstances that you had been blatantly guilty of gawking at her?

"I see." She sat primly on the edge of the bunk. "Brother, they have brought you clothing as well."

"I am shocked you would choose to appear before the captain in anything less than your ball gown." Had that carping tone of a fishwife come out of his mouth?

"Mr. Bingley," she snapped. "Eventually we will reach our port of call where I will need to present myself at my best. I will ask the captain this evening for a needle and thread to repair my gown so I will not appear threadbare and tattered. I am guessing that our distant Bingley cousin, if indeed he is the client, has not seen us for a long while, if ever. I would not want his first impression to be regretful of his relatives."

She was completely in the right. Needing to rethink his reactions to her, he changed tactics.

"Are you anxious?" he asked, his hands rubbing down his thighs.

She looked him directly in the eye. "I am."

Nodding, he said, "I would be as well."

"Sir, rather than imagine the worst of the situation, I chose to believe Master Hackett, that Captain Bartholomew is a fair man. Therefore, my goal is to obtain as much information about our situation as possible."

"Your plan is sound." Unlike her, his inclination was not to consider her invitation to dine as an opportunity. Nevertheless, he was in a circumstance for the first time in his adult life where he had absolutely no power. Thus, he needed to consider all available options.

"For yourself," he inquired, "what is it you most wish to know?"

She hesitated before answering. "I long to know the estimated length of the trip. I want to know, since I was not the intended target of the kidnapping, what does the captain see as my future? These matters fill my mind, sir."

He nodded.

Elizabeth continued, "I also am curious about this client Captain Bartholomew mentioned. Who stands to gain from Mr. Bingley's presence? Who from the Carolinas even knows him? If it is his distant cousin, why would he want to do Mr. Bingley harm? Do you wonder the same?"

"I do, indeed." Darcy carefully ran his hand over his battered jaw. "In addition, I want to know if my valuables will be returned to me. If they are, I will have a means of identification as the Darcy seal on my signet ring coupled with my signature is well-known in the business world of the Americas. I want to know if there is anyone on this vessel who is truly trustworthy. Also, I am concerned about the terms to be enacted by the man who wanted Charles in the Carolinas. His motive cannot be anything other than nefarious or he would have extended a polite invitation to Bingley and waited for a response."

"I agree." She gnawed at her thumbnail. "Mr. Darcy, I mean, Brother ... would there be a request you would like me to make on your behalf should the opportunity avail itself? I feel it would be correct to assume that some time on the above decks would be welcome so you can stand erect rather than sit?"

He nodded. "Yes. It would be most welcome."

He deeply appreciated her kind consideration of his needs. Perhaps, he could return the favor.

After much consideration, he said, "Elizabeth, I have been thinking of ways you can protect yourself if the captain should overstep the bounds of a gentleman." He stood as best as he was able. "Would you face me, please?"

She did not hesitate to stand.

"Very good." He reached for her hand. "Make a fist like you were going to strike me."

"Strike you? I could not!" Despite her words, her fingers curled into her palm.

"No, not like that." He pulled her thumb from underneath her fingers, placing it correctly. "You could cause more injury to your-self than to another if you followed through with a quick swing. You could break your thumb."

"Like this?" She waved both of her fists at him, instinctively stepping into a boxer's stance.

"Well done." He grinned. "Now, I need you to think. Where on a man's body are we most vulnerable?"

She looked him up and down. "Where there are no bones, I would suspect."

"Exactly. To strike a man in the chest or the knee is rarely effective. Therefore, you need to aim for his nose, his eyes, his throat, or his groin so your blows have the greatest impact."

"Sir! I could never!" Elizabeth's hands dropped to her sides, her fingers wiggling to loosen them from her position of defense.

"No, Elizabeth. You must learn this for your protection. Both my cousin Richard and I taught Georgiana after an ordeal she went through this summer. She was left susceptible because we unwisely believed we needed to protect her sensibilities. Had she known how to adequately defend herself, she might not have felt vulnerable." Darcy put his fists up like she had done. "Pray, bear with me as I demonstrate how best to move."

Instead of swinging at Elizabeth, he grabbed her, pulling her to his chest as close as he was able in the low-ceilinged room. *Good*

*Lord!* She smelled far better than Richard. The way she felt in his arms? He could barely ... wait, what were they doing?

She squealed. Then, she squirmed, shooting fireworks from his toes to the tips of his hair.

*This had been a poor idea.* Darcy gulped, dangerously close to lowering his mouth to taste ...

She pinched him—hard, recalling him to his senses. Blast his weak flesh when it came to this woman!

Inhaling deeply, he slowly exhaled, all the while enjoying the feel of her against him. 'Self-defense! Self-defense! Self-defense', he chanted to himself. To her, he said, "Elizabeth, recall where I am most vulnerable. If your hands are not free, use your forehead or your elbows. Use the heel of your foot on the arch of mine. Your knee is your best weapon against a man's most sensitive parts."

She was a woman of action. He jumped back in time to protect his future children and his chin. She followed with a quick jab of her fist that smacked him in the temple. Before he could recover, she used the heel of her foot to crash into the top of his.

"Stop!" His voice rose three octaves. He had been battered enough. Nonetheless, he was exceedingly proud of her, and told her so.

"Well done, Elizabeth." He bowed, as much for comfort as for manners. "You have, as I have learned you always do, exceeded my highest expectations."

She chuckled as she waved her fist at him. "A lady does need to hone her accomplishments, does she not?" Then, she sobered, "In all seriousness, I will admit that I was far more defenseless until I remembered your advice." Her cheeks glowed red.

"I am happy to be of service."

Opposite of his words, he was miserable. Having her in his arms, despite her struggling for escape, was a delight. Having to let her go alone to the captain was a torture he feared he would suffer from for the rest of their journey, or a lifetime.

## 6

E lizabeth pulled the roughly woven shawl around her
shoulders. The chill from the weather was nothing
compared to her nerves. She had no idea what to expect.
Jonah was a ball of energy with no fear of what was to come.
Instead, he seemed rather joyous that she would be spending time
with his beloved captain.

When she had greeted him as "Master Hackett," he had shyly
asked her to call him by his first name. He told her nobody had
done so since his mother.

Taking the boy's hand in her own, she admitted, "I am frightfully nervous, Jonah. Pray realize that it is not that I do not believe
your opinion of your leader. It is only that this situation is strange
to me. I am unaware of the ship's protocol. Do I curtsey as I would
to a gentleman? Do I salute as a soldier does to his colonel? Do I
do nothing like I do to my father?"

"Why, Miss Bingley, he tis a wild sea monster sportin' fangs an'
a long sword ta carve ye in two fer his supper." His angelic smile
belied his mischievous intent.

"You imp!" Elizabeth pulled him towards her until her hip

bumped him off balance. He giggled like one of her younger sisters. Her heart squeezed at the thought. She missed Jane, Mary, Kitty, and even spoiled Lydia, dreadfully. What must they be suffering at her disappearance? How long would it be before she would see them again? What would her circumstances be when she did?

The weight of all that was riding upon the information she might be able to solicit from the captain settled upon her shoulders. Glancing at the boy next to her, she had to believe that he was honest in his appraisal of her situation.

His mood went from jovial to serious prior to his rapping on the wooden door. At the captain's "Enter", Jonah stepped aside, waiting for Elizabeth to walk into the room before he followed.

"Miss Bingley, how good of you to join me." The captain had changed to the uniform of an American naval officer, the dark blue of his coat covering the fine white linen shirt, vest, and cravat. The colors were the perfect foil for his features. Rarely had she been in the company of such a stunning figure of authority. His smile showed evenly placed teeth not turned yellow like some of her acquaintance. His jaw was squared, his nose perfectly straight, and the hair pulled back into a queue revealed no hint of early baldness.

Despite his good looks, what sort of man was he? Unbidden, her mind flashed to Mr. George Wickham, the gentleman whose sufferings had instigated the argument with Darcy while on the dance floor. He, too, was a pleasure to gaze upon. Unlike the captain, Mr. Darcy and Mr. Wickham had dark hair and eyes.

Shaking off the thought, she gave her full attention to the officer in front of her.

"I thank you, Captain." She glanced around the room. To her right was an alcove filled with a large bed, a shelf of books, and a washstand. To her left was a cabinet with long, narrow drawers. At the top was an opened map with odd wooden and metal tools placed randomly on its surface. In front of her was a small table surrounded by four chairs. The table was set for two. At least she was not completely alone. She had Jonah to ...

"If I may be excused, Cap'n?" Jonah asked before quickly vacating the room, closing the door firmly behind him.

The blood flowing through her veins started pumping faster. "Are we to dine alone? Are there no other officers onboard this vessel with whom you routinely break your fast?"

She could not tell if his response was a smile or a smirk. Either way, she was as unsettled as she had ever been.

FOR THE FIRST time since he woke, Darcy's mind functioned properly. The benefits of his temporary stint in the fresh air outside the cabin and not having Elizabeth near had cleared his thoughts until a myriad of details poured into his skull. With little room to pace, he sat on the bunk with his feet pressed against the opposite wall. To the swaying of the ship he flexed his calf muscles, keeping himself upright. He extended his fingers, then pressed them into his palms.

If they kept their true identity hidden from the ship's captain and crew, he would be protected, but Elizabeth would be vulnerable. If he explained that they were not the Bingleys, would they be believed? How would the captain and crew respond? Would they both be pitched overboard to come to their end in the frigid cold of the Channel? He knew from experience that the distance from London to the open ocean could take days. Once they reached the waters of the Atlantic, the ocean would be even more deadly.

His heart pounded as he considered every scenario that came to his mind. Within moments, he knew exactly what to do.

Banging on the door, he yelled for Jonah Hackett.

"Miss Bingley, your dowry is how much?"

Elizabeth knew she was in trouble as soon as the words left Captain Bartholomew's mouth.

"May I ask to what this question tends?" Her response was a mere ruse to buy herself time. Elizabeth and every other unattached female in Meryton knew the amount of her dowry. Miss Bingley had often boasted of her twenty thousand, knowing Elizabeth and her sisters would receive a meager fifty pounds annually as their portion.

What was his purpose? How should she reply?

The captain stepped closer to her, his hand raising to lift her chin. Looking Elizabeth directly in her eyes, he answered, "At this point, your future is very uncertain, Miss Bingley. As I told you before, my client had not included you in his negotiations. Should he not offer hospitality, you, my dear, will be left entirely on your own. On the other hand, I might be induced into the holy state of matrimony should you come with enough cash to make it worth the loss of my freedom. Not only would it protect your virtue and your future to be the captain's wife, but our union would make the Atlantic crossing much more ... ah, pleasurable for us both."

"I ...," she swallowed, then closed her eyes and inhaled. Remembering her lesson from Mr. Darcy, her courage rose. "Unhand me now!" Her glare would have melted ice. Stepping back, she slapped his hand away from her. Should she hit him with her fist as she had done Mr. Darcy, or should she poke him in the eyes? Her hands itched as her fingers flexed then fisted.

Before the captain could respond, the door to his quarters slammed open. Into the room rushed an enraged Fitzwilliam Darcy.

"You do not touch her!"

Elizabeth was both relieved at his entry and surprisingly upset.

Here was her first opportunity to practice what she had been taught, and she was being rescued by her instructor instead.

Darcy's approach was swift and aggressive. Placing himself in the narrow gap between Elizabeth and Captain Bartholomew, he hissed, "We are not the Bingleys. I am Fitzwilliam George Darcy, master of Pemberley in Derbyshire. My mother was the daughter of the Earl of Matlock, and I am nephew to the Archbishop. My cousin is a decorated colonel in His Majesty's army who earned his rank on the battlefield. Should anything befall myself or my sister at the hands of you or your crew, he will hunt you down and see you hang, no matter where you try to hide."

Captain Bartholomew glanced at Elizabeth before taking a step back to stand by the table.

"What? How is this possible?" His brow rose. Turning away from both of them, the captain paced the floor. "Tell me, Is she truly your sister?"

Darcy ignored the question. Instead, he turned to her to ask if she was well.

"Well enough," she whispered.

Darcy took her hand in his, gently squeezing her fingers.

"Captain, I ask you to check the signet ring you stole from me. There you will find a "D" for Darcy along with a quill and a sword, the Darcy coat of arms."

The captain threw his hands into the air. "I am not a poacher to set his sight upon another man's goods. I certainly did not steal anything from you, Mr. Bingley or Mr. Darcy, whomever you are. You are as you were delivered to me."

"Then who?" Darcy growled.

The captain shrugged. "Does it matter now? Whoever was hired by my client apparently decided to supplement their fee. I suspect your ring is in some London pawn shop with the money already spent." Pulling a chair out from the table, Captain Bartholomew gestured for them to be seated.

Elizabeth hesitated. Darcy did as well. The captain had gone from aggressor to passive. She did not trust him at all. However, recalling his earlier threats about the penalty for disobedience, she moved to the table.

Darcy assisted her to be seated then dropped into the closest chair, his forehead in his palms. "Then neither my sister or I have any means of identifying ourselves to you or to your client."

What? This was in every way dreadful.

"Hm ... yes, I can see your problem." With an economy of movement, he returned to the stand next to his bed and came back with a bottle and three cups. Elizabeth rejected his offer when he lifted the bottle to her. She needed a clear head and so did her 'brother.'

Pouring two fingers into two mugs, he sipped while Darcy only stared at the container.

Darcy murmured, "I have no shoes, no money, or nothing to sell. Blast! What a mess."

Captain Bartholomew offered, "Are you certain you are not Mr. Bingley? It is unimportant to me, but it will be to my client. You see, I was paid in advance to transport one passenger to the Carolinas. The men he hired were to deliver you to the *Peregrine* before slack water. This, they did, after telling Boone that you drank too much and had passed out on the way. As I was instructed, I had my quartermaster hand over the purse to them, and you were brought aboard. It was only later I discovered there were two bodies inside the cabin. Imbeciles!"

"Could we not turn back?" Darcy pleaded.

"We cannot." The captain swallowed the brandy in one gulp. "We are soon to enter the southbound Canary Current, which should get us quickly past the coast of France and Spain. Unless we are met by the heavy guns of Napoleon, we will be two weeks until the Equatorial Current carries us to the Gulf Stream. If the weather holds and we meet no enemies, we could be in Charleston Harbor in a month."

Darcy's head shot up. "Could we not venture to Boston or New York? I have business contacts there who could easily verify my identity. I would gladly pay double what your client is paying you."

"Ha! I imagine you would." The captain slid his cup away from him. "This time of year, the weather fluctuations along the northern Atlantic Drift are dramatic. Not only would we be fighting the current, the wind, and the cold, we would be pushing against the clock to get you delivered on time should we adjust our headings due west. No, it cannot be done."

Darcy nodded slowly, his shoulders dropping slightly. "Then our die is cast."

"Julius Caesar."

Elizabeth looked at the captain with a start, for she had thought the words as the captain had said them. She could not keep from asking, "You have read Suetonius?"

"I might ask you the same, Miss Bingley, or is it Darcy?"

Darcy reached over to grip her hand tightly as a signal to follow his lead. "My sister has been," he cleared his throat, "Mrs. Stephen Bennet of Longbourn in Hertfordshire but a few months."

"I sense your hesitation," the captain noted. "You disapprove."

"He is not the man I had hoped my sister would wed."

Mr. Darcy's story was quite inventive—and effective. It would instantly lessen her appeal to the captain or any other man on the ship.

Now that the immediate danger diminished some, Elizabeth studied the two men. Captain Bartholomew leaned back in his chair; one foot crossed over the other. While his pose was relaxed, his eyes shot between her and Darcy. On the other hand, tension poured off her new brother.

At a noise from the doorway, the captain barked a command. "Not now, Hackett. Close it and get back to work."

Elizabeth caught the boy's eyes before he obeyed his master. There was a hint of sadness before a saucy wink made her smile. *What a lad!*

Boldly, Elizabeth spoke. "Sir, young Master Hackett claims you to be a fair man. My brother ..." she came to an abrupt stop when the captain slammed his hand on the hard surface of the table.

"Why?" he demanded. "Why would you allow me to continue in ignorance? Why did you not tell me immediately that you were not the Bingleys?"

Darcy's answer was simple. "We do not know you, Captain. We were drugged, kidnapped, and robbed. I was pummeled while who knows what offenses were committed against my dear sister. Jonah Hackett may admire you, but I have witnessed nothing up to this point to earn my respect."

The captain nodded. "Kidnapped! Of all the foolish things for Silas Bingley to do. That he has brought this black stain upon my ship is unconscionable."

"Did you think you followed the law when a crime resulted in our being aboard? And what of my sister? How did you not realize by her presence that our capture was nefarious? I cannot believe you gullible enough to think you did no wrong." Darcy insisted. "I will pay you for your time or any late fees you accumulate should you return us to London now."

"It is not that simple, Mr. Darcy. I have a contract to deliver a healthy, wealthy gentleman to Charleston, one I will not break. I will admit to some surprise that there was not one person but two. The tale I was told by the men who brought you to the wharf was that you were with a group of friends at your club in town. I take it that you were not in London then?"

"No, we were in Hertfordshire." Darcy glanced at her. "Charles Bingley is a long-time friend who was hosting a gathering in celebration of leasing his first property. As well, he was and is desirous of attaching himself to Miss Jane Bennet, the eldest sister of my brother-in-law."

"*Blast*! I should have known the men were up to no good. Never hire a stranger to do a trusted man's job!" The captain shook his head, then continued, "I cannot know what Silas Bingley has on his mind. The arrangements for the men to bring you to my ship were made by him through an agent I was to give a letter to upon reaching port. Also included was a packet of two missives, both addressed to Mr. Charles Bingley. My assumption was that they were an invitation and an explanation of why he was needed quickly in the Americas. Bingley gave me the name of the agent. I took care of the task personally. That it was such an epic failure reflects poorly upon me." He slammed his fist on the table. "I will not have it!" He brooded. "At least tell me this, is the real Miss Bingley well-dowered and unwed?"

Elizabeth chuckled. "She most certainly is. Despite using every ploy imaginable to gain my brother's attention, she with her lovely appearance, fashionable wardrobe, sharp tongue, and twenty thousand are available. Should you choose to turn this vessel and return to London, I guarantee you that the two of us would be pleased to provide an immediate introduction."

When the captain smiled at her comment, she was relieved to note no lascivious gleam in his eye.

"I will need to hope Miss Bingley is still available in several months' when next I am in London, since I cannot and will not reverse our course." He slid Darcy's cup closer. "Drink up, my man. You will, of course, join us for a meal?"

Darcy grumbled. "For a certainty."

## 7

Darcy was extraordinarily proud of Elizabeth's quickness and willingness to support his blatant falsehood. Any sort of disguise was his abhorrence. Yet, under the circumstances, the lie that she was his married sister was his best means of protecting her. She was as demure in front of this stranger as a lady should be. He was grateful she used her smiles judiciously. She kept silent, listening, and absorbing the conversation.

How unlike the ladies of the *ton*. They flirted and gossiped behind their fans like silly children, begging for attention. Elizabeth's quiet dignity under stress elevated her above any female he knew, definitely above Miss Caroline Bingley. Darcy admitted, if only to himself, that his mother would have approved of Miss Elizabeth Bennet as a family friend, the highest compliment of which he could conceive.

As soon as Darcy and Elizabeth successfully met the challenge of keeping their plate, cup, and utensils from sliding across the table with the rocking of the ship, the captain cleared his throat.

"You say you do not know me, and this is true. First and foremost, I am a businessman—an honest businessman. I learned from my father and grandfather before me that my word is my greatest asset. I try to surround myself with trustworthy men. However, I know that what drives a man to the sea is often a series of tragedies or errors that cannot be tolerated in landed society. Of this, I care nothing. A person's value as a crew member is his quick obedience and loyalty until his wages are paid. Once the crew steps foot off my ship, I care naught for what they do. Nor do I concern myself with what brought them to me in the first place. I will not tolerate laziness or slackness in their work as I do not tolerate it in mine. I have a healthy respect for the law of whichever sovereignty I am in. I enjoy the company of men and women from every race or nation. Therefore, I abhor the slave trade or anyone who promotes such a heinous practice."

"Yet you aided and abetted a kidnapping, which is punishable by hanging," Darcy challenged. "As master of Pemberley, I have hundreds of people in my employ. Anything done by them on my property is my responsibility. Like you, I care not what they do on their own time or away from my property. Nevertheless, once I become aware of wrongdoing or an injustice, I act quickly to rectify the matter, seeing that the guilty are punished, as well as reparations made to the innocent."

"As I will as soon as we arrive in Charleston harbor." The captain looked him over. "I have valuable commodities below for which I will receive double if they are delivered before the twenty-fourth of December. In a private agreement with the wives of my usual customers, myself and my crew will receive bonuses that will fill our coffers, but only if we tie up at the docks no later than noon on that date. Each man aboard agreed to go without hot meals until we reach Charleston harbor. Thus, after expenses, the profit will be even greater for each man. I cannot nor will not go back on my word to those women. They are the ones who demand the goods from their husbands. They are the ones we will please, not you."

Darcy's mind spun with the implications. There would be no turning back. Any attempt could bring mutiny, which would cause more harm to Elizabeth and himself.

Elizabeth raised her eyes, then said, "My father taught that honesty and the treatment of others in a fair manner is the mark of a decent person. Pray, might I ask, sir, this client of yours does not have slaves on his property, does he?"

"Not that I know of," the captain shrugged. "With that said, there are ... gentlemen, as they call themselves, who cautiously hide who and what they are. This was my first time doing business with Mr. Silas Bingley. My initial impression was that he appeared an agreeable sort. His money was good. Our arrangement was that I would pick up a passenger in London to be transported to his plantation in the Carolinas. As an incentive for a timely return, I carried several tons of the finest cotton and dye produced in the Americas, which quickly sold for exorbitant fees in England. Although the bulk of the profit belongs to Mr. Bingley, the *Peregrine's* share was substantial. The transaction appeared straightforward. As I already mentioned, I was not aware until we were already at sea that one of you was female."

"Then, the clothing I am wearing was not brought aboard for my use?" Elizabeth asked.

"No, not at all. I have a small trunk with practical clothing items for the few passengers I carry."

"I noted you provided clothing for my brother. Fine fabrics appropriate for a ballroom will not last a month at sea and beyond. Therefore, I thank you."

Darcy's heart warmed with her care. If he did not know differently, even he would have believed she was a relative by birth.

The captain looked Darcy up and down. "It will not be what you are used to, but you are welcome to the pile. There are needles and thread if you have the skill to make adjustments. There might even be a pair of boots that fit, or not."

Darcy nodded appreciatively. "The man who first opened our door this morning had some polish amidst his sailor slang. Is he one whose background you choose to ignore?"

"Ah, you refer to Augustus Gerald Hollingsworth the third, my quartermaster, whom we respectfully address as Boone." The captain straightened in his chair. "I am aware of his background, and so might you be if you know New York society. However, speak to him of his past or call him by anything other than Boone at your peril."

"I see." Darcy attended the comment with all seriousness.

"I hope you do, for he beat the last man who dared call attention to his family to within an inch of his life. The only thing that stopped the thrashing was Boone's becoming aware of the presence of Hackett. There is no one onboard who protects my ship's boy with more fierceness than Boone. Be warned and keep away from him. The journey will be much more pleasant if you do."

"Duly noted." Darcy said.

For an hour, the captain regaled them with one adventure after another in various ports of call. The life of a sailor sounded exciting, but Darcy knew that what the man did not address were the lonely weeks and months away from society other than a motley crew, a constant shortage of rations, and perpetual boredom.

After a cold dinner of meat, cheese, and sliced fruit, the conversation turned out to be unexpectedly pleasant. The captain allowed Darcy and Elizabeth a few moments above deck. Walking was perilous as the ship tilted forward and back, occasionally lunging from side to side with the movement of the sea. Dusk had fallen.

The night was unusually clear for a late November evening. The breeze that flapped the sails was icy. Darcy could not keep himself from looking longingly towards where the distant British shoreline would be. Glancing across the deck to the other side, none of the lights on the coastal ports of France were visible. They were still in the channel.

Within a few days they would taste the salt spray of the open ocean. Straining his eyes to see what might be his final glimpse of England for a long while, a flicker of hope rose in his chest.

"Can you swim?" he whispered into Elizabeth's ear.

She nodded, quickening his breath.

He had no shoes to weigh him down. It would take mere seconds to strip off his coat. Anything of value he had carried in his pockets or on his person at the ball were gone. Vaulting the railing would be an easy task compared to the many high fences at Pemberley he had leapt over.

Darcy stared at the shore, mentally calculating the distance over the water and the length of time it would take to reach safety.

The times he had been on a ship with his father allowed him to learn something of the water. "From the speed we are traveling, I would guess we have an ebb tide. The current of this arm of the Atlantic is fast."

"And freezing," she added.

That one fact brought his hope for a bid for freedom to a halt. They would never make it.

Disappointment enveloped him like the frigid water would have done had he followed through. As much as he wanted the two of them back on British soil, he would never endanger her life if it was within his power.

"Brother, I will admit for your ears alone that deep water scares me. I have read enough of father's books to know of whales, sharks, and eels that lurk below. I simply cannot believe the Channel would be kind to the two of us if we were without the protection of the fine crew aboard the *Peregrine*."

Her message was clear. She, too, felt the danger was not worth the risk.

Elizabeth looked to the heavens. "The moon is waxing gibbous. I will guess two more days until it is full."

A gruff voice startled Darcy from behind. The unknown sailor said, "Three, ma'am. It'll be shining so bright ye can see yerself in ta drink should ye peer overboard. That is 'less the clouds cover it with theys silver shrouds."

With the celestial light hovering above the horizon and him in their shadows, the man was cloaked in darkness. Elizabeth dipped her knee. "I stand corrected, sir. I thank you."

"Welcome, ma'am."

The unknown sailor disappeared as stealthily as he had arrived. Darcy shivered. "I had assumed that after being crept up upon at Bingley's ball, my senses would be heightened to having someone sneak up behind us."

"In truth, I was also unaware of his presence," Elizabeth admitted.

A gust blew salted air into their faces as the bow slipped down to the wave below. She did not shy away from the assault. Instead, Elizabeth lifted her face to the wind. In Darcy's mind, the action defined her character. She was bold enough to face her challenges head-on, fierce enough to believe herself equal to the force of the wind, and insightful enough to find delight in something fully out of her control.

He leaned against the railing. "You have studied astronomy then?"

"Shall we play 'Do you remember?' We have not done thus in years." Elizabeth's voice rose, the stiff breeze carrying her words far and wide. "Surely, you are not so old that you have forgotten my favorite childhood game?"

The lilt in her voice delighted him. At the same time, he wondered what she was about.

"I will begin. Pray, do keep up, Brother." She tapped her chin with her finger. "Let us see, you asked if I studied astronomy. I will have you know that while you were away at school, I read many of our father's books from the library. As you are aware, he loved climbing to the highest point on the estate with his telescope in hopes of identifying the constellations and planets. When you were gone, he would have me join him. I loved those times with him alone with a sky full of wonder. On occasion, he would leave the telescope at home. Instead, he carried one blanket to lie upon and one for me to snuggle into. We would spend hours at Oakham Mount watching the movements of the heavens. I cherished those memories."

Her clever weaving of what was true and false, making her story cohesive, was brilliant. Both of their fathers were educated men. Both had extensive libraries. Apparently, both loved the stars. However, Oakham Mount was at Longbourn, not Pemberley. Her father was still alive, undoubtedly frantically searching in hopes of finding his favorite child. Darcy's father had been in the grave for five years.

He chose to play along. "Father did the same with me before I left for Eton. You were too little to tag along and too young to be that far from your nurse."

"Bah!" she harrumphed. "That is solely your justification for not including a curious girl on your excursions with Father."

This odd sort of sharing was a delight to Darcy.

A rogue wave sent an icy spray of water over the bow, sending the two of them scampering for the lower deck. Jonah Hackett appeared lugging a wooden box, a lantern, and a wooden beam as Darcy reached to open the door.

"Cap'n says ye can come an' go as ye please. A bar can be dropped ta lock ta door when Miss Bingley ... no, Mrs. Bennet be inside alone."

"I thank you, Master Hackett." Darcy bowed, then looked to the sky for a final glimpse before the torture that awaited him in the small room.

"Might I have a moment, Jonah?" Elizabeth asked. "My brother will need privacy to change."

On the surface, Darcy had no concerns about Jonah Hackett. The lad appeared to have attached himself to Elizabeth like a chick to a hen, a comparison Darcy inherently knew Elizabeth would not appreciate. Nevertheless, the rest of the crew were roaming the decks. They had already proven their stealth.

Grabbing the homespun shirt and pants that had been earlier left on their bunk, he quickly changed. Although the fabric was coarser than his formal garments, the cloth was thick and warmer than the fine linen of his shirt. Hanging his coat, shirt, cravat, waistcoat, and trousers on a peg next to where Elizabeth's ball gown was draped, Darcy considered the other ways they would be side by side for the next several months.

A tap on the door interrupted his thoughts.

"Brother, are you ready for me to come inside?"

Darcy opened the door to Elizabeth hugging young Hackett to her. The boy wrapped his skinny arms so tightly around her that her eyes popped open wide.

"Have a restful night, Jonah." She squeezed the boy's hand once he stepped away from her. "I hope to have my first lesson in the morning."

"Aye, aye, Mrs. B." With a snappy salute, the lad bounded up the stairs to the deck above.

Elizabeth attempted the same gesture with far less success.

"Mrs. B?" he could not keep from asking.

"Aye, aye, Brother!" Stepping into the room, she sat on the far corner of the bunk. "He is a good boy."

"I hope so," Darcy mused aloud. "What are these lessons you start tomorrow?"

"Brother!" she exclaimed.

He glanced around the room, looking to see what had startled her only to find her eyes upon him.

Darcy cleared his throat loudly. "Yes, I fear my borrowed clothing does not fit me as well as yours does you. While a needle and thread might help your skirt and blouse, I do not believe there is anything that can be done with pants and sleeves measured to fit a much, much shorter man."

He held his arms in front of him. The ragged-edged sleeves reached the middle of his forearms. The pants were the same length as worn by Jonah and the crew, showing a fair amount of leg.

"I am jealous," Elizabeth admitted with a grin. "Your thick wool socks must be divine. It is a rarity to find a single pair that displays so many different colors at one time."

"Ha! Then you will be happy to note the pile contained another smaller pair that I believe will warm your toes sufficiently."

He dug through and handed them to Elizabeth, who held them up to the lantern's light.

She laughed. "I will look like a leprechaun chasing the rainbow on my own feet."

Darcy shook his head. She was an imp. He studied her from head to toe. Despite the rough garments, she was lovely.

"What?" It was her turn to look around for something wrong.

"You, Elizabeth. You are a wonder to me," he stated with no hesitation.

She hesitated, her smile fading. "I do not understand."

Seating himself next to her, he explained. "What I have learned to appreciate about you in addition to your intellect is your ability to find delight in the mundane. No one in my world does this. Rather, they hope to draw attention to themselves by holding their jaded opinions up as superior to others—and they want to be admired for it, I fear. Your joy, Elizabeth, sets you apart, far higher than others could ever attain. And, yes, before you ask, I am one of those others. I believe you said that my life has been mired in selfish disdain for the feelings of others. Is this correct?"

Her cheeks flushed a rosy hue as she nodded.

"Pray, do not be distressed, Sister. My purpose is not to cause you discomfort," he admitted. "Rather, I am keeping in mind the covenant we made, that we would pursue peace in our quarters. Since nothing we discussed earlier was apparently repeated to the captain, I believe we can have freedom of speech here. None-theless, once the door is open, we will both need to be on guard."

She nodded. "I sincerely thank you for expressing yourself openly. In the same spirit I will admit that my emotions are churning to the same rhythm as the sea. Those times I express my happiness are like the ups. With that said, there are far more downs that I am sinking into. Through no fault of our own, our lives are permanently changed. I both resent this lack of control and fear it."

"Would you share your fears? It might lessen the burden slightly."

She sighed, pushed a curl that had escaped in the wind behind her ear, then looked directly at him. "I worried about the sort of man Captain Bartholomew was until the conversation tonight. Now, I see that he is exactly as he says he is, a businessman solely interested in trade. Too, I worried about being alone with you. Oh, I trusted you to act as a proper gentleman." She fluttered her hand at him to dismiss his intention of explaining himself. "Do not fret, sir. I worried we would kill each other within the first hour. I am pleased to find that we did not." Her smile was brief. "However, my greatest fear stems from what might be happening at Longbourn. You see, last autumn, Papa was helping with the harvest as was his custom. At the end of the third day of tireless labor, he appeared at the table with pale skin, clammy hands, and an ache in his chest that would not go away." Her eyes closed as she inhaled deeply. "Oh, I know what you see when you look at our fields and my father, whose name, by the way, is Thomas Edward Bennet. He appears indolent and uncaring. The reality is that we learned a year ago that his heart is failing. What my kidnapping will do to him, I can only imagine. I worry ..." her voice quivered. She rested her head back against the wall. "I fear I will never see him again."

Darcy yearned to take her in his arms to comfort her the way he had done with Georgiana when their father died. At the time he tended to his sister, he had no clue how he would survive the devastating pain of loss nor bear the burden of all that was Pemberley.

He wanted to hold Elizabeth's hand. They had made tremendous progress since they woke earlier in the day. Nevertheless, he easily recalled her harsh words describing him as arrogant and rude. She did not like him. More specifically, she loathed his supposed denial of his father's will toward George Wickham.

*Wickham!* What a sorry excuse for a human being. That the rogue had been in company with Elizabeth, that he had spoken to her, even planned to touch her hand while dancing made him want to slam his fist into the wall.

Instead, he ran his hand over his battered face. She was hurting far too much about her immediate family to burden her with an exposé of Wickham's foul deeds. Additionally, to protect his sister he had vowed to Georgiana and their cousin, who shared her guardianship, that he would never speak of the reason he despised Wickham with a passion. What had happened to Georgiana four months prior at Ramsgate was unspeakable. No, he would need to prove his character without revealing his actions with George Wickham.

When from the corner of his eye he spied Elizabeth weeping, he knew it was not a mistake to keep silent on the matter. She already had enough heartache. Learning that her favorite was a rake would be a devastating blow. Darcy cared far too much to deliberately cause her additional pain.

## 8

Elizabeth rubbed the end of her nose, which had lost blood flow from being firmly pressed against the wall. She was afraid to move, afraid to breathe. The air was bone-chilling cold. Nonetheless, despite her misery, she yearned to press herself even closer to the hard surface, away from the warmth at her back. Could she be any more uncomfortable? She thought not.

Even though the arrangement to share the bunk had been mutually agreed upon, the reality of being in such close contact with a man who completely unsettled her robbed her of the ability to sleep. She doubted he fared any better.

Like the ocean, the day certainly had its ups and downs. Meeting Jonah Hackett was a bright spot. Even spending time with the captain had been pleasant, once Mr. Darcy had joined them and they had been able to sketch his character.

She sighed. If the captain was correct in his timing of this journey, Elizabeth and Darcy would be stuck together for a minimum of two months to the Carolinas and back. Would the two of them be able to pass the time without tossing the other overboard? She had no clue. Of course, the great unknown was the reaction of one Mr. Silas Bingley. Their current situation proved that he was impetuous, that he insisted upon his own way, and that he was not above using evil arts to achieve his desires. What did he want with Mr. Bingley? When he became aware of her presence, what would his reaction be? What would he do with her? Would he keep Mr. Darcy and leave her to her own resources in a foreign land?

All of these unknowns added to her confusion with the man sharing the bunk. One minute he infuriated her. The next, he bordered on being tender. Was he so mentally adaptable that he actually thought of her as his sister to the point he treated her as his own? How could that be?

Caroline Bingley praised Georgiana Darcy's talent, wisdom, and looks until Elizabeth concluded she was a fearsome thing. Added to the comments from old family friend, Mr. Wickham, that Miss Darcy had once been a sweet girl but now was as arrogant as her brother, Elizabeth could not in her deepest imagination believe there was even a modicum of tenderness in the Darcy family, not even to each other.

Yet ... Elizabeth could not deny that Mr. Darcy had placed himself between her and the captain until the threat was over. He had given her his coat. He had held her hand. He had admitted his faults and apologized more than once.

*Who was this man!*

"Are you awake?" he whispered.

"I am."

The gentle rocking motion of the ship was disrupted by sharp movements from behind her. He bumped her back. Her knees were pushed into the wall. Then ... warmth. Blessed warmth as he snuggled against her in the same manner as she and Jane did during the bitter cold winter months. Except this was far different from having Jane spoon against her back. What was normal between sisters was outlandish with a man she hated.

The relief warred against her affront. How could he, a man who easily caused offense, seek comfort with her? He must have felt the cold to his bones as she had. When his arm snaked over her bringing his thin blanket along with it, she did the only sensible thing in the fierce chill, pulled him closer to her.

Then, she held her breath. Were they going to be struck down for blatantly placing themselves into a compromising position? Was the Lord that cruel? Of course not! If he had not wanted his sheep warm and cozy, he would never have created them with their thick coats of wool. She wanted to snort. Her ridiculousness was running away with her.

What was the proverb? One may as well hang for a sheep as a lamb? Inhaling deeply, she closed her eyes before twisting and turning to her other side. Instead of her nose pressed against the wood, now it was back where they had started the day, rubbing the fabric covering his chest.

Without a word, he settled her into his embrace. By the time he lay back with a sigh, her head rested on his shoulder, her face tucked in the nook of his neck, her right arm was at his waist and her feet had one of his wool-covered ankles anchored between them. Heat radiated from his whole body.

His hand rubbed her back, leaving a trail of exposed nerves everywhere his fingers touched. She thought to complain about his familiarity, but the warmth left behind was wonderful.

"Elizabeth, just sleep, I pray you. We can argue about this in the morning."

With those sensible words, she closed her eyes, relaxed into him, and slept.

HE WOKE to a light tap on their door.

"One moment," Darcy mumbled as he unburied his face from

his pillow. Except ... *good heavens!* It was not a pillow. It was Elizabeth's ... *upon all that was holy!* He was a pious hypocrite for his inclination to return to his soft haven instead of running from the temptation.

The morning sun's rays lit the far wall, leaving his sleeping companion shadowed in the dawn. She lay on her back, her face turned slightly to the porthole. She was lovely. And she was crowding him off the mattress. How could someone so much smaller than he take up the majority of the bunk?

He smiled before carefully beginning the task of loosening himself from Elizabeth so as not to wake her. Her left arm was hooked around his neck, holding him in place. If he tilted his head just so, his lips would brush the softness below her ear.

No! He would not dishonor her by pursuing his own desires. He was a gentleman!

"Elizabeth, we are being summoned."

Her eyes popped open, slightly unnerving him. Within a breath, she had released her grip on him.

"Mr. Darcy, ye be needed on deck, sir." It was Jonah Hackett.

Looking back to make certain Elizabeth was modestly arranged, Darcy opened the door.

The scamp darted past him into the room to grab the chamber pot from under the water stand.

"Ye won't be needing this no more though we'll keep it in here just in case. Wait fer me, sir, an' I'll show ye the head. I'll be taken Mrs. B to the cap'n's water closet fer her use first." He glanced at Elizabeth. "Come on. As soon as yer finished, we can start yer lessons."

Elizabeth scrambled off the bunk to follow the boy. Darcy stepped back to let her proceed.

The lad spoke over his shoulder. "Mr. Darcy, I'd be taken' off me stockings if I were ye. The deck is as wet as a rain cloud an' ye don't want ta be bringing the stink of the head back ta yer quarters."

Darcy was mortified at Elizabeth's hearing the lad speak of something *never* discussed in the presence of a lady.

When Hackett showed him where and how he would be easing nature, he was shaken.

There were two holes, one on either side of what Hackett called a bowsprit. Alongside each was a bucket with a sponge. The downwind smell of the area was atrocious. Since there was no protection from the elements, Darcy wondered at the logistics during stormy weather. Needless to say, there was no privacy as one hole was already occupied.

"Ye get used ta it." The boy shrugged. "Just be careful when the salts are up in the riggin' since it be impractical to run up an' down the lines. So when they yell 'look out below" ye best be gettin' outta the way cause ya don't wanna be wearing what they be sprinklin'."

Darcy immediately looked up into the upper sails knowing he would need to warn Elizabeth. Last evening's foray might be her only chance to feel the ocean breeze. She was bold. Yet, she was intelligent as well.

"Hackett, what sort of instruction will you be sharing with my sister this morning?"

The lad stood tall. "Ye can call me Jonah too, just like her, sir."

Darcy bowed. "I thank you for the honor."

"Oh, it be no honor," the youth reassured him. "Tis just that it be so long since I heard it. Hearing Mrs. B say it sound almost the same as when me ma would yell at me ta fetch this or that. So, Mr. Darcy, I guess that be yer name?"

He nodded. "I am Fitzwilliam Darcy."

It was the boy's turn to nod. "Did ye find the cap'n to be a fair an honest man like I told ye?" Jonah shaded his eyes then dropped his hands to his sides, his mouth gaped open. "Ship ahoy!" he yelled. "Ship ahoy, starboard side!"

Never could Darcy have imagined the organized chaos that ensued. Moving as quickly as he was able, he approached the helm. There, the captain and Quartermaster Boone had been in deep conversation. Now, they were taking turns looking through a spyglass and barking commands to the crew. "Hold her steady." "Ready the guns." "Prepare to strike the colors."

Nothing in Darcy's life had prepared him for the activities common aboard a threatened ship. When Captain Bartholomew commanded him 'below decks,' Darcy did as was suggested.

Elizabeth stood outside their quarters, her hand holding her steady by grasping the doorknob. She asked, "Does 'ship ahoy' mean what I think it does?"

"It does." He covered her hand with his to open the door. "Until we know if the approaching vessel is a friend or foe, we are safer inside."

In the time it took to reach their bunk, the *Peregrine* began to turn hard towards the shore. There might be hope for them yet.

## 9

D arcy and Elizabeth took turns looking out the porthole until they spotted the approaching ship. It was too far away to see if it flew the flag of Napoleon.

"What will happen to us?" Elizabeth moved away from the window; her hands clasped tightly at her waist.

"I cannot know for certain." Darcy rubbed his hand over his chin. "If it is British navy, we can beg for protection. However, this is not without danger."

"How so?"

Darcy was torn. If he told her too much, it would increase her fear. If he did not tell her enough, she would be completely unprepared for any eventuality.

"Without any means to prove who we are, I am subject to impressment."

"No! That cannot happen," she insisted. "I know what that means. My father has shared his circulating papers with me since I first learned my letters. You could be pressed into service for years and years. I read the list of names of battleships lost at sea. I also read list after list of those who are captured or missing in action. They could keep you away from England under their servitude until Napoleon surrenders. No, we cannot allow this to happen." She faced him, and asked, "Pray forgive me for being entirely selfish, but if they forced you to sail with them, what would happen to me?"

"I do not know what will happen to either of us." He hedged. "Elizabeth, it is possible we have another American merchant approaching. In that case, I believe they will signal with flags and pass by with no trouble."

"If it is French?"

"Rarely does Napoleon send his fleet into the channel. No, his success lies in victories on the open sea where he uses his ships of the line against smaller vessels. However, should his tactics have changed, then likely we will be captured together. Napoleon will seek a ransom which my family will pay. When the timing is right for negotiations, we will be released."

"I have read that Napoleon treats his aristocratic prisoners well. Let us hope it is a French or American ship approaching."

"Yes. We can hope." Although he said the words, he did not believe any of them to be true. Reports of interactions at sea were rarely beneficial to innocents. Unlike Elizabeth, he was not the type of man to put stock in good wishes and happy outcomes. An orphan rarely had the option, whether rich or poor, to believe in their heart that matters would always turn out well.

Therefore, he was the type of man to prepare for the worst and hope it was not so bad as it could be. Were they back in England, he had innumerable resources to draw upon. However, on a ship he did not own, he had no control.

*Blast!*

The thought of being separated from Elizabeth with her under the power of strangers was abhorrent. His heart pounded. His palms were damp. He wanted to fight every single one of them, but his death or capture would increase her vulnerability.

If only they were back at the ballroom arguing over Wickham. It would have been a relief. How silly that disagreement seemed now.

Sitting next to her, he considered his words carefully. He loved her intellect. He loved her ability to see good in bad situations. He loved her kindness to young Hackett.

He loved her. *Good heavens!*

He was in love with Miss Elizabeth Bennet.

The timing for reaching this conclusion could not have been worse. He was possibly in the throes of the most perilous physical danger of his life and hers too. He needed to think.

She slapped her hand down on the hard mattress. "Might I suggest that we attempt to look the part of who we really are. The British Navy might have no interest in you as a landed gentleman. Certainly, you must be aware of accounts where the Admiralty has been applied to for proof that a captive is master of an estate. Several times the man has been set free. If they are French, it would be a good idea as well to present ourselves as gentry."

"Brilliant!" No wonder he loved her.

Turning their backs on each other, they outfitted themselves in the clothing they came with. The two of them would be frayed, stained, and wrinkled, but they could stand tall to meet their future.

He desperately needed a shave. During the thirty hours or so they had been missing from Hertfordshire, his whiskers had sprouted a dark shadow that made face and neck itch. In a matter of a few weeks, he would have a full beard, making him fit in with everyone on the crew except the captain and young Hackett.

Elizabeth fussed with her skirt, then turned attention to her hair. When she finished, she handed the battered brush provided in the captain's box to him.

He cleared his throat, suddenly embarrassed.

Before he could utter a word, she asked, "If you would fasten my buttons, I will straighten your neck cloth."

She turned and ... he almost swallowed his tongue.

The smooth skin of her back and shoulders above her chemise and stays glistened in the early morning light filtering into the room.

His fingers quivered as he reached to pull the edges of her gown together. Hours seemed to go by as he fumbled with one button then another. When he finished and she raised her arms to assist him, his knees threatened to collapse.

*He was an idiot! He was an idiot! He was an idiot!* By the time she finished, he had chanted the truth no less than a dozen times. When her fingers brushed his throat to straighten his hastily tied knot, he was shocked that he had not gone up in flames.

"There." She patted his chest. "You look the part of an English gent sans shoes and jewelry. I am a tattered and torn British lady who is far more at home in a ballroom than a ship."

A sharp rap on the door interrupted his desire to prolong the domestic scene by pulling Elizabeth into his arms. No doubt, she would have scratched and clawed him to threads had he tried.

Boone shoved the door open and tossed some items on the floor. "The Captain requires you both on deck now. Hurry!"

There before them were his shoes. Shoving his feet inside, they rushed after the quartermaster.

Wondering what else of his 'lost' possessions would suddenly appear if needed, Darcy clasped Elizabeth's hand in his to steady her on their way. They followed the officer up the stairs to the deck. Darcy's eyes went from bow to stern, wondering if it was the same crew they had glimpsed the day prior. Instead of ragged sail-cloth garments, the men were dressed neatly in degrees of blue and white. Even Jonah Hackett looked smart in his uniform. One glance at Captain Bartholomew showed him in a coat far less decorated on the lapels and shoulders than the one he wore the night before. The tails were longer. The sleeves were heavily trimmed in gold braiding.

"Come," the captain commanded as they approached the helm. "We cannot yet see if they are flying the Union Jack, the 15 stars or Napoleon's blue, white, and red ensign. I doubt a Frenchie would be this far up the channel, although it is possible. No, I suspect we are about to meet one of Britain's mighty fleet. You had best look sharp, Mr. Darcy, or the press gang aboard will have you on your knees with a holystone for the rest of the war. If it is the French, we will draw our guns and fight."

"Yet you turned towards the French shore." The movement had puzzled Darcy.

"Aye," the captain nodded, as he peered through the spyglass. "We are smaller than that battleship. The eddies will pull us closer to shore than he could safely navigate. We will remain on this course. We still head west-southwest. We should be able to slip right by whomever it is by hugging land. My goal is the Azores, then New Providence Island in a few weeks to restock supplies before we hit the Eastern Seaboard. I mean to do all I can to get there on time."

Jonah tapped Elizabeth on the arm. Whispering, he said, "Ye might be wonderin' at the holystone. It be a limestone brick for cleanin' the decks. The Brits still do it every day. We be scourin' every fourteen days. It be tough work, even fer me."

She dipped her chin in acknowledgement, then reached for his hand.

"Have you seen battle, Jonah?"

"Not so much." He scuffed his feet. "Mostly, the cap'n trades goods. Then we don't have to fight. Since all the crew be partners in the cargo on this trip, we wanna keep as much as poss'ble. The cap'n says if we keep our 'penses down by not askin' fer hot food an' rum, we'll make a fine killin' once we get back ta Charleston harbor. Why, Mrs. B., I'd be pleased to buy ye a perty dress."

"Oh, Jonah," she sighed as she brushed his cheek with her fingers. "What a delightful lad you are. You look smart in your uniform, young man. Why, even the buckles on your shoes are shined." Her smile vanished. "Stay safe, I pray you."

"Don't you worry none, Mrs. B. I'll protect ye. Mr. D. too." With a grin and a smart salute, he ran off to perform whatever task he had been assigned.

Mr. D? Never could Darcy recall having a nickname he was more pleased at hearing. Certainly, his first name had been a source of many attempts at brevity. When they were young, his cousin Richard had called him Fitz, Fitzy (which always generated fisticuffs), William, Willie (which also was like waving a flag at an angry bull), and Will. *Mr. D?* Yes, he could happily live with that moniker from Jonah.

"Brother," Elizabeth leaned closer to him as the vessel rose and fell. "There is a shocking amount of quiet amongst the crew, is there not?"

Gathering his thoughts, Darcy focused, not on the immediate concern for Elizabeth and his safety, but on the whole of their surroundings.

She was correct. The sparsity of movement and sound other than the hull slapping against the waves and the sails flapping was odd. Since this was his first opportunity to study the frigate in the light of day, he was surprised to see a merchant ship so heavily armed.

On the port and starboard sides were eight cannons being silently readied for action. The stern held two cannonades. From an economic stance, this made little sense. The iron alone of the armaments must have weighed several tons. That Captain Bartholomew, who was a self-admitted man driven by monetary gain, would choose to lose that much capacity for goods did not seem a reasonable decision. Something about this situation was not right.

"Look," Elizabeth whispered as she nodded towards Boone.

The quartermaster was hunched down with his back to the bulkhead, rubbing his hands together in anticipation. As Darcy's gaze moved from bow to stern, he saw the same eagerness in the rest of the crew. If he did not know better …

All of the sudden, bits and pieces of the events over the last twenty-four hours began to paint a picture that was quite daunting.

Touching Elizabeth's elbow, they moved as far away from the captain as the ship allowed. He leaned down so his mouth almost touched her ear. Chills, not from the weather, shot down his spine. Ignoring the surge of emotions, he said, "Keep on the watch, Elizabeth. I fear that there is more to this crew than we have been told."

She turned her face towards him so quickly that he had to jump back, or his mouth would have met hers—not something he wanted under the watchful eyes of the captain.

She asked, "You noted the change of uniforms then?"

He had. Last evening at their meal the captain was in full American Naval dress. Today, the whole crew were British. The guns belied the claim of being mere merchants. In all of the journeys to Ireland he had made with his father, there had been fewer than twelve crewmen on board each merchant ship. The *Peregrine* had six times that amount. Jonah's mention of signing 'articles' and the solid black of the flag that was now waving high above the deck told Darcy all he needed to know. However, the most telling was that they were headed towards the hotbed of unsavory ships, New Providence Island, a Bahamian island that had long been at the mercy of rogue mariners who followed the laws of no man or country.

Darcy's stomach plunged to his toes.

No wonder his repeated plea to provide their own ransom had fallen upon deaf ears. Captain Lucien Bartholomew was no simple businessman looking to make an honest shilling. He was a pirate.

## 10

Never in his lifetime had Darcy been in a position where one decision would mean life or death, survival or misery of the acutest kind. Sweat trickled down the middle of his back. Beads of moisture gathered under the whiskers shading his upper lip.

If the battleship were French, then the whole of the *Peregrine*, including Jonah, was in danger. If it were American, much would depend on its intentions. Article after article in the circulating papers reported on ships' captains from every continent who used the permissions of a letter of Marque to steal, capture, and enslave anyone deemed healthy enough to work aboard their own vessel. These crimes against mankind were rarely brought to justice. With minimal effort, a captive could easily disappear forever overboard. The fate of those pressed into service was often inhumane. Men and boys were kept below-decks in squalid conditions until they begged for the 'freedom' of duties in the open air. Women, even young girls, were treated as playthings by the captain, then turned over to be used cruelly by the crew.

Darcy now knew in his heart that had the second body

brought aboard with his kidnapping have been male, the man would be bartered to whatever ship approached, likely never to be heard from again. He would live out his years in abject slavery.

Pressed to a British vessel could be nearly as bad. According to the general information Darcy had learned, conditions aboard were little better than on any other ship. Inevitably, spillages from the galley seeped down to the bottom of the bilge. This created a horrid stink that permeated the whole vessel. Routinely, Darcy avoided the London docks since the smell and vermin were offensive at every level. To be held as a captive meant no wages for the labor performed until the ship was blown to pieces in battle or it limped into port where escape was rarely possible. At least, he would have the option, should the ship survive battles, to return to England when the war eventually ended. But he would not be able to take Elizabeth if he were pressed into service. The muscles inside his gut pulled taut at the idea of leaving her behind with Bartholomew. *Never!*

If he lost his life or was taken, there would be no one other than a ten-year-old boy to defend her, which meant she had no protection at all.

He wanted to vomit.

He had no weapon and he doubted, even if he did, whether the rules of engagement he had learned at Gentleman Jackson's would be observed by enemies aboard ship. He had no way of proving who and what he was. His investment and estate management skills honed by nearly twenty-eight years at Pemberley were useless at sea. In addition to English, he was fluent in Ancient Greek and Latin. He was more than passable in French and German. He knew not one word of Portuguese, should they survive to make it to their first port before New Providence Island —the Azores. He had no money, nor anything of value except the clothes on his back to sell—and they were as tattered as Elizabeth's gown. *Blast!*

Then there was Elizabeth. How in the world was he to protect her if he could not protect himself? He was the man. He was the one to be relied upon for care.

A chill wind blasted the starboard side of the ship, whipping the sails, almost knocking him and Elizabeth off their feet. The vessel swung dangerously towards the shoreline, which was now easily discernible.

Grabbing Elizabeth to himself with one arm, he leaned against the railing, his right arm grasping one of the lines leading up to the center mast. She buried her nose in his neck, her temple resting on his shoulder, her arms tightly wrapped around him.

Closing his eyes, he breathed in the memories of every word she had spoken, every smile she had given to everyone but him, every lift of her quizzical brow, and every tilt of her chin.

"Elizabeth, I will do my best." His words were as weak as the foundation upon which they rested. His body shook as sweat beaded at his temple and upper lip. Their odds of enduring the confrontation with the other ship with their dignity intact and without harm was little to none. Their chances of survival were minimal.

"I know."

When she lifted her eyes to him, he could see her fear. Inside, he knew her trembling was not solely from the cold. Their terror was real.

Another blast of wind seemed to shoot the heavily loaded vessel across the top of the waves toward the beach. Darcy pulled her even tighter as he turned his back to the gale. The next gust of air hit them hard and never let up. Instead, the raging wind battered the ship and raised the waves in the channel to mountainous peaks and valleys.

"We went right by them," Captain Bartholomew yelled above the noise. "Let's batten down."

To Darcy, he barked, "Get her below. All hands on deck."

Nodding, he turned them towards the staircase, only to be met by a heavy curtain of frigid rain. Within seconds, they were soaked.

ELIZABETH'S TEETH CHATTERED. She wondered if she would ever be warm again. Rivulets of rain streamed down her cheeks. She reached up, surprised at not finding icicles on her jaw.

Darcy kicked his shoes off into the corner next to the water stand. "Turn around," he ordered Elizabeth. "We need to get you into dry clothes before you catch a chill."

While her mind was ready for action, seeing the reasonableness of his request, her body shivered uncontrollably.

He spun her around to start working on her buttons. His fingers were colder than the air. He spoke in low tones the whole time he was about his task.

"Elizabeth, I surmise you have reached the same conclusion as I, that we are aboard a pirate ship. We need to be alert to any changes in the attitude of the crew. Look how quickly they went silent." He fumbled with the final button, then noted, "You are damp underneath."

She felt him pull at the knots on her stays.

She wanted to protest. Not even her father saw any of his daughters in their undergarments. Here this man, this stranger, no ... that was not correct. He was more than a stranger.

She had to remember that this was not the first time she had changed clothes in the same room with him. Of course, she had kept on her petticoat, stays, and chemise. As well, they had their backs turned to each other so nothing was seen that should not have been. On this occasion, once the strings were loosened, he would have in front of him a view of her bare shoulders and chemise. That was a husband's privilege.

She groaned, causing his fingers to stumble even more.

"Pray accept my apologies. I am moving as fast as I can."

Adding the rocking of the ship to the mixture unsettled her further.

Finally, he ripped the ties apart. The usual relief of freedom was quickly followed by him thrusting the rustic garments she had worn earlier into her arms.

"Here!" his voice was gruff as he handed her the wool blanket from the bunk. "Wrap in this to warm you."

She should not have looked back to thank him.

He had hastily stripped off his shirt and was reaching for the homespun cloth to dry himself. The powerful muscles of his back rippled. His skin glowed.

*Goodness!*

Her blush heated her cheeks. She was shocked at herself for gawking at Mr. Darcy, of all people. Even more shocking was when she decided to follow his lead by removing the rest of her clothing, so she could put on a dry garment to finally be warm.

"Elizabeth, can I turn? I dare not risk the captain's ire by remaining below."

"You may." Wrapping herself in the blanket, she sat on the bunk, then scampered back to be out of his way.

"Pray, bar the door behind me. I cannot leave without knowing you are safe. I will return as soon as I can." With those words he was gone.

The void he left behind as soon as the door closed stirred Elizabeth to rehang her ballgown and his clothing on the pegs. Never had she touched a man's garments. Well, in truth, she had likely done so as she toddled from her mother to her father in her infancy. Her hand lingered on Darcy's waistcoat. It smelled like him.

She was ridiculous. After a month at sea, neither of them

would smell like they knew the value of a bath. She shuddered, disgusted at the thought.

Lifting the box that Jonah had carried so easily, she dropped it on the bunk and opened it. On top was a man's leather boot. Elizabeth set it aside, determined to clear her mind from pondering the intimacy of having tended Mr. Darcy's clothing.

Searching through the rest of the box, Elizabeth found a treasure. Some kind female who had traveled before had cut rectangles of fabric and hemmed them for a lady's personal use. There were four quilted cotton pads, which meant she would still need to rinse and dry them when the time came for her courses to start.

Setting those aside, she pulled out three packets with lengths of white, black, and blue thread, each sealed by a sewing needle stuck through the fold. Below them were another pair of large socks, two men's shirts and trousers, a lovely fringed paisley shawl, and the other boot, possibly the pair large enough for Mr. Darcy's feet.

Returning the items to the box proved challenging as her hands still shook from the cold and the boat seemed to swivel in a complete circle while still rocking up and down and from side to side. The rapid change in motion upset her stomach. Lying flat on the bed did not help. Within minutes, everything she had eaten had been violently cast up into the chamber pot. Once her stomach started its rebellion, it did not want to stop.

If only the sea would calm. If only she was back in her bed chamber at Longbourn. Only then could she find relief.

Misery swamped her until she was too weak to do more than roll on her side to heave, hoping any dregs from her stomach would reach the bowl. When the ship took another turn, the chamber pot began to slide towards the far wall. Only desperation to not have the contents covering the wooden deck spurred her to climb off the bunk to secure the container in its rack. With nothing left to do, she pulled the blanket off the bed and lay down on the floor.

Elizabeth woke hours later to Darcy charging through the door, bringing the cold rain and blessedly fresh air. She had forgotten to bar the door.

"Oh, Elizabeth," he flinched as the smell from the bowl must have hit his nostrils. "You are a mess."

Jonah spoke from the doorway. "I got it, Mr. D."

If Elizabeth had ever been more embarrassed in her life, she could not recall the circumstances. The look of empathy on the lad's face at seeing her on the floor brought tears to her eyes.

"Mrs. B, don't ye be frettin'. Many a hardened sailor gets green around the gills. Why, the first time I rode the jagged buckin'-horse motion as she fell off waves and plowed into the swell, I know'd I was gonna die. I didn't though." He smiled as he splayed his hands from his sides. "I'm still here."

"I thank you, Jonah," she rasped, her throat feeling like the inside had been scraped raw. She was far from reassured.

"The rain has let up, though the wind still be blowin' like a banshee. If ye can make it up top, the sight o' land seems to settle yer gut." He stepped around Darcy to grab the chamber pot. "I'll dump this so we can clear the air."

He was gone in a flash.

"Come, Elizabeth," Darcy held out his hand for her to take.

"Pray allow me a moment." Surely, he understood that movement of any nature was torturous.

She felt the ship rising up to the top of a wave, knowing what would follow. The plunge to the bottom of the next wave would bounce her body against the wooden floor. Her stomach would protest, and whatever bile had pooled inside her would spew forth.

"Come." This time, he did not wait for her reply. Instead, he grabbed her under each arm and lifted her as if she were feather light. Holding her close to his side, she shivered. He was like a solid block of ice. Pulling the blanket from her, he tossed it onto the bunk.

She was at first angry. Then she thought of how much she would appreciate its warmth once she was allowed back in their quarters.

The ascent to the upper deck was precarious. Several times they were hurled against the stair rails as the ship rocked back and forth. Once she reached the side of the ship, she opened her eyes and saw land.

"Do not look away, Mrs. B. Keep yer eyes fixed on that sight til your stomach settles, and it will, I promise." Jonah reassured. "The cap'n says the wind be blowin' us closer an' closer ta the Atlantic than we would be had we sailed on our own. We still be on schedule."

Hanging onto the ship's railing with all her might as each wave threatened to fling her onto the deck, Elizabeth attempted a smile at the boy. He was again dressed in his sailor togs. She suspected they were his daily clothing. It was no wonder they were streaked and torn.

"It is a fine thing to still be on schedule." She glanced at the lad to find there was not one ounce of fear on his face, which the water had washed blessedly clean.

"Cap'n Bartholomew, he says we will be in calm seas within a week. Just hang on there, Mrs. B. Ye will be just fine, I suspect."

She had no doubt that his words were meant to encourage, but ... a week? *Ugh!* She would never make it. Elizabeth knew a body could survive without food. Water intake was needed to continue living, however at that moment, even the idea of taking a sip made her stomach roil.

Closing her eyes against the salt spray, the bottom seemed to have been pulled out from underneath her.

"Whoa! That be a wicked wave, Mrs. B, but don't ye worry. The captain says we be like a cork floatin' on a pond. It be almost impossible for the weather ta sink us."

From a distance, she heard a man yell. Others took up the call. Opening her eyes, she turned along with Darcy and Jonah to see the reason for the panic.

Captain Bartholomew and Boone had grabbed the ship's wheel, the muscles in their necks straining with their effort to turn the *Peregrine* into the largest wave Elizabeth had ever seen. From above, the men were scrambling down the ladders, one man jumping to speed his descent. Wooden crates which had been loaded with cannonballs were sailing across the deck.

The chaos temporarily distracted Elizabeth from her own suffering. When the water began lifting the ship like it was a toy, the quick roll to the side forced her to hang onto the railing even tighter. The *Peregrine* balked at the mistreatment. Despite the cries of encouragement and the curses coming from the crew, the vessel tilted almost beyond recovery.

Elizabeth's fingers were ripped from the rail as her side of the ship dipped into the frigid water until the wave hit her in the face, robbing her of breath. Jonah's slim arms surrounded her middle as strong arms held them together from behind. Within a second or less, they were engulfed by the churning ocean pulling against their limbs, trying to separate them or break them into pieces. Instinctively, her feet started to paddle as they rolled over and over from the force of the sea.

Kicking as hard as she humanly could, her feet tangled with Darcy's longer legs. With each move forward, they seemed to be pressed further into the watery deep. Her lungs were screaming for relief. Tears were fruitlessly pouring from her eyes. The weight of the water pulsing around them seemed to squeeze every drop of hope from her.

Was this to be it? Was her life to end without notice? *No!* Desire to live life to the fullest welled within her until any residual weakness from her motion sickness disappeared as a burst of energy filled her soul. Kicking with all her might, she fought against the current, the wind, the waves, her bulky skirt, and her lack of air to push toward the surface.

Whatever struck her at her temple was unknown. One second she could see the blessed light of the wave's crest, the next she saw black.

---

## 11

Darcy caught sight of an incoming empty crate out of the corner of his eye just before it crashed into her. Jonah was enough shorter than Elizabeth that he escaped injury.

*Elizabeth!* His mind screamed, horrified that she had come to harm under his care.

Now, holding her limp in his arms, he knew they would all die if they could not reach the surface. Darcy could not tell which way was up. They had been so close to the surface when another large wave buried them into the depths of the churning sea. The water was pitch dark, stinging his eyes as they tumbled under the pounding waves. The sea tossed them around like flotsam, holding them under the surface, keeping them imprisoned to its awesome power. Afraid to let go of Elizabeth and concerned with hanging on to Jonah, he had only his legs to propel them to the surface.

Fear surged through him. They were completely vulnerable against an enemy who held all of the weapons. Darcy felt his own insignificance with his whole soul. He was nothing against the mighty natural forces.

All of the air had been ejected from his lungs on first impact with the water. Now, the temptation to inhale taunted him with a lie. *Just a little inhale and the pressure in your chest will ease. No!*

Biting the inside of his cheek, he pushed with his full strength only to be battered back into the depths. Freedom to breathe seemed even further from his reach.

Visions of running free at Pemberley teased him. His feet firmly on the ground, he rushed through the gardens down the hill to the lake where he stood breathing safely on the shore. When he was the same age as Jonah, he had been swimming at the deeper end with Wickham. Thinking his actions were funny, George, who was considerably bigger at the time, delighted in holding Darcy's face under the water until he feared he would drown.

Darcy fought that same helplessness. There was no one to come to his rescue like one of the gardeners had done in his youth. Any hope of escape was on his shoulders alone.

Panic filled him from head to toe as the dark, murky depths seemed to draw his focus away from a life worth living. If he relaxed, if he quit fighting, he knew in his treacherous heart that it was warm at the bottom of the watery deep. If he let go, they would all be cozily nestled as the salty brine rocked them into a permanent sleep. He only needed to stop trying.

*No! Never!*

A thread of yearning to grow old with the woman he held wound around his heart. He longed to see Georgiana happy as she grew in confidence under Elizabeth's tutelage. Even Jonah's future pressed in upon his consciousness. Despite the muscles in his calves and thighs burning from strain, he pushed them towards where the water felt most violent. Every single muscle and tendon in his whole body reacted to the hope of survival. As the waves pushed and pulled at them, he forged a path by forcing his legs apart then snapping them quickly together as his feet paddled frantically against the current's pull. They would *not* die today!

It was then that he saw it, that band of luminescence indicating they were within ten feet of being able to safely inhale. Using the last of his energy, Darcy gave one final mighty kick. The light filtering through the water instilled hope. With this last thrust, they burst through the wave.

Air, glorious, glorious air. Darcy filled his lungs before the next wave hit them. Lifting Elizabeth above his shoulder, he was thrilled they had made it. Then, he was horrified when she coughed and sputtered.

No! Pray, God, that she had not sucked water into her precious lungs, No!

Desperation surged through him, fueling his will to survive and rescue his fair lady. Yelling at Jonah to kick, they caught the next wave, riding it towards the shore. His heart pounded in his brain as he kept spinning her on top of him so she could breathe air instead of water. Only when he became lightheaded did he cover her mouth and nose with his palm. He turned them over so he could breathe.

It was a wicked journey to the beach, taking both him and Jonah to get Elizabeth out of the grasping grip of Poseidon. Darcy pounded her back until she vomited the sea water she had swallowed onto the sandy soil. Her breathing was rough and unsteady as she gasped for air. His fingers traced the gash over her left ear. Her hair was matted with blood. He pressed his palm over the wound desperately hoping to stop the bleeding.

She was pale except where blue ringed her mouth and eyes—too still for his Elizabeth. Please, God. Please let her live, he unashamedly begged.

As he had done in their quarters, he lay alongside her, his cold flesh as close to hers as possible to share his warmth. His mind supplicated his heavenly Father while his heart beat for her. When he finally felt her steady breath on his cheek, he wanted to sob in relief.

He had not thought they would survive. In his lifetime, he had never been that close to death, not even at the lake with Wickham. Yet, not once had he considered letting go of Jonah and Elizabeth. They would all survive together, or they would not. His life would have been meaningless without her.

God, but how he loved her.

Her chest lifted from a coughing fit she could not control.

They needed shelter and warmth both inside and out.

Glancing at their surroundings, there was sand along the shoreline as far as he could see in both directions. Not another human was in sight.

Despite being out of the sea, they were still in danger. The ship's proximity to France when they went overboard meant they had landed on enemy soil. They were soaked through with the air temperature hovering close to freezing.

The lad stood at the water's edge, searching the horizon for any sign of his friends. Nothing but pounding waves, brown from the stirred-up mire from the Channel's bottom, were visible. He shrugged, then walked back to Darcy and Elizabeth.

"Mr. D, it don't look like nobody else o' the crew were tossed overboard, which be good for the *Peregrine*, I guess. Yeah, I guess they'll do well enough without me." He dug his toes into the sand.

The sorrow of the boy tugged at his heartstrings. The lad looked like he had lost his favorite dog. Darcy vowed to comfort him later. They had far more pressing needs.

"Jonah, we need to get Elizabeth to safety. Do you speak French?"

The boy lifted his shoulders. "'Bout as good as I speak English." He shrugged. "If only we'd landed on one of the

Channel Islands. They speak French and English too and some sort of other tongue native to 'em."

"I cannot help but wish the same."

Darcy stood then bent to lift Elizabeth. He swayed, his unsteady legs threatened to give out underneath him. His arms were as weak as a ninety-year-old's. Jonah helped as best as he could. Gathering his reserves, Darcy pushed with his calves, the muscles quivering as he stood with her in his arms. He held her close to him, his whole body shaking from the strain.

"Mr. D." The boy pulled on his sleeve. "When the salts been drinkin' too much, it be easier to sling their cargo over they's shoulder. It will help get the water outta her lungs. Mrs. B won't know an' I certainly won't be tellin' her."

The lad was correct. Adjusting her position, they were able to make progress over the sand until they reached a small grove of trees. Gently easing her to a narrow patch of grass, Darcy brushed her hair from her face.

She was so lovely. How had he not noticed before they had been forced together? Not pretty enough to tempt him? He was an idiot.

"Mr. D, I'm gonna wander around to see if I can find us someplace ta shelter."

The absurdity of being under the care of a ten-year-old pierced his core. He was Fitzwilliam Darcy, caretaker of a multitude, who depended upon no one. *Lord!* He had no choice but to let Jonah go alone. He would not leave Elizabeth without protection.

"Take extreme care, Jonah." Darcy offered his hand, which the boy grasped and shook. "We are the enemy. It appears we landed in a cove. Smugglers could be about. Use caution, I beg you."

"Aw, don't ye worry none. Nobody pays much attention ta a scruffy kid." With that piece of brilliant observation and a snappy salute, the lad walked away.

Leaning his head back on the tree trunk, Darcy pulled Elizabeth closer, holding her wound to his shoulder. Their circumstances were dire. They had no money and nothing to sell. They had no means of identification to prove who they were. They were dressed like the poorest of paupers. They were nearly frozen and soaked through, and they were in the land of the enemy.

For the second time in his life, his wealth meant nothing. His purse had no effect on Captain Bartholomew. This ... this being only a Channel away from accessing enough funds for any sort of assistance, the best physicians for Elizabeth, the warmest clothing, and the most comfortable housing for the three of them was another blow. Until they were kidnapped from Netherfield Park, his money had never failed to provide his needs and more.

Wispy tendrils of darkness weaved their way through the farthest reaches of his mind. The bitter humiliation of not protecting Elizabeth from harm and being dependent on a child with little education was a challenge to swallow. He was the man. He was the provider. He was the one to whom others turned when in need. Even his impressive cousin, Colonel Fitzwilliam, had come to him more than once during their adult life seeking aid. However, not today or the day before. Not since they left the safety of the Netherfield Park ballroom had he been in control. The loss shook him. He was as powerless as a swaddled babe. The fierceness of the ocean, the vastness of the sky above, reminded him how small he was in the whole scheme of things.

Closing his eyes, the burn behind sent a tear down his cheek. Swiping it away, he considered; what was he going to do next? If harm came to the boy, if he lost Elizabeth, he did not know how he could manage to put one foot in front of the other to save himself.

He rubbed her back, then up and down her arm. The coldness of her skin was distressing. The fact that he could do nothing to assist her...was there no hope? Frustration at their circumstances ate at him. The bleakness of his thoughts had him completely undone.

This time, he ignored the tear making its way down his cheek to rest in his growing whiskers. *Why,* he yelled to the heavens. Why him? What had he ever done to deserve ... no! He refused to allow his mind to go there. Circumstances dictated their current situation, not poor decisions on his part. Being in the right place at the wrong time or the wrong place at the right time had been their only error. Had it been Bingley and his sister on that balcony, he would have lost them both; neither knew how to swim.

Opening his eyes, he inhaled deeply. Resettling Elizabeth, he cradled her face in the crook of his neck. Could he help it if his lips brushed her forehead? Not on his life!

Whether he had the papers or his signet ring to prove it or not, he was Fitzwilliam Darcy, master of Pemberley. He was an educated man with a quick mind. He was respected by his peers. Determination vanquished the blackness of self-doubt. He would do whatever he needed to do or become whomever he needed to become to see his two charges safe.

# 12

---

What seemed like a long time later, Jonah reappeared. "Come on, Mr. D. I've found us a place. It ain't a palace fit for a king, but it be warm."

"I thank you." Darcy did not think he would ever be truly thawed again. He had rubbed the bottom of his feet against the sparse grass and huddled with Elizabeth as best he could. But he was frightfully cold. Elizabeth had yet to wake.

A little of his strength had been restored from resting under the tree. The muscles of his arms and legs no longer quivered from fatigue. Elizabeth's figure was light and pleasing but an unconscious form seemed to weigh more than one who could hold herself up by wrapping her arms around his neck.

When she was much younger, Georgiana hated when her boots were wet after playing in a puddle. She insisted that her brother carry her when it rained. Darcy barely noticed the burden. However, when she had fallen asleep in front of the fireplace in the library and he needed to carry her to her chambers, she seemed much heavier.

Darcy's legs tingled and burned.

It was with relief that he spied their goal, a thatched-roof cottage barely large enough to contain needed room for a solitary occupant. That three were adding to the space would be a hardship. There was no barn nor any out-buildings other than a rickety lean-to and a shed for a single cow. A narrow overhang for wood storage was at the back of the house. It appeared nearly empty.

Jonah stopped him before they could approach, his countenance exceedingly uncomfortable. "Uh, Mr. D., it appears the lady be a widow. She looks like the sort who be preachin' and prayin.' So, I mighta told her ye an' Mrs. B be man an' wife since I suspect ye be bunkin' together."

Darcy was unconcerned. He knew where his heart's loyalty rested. He also knew they would need to marry as soon as they were back in England, if not before.

"Is that all?" he asked.

"Well," the lad scuffed his feet. "I mighta also told her that ye be a mute from Charleston like me. Well, not that I's mute. But she told me she hated the Brits. One word from yer mouth an' she'd know for certain that ye and Mrs. B is the enemy."

"I see." Darcy considered the danger of the house they were approaching. "Did you see evidence of men in the area?"

"Nope, I didn't. She didn't let me inside the house." Jonah grinned. "An' I doubt any is about since the first thing outta her mouth was to question whether ye was a strong fella who knew how ta work. Now, I know'd ye had a hard time aboard ship with the gear an all, but I think ye could handle an axe or a shovel just fine. I thought to tell her ye was a pitiful lookin' man, but I do try not to lie when I can."

Darcy grinned. "I thank you for that much, Jonah. Was there anything else?"

The boy fairly skipped up the path. "I be suspecting she be hard a hearin' or her French is worse than mine, since she called me Christophe. When I first joined the *Peregrine*, we had a first mate named Christophe. He were a black man from Port Royale with a musical way a talkin' and a temper worse than Boone's. I learnt my French an' how ta keep from gettin' into so much trouble from him." He stopped, waiting for Darcy to catch up. "Come on," Jonah hurried. "I understood the lady enough to know she promised hot soup once we returned."

"Very good, Jonah." Darcy considered, "What did you tell her of our circumstances?"

"Well, except for the married part an' that ye is mute, I told the truth." Jonah shrugged. "Tis far easier to remember than a lie."

"A valiant principle to live by," Darcy whispered to himself, thinking of the lie he told the captain and crew about being brother to Elizabeth. Did her safety justify his dishonesty? He could not regret his decision, despite the fact that there might have been a better way had he had the time to give it a thorough consideration.

ELIZABETH'S EYES FLICKERED OPEN, her lids blinking rapidly against the light. Her head pounded. Her stomach churned. Her throat and lungs felt like hot knives were being stabbed over and over inside of her until she would surely bleed to death. Drool ran up her cheek. Up her cheek? *Good heavens!* She was hanging upside down. Her arms were swinging until the tips of her fingers nearly touched the ground. Her hair fell inelegantly to drag across the sandy soil. Her view as she considered her surroundings was the backside of a well-formed man.

Even sodden, she recognized those clothes. Mr. Fitzwilliam Darcy, master of his domain, had flung her over his shoulder and was carrying her like a sack of field potatoes.

She wanted to kick him.

Pinching a few dark hairs coating his calves between her fingers, she pulled, bringing him to a sudden stop.

"What? Elizabeth?" He gently held her waist as he slid her from her perch. "Thank God, Elizabeth, you are awake!" Kneeling beside her, he brushed her hair from her face, then held her arms to keep her from collapsing fully to the ground.

The warmth of his eyes, the tenderness of having his brows furrowed out of concern for her, melted the last of her irritation with him. Her most recent memory had been of falling overboard into the sea. He had saved her life. Likely, he had saved the life of ...

"Jonah!" Her voice was raspy. "Where is ... ? Did he ...?"

"I be right here, Mrs. B." The lad stepped into view. "Tho, I need ta get used ta callin' ye by yer birth name since I told the old lady o' the house that ye be the wife o' Mr. D instead o' his sister."

Unbidden, salty tears streamed down her face. "I could not have borne it if something had happened to you, Jonah." Stretching out her hand, she gathered his fingers in her own as he stepped closer. "I have no doubt you would rather be with your crew sailing the seas, my dear young man, but I am absolutely delighted you are here."

"I thank ye," he blushed crimson. "We best get ye inside the house, Mrs. Darcy. Say, Darcy sounds sorta French-like. Maybe we ain't in such a bad situation after all."

He bowed, pretending to sweep a hat from his mop of hair. *"Bonjour, Monsieur et Madame Darcy. Bienvenue chez moi."*

Despite their circumstances, she could not help but smile. "Pray help me to stand. We may be on our way to said house; three vagabonds in search of a warm fire."

Her will was far stronger than her body. She had no sooner been helped to stand than her legs wobbled like a new calf until she needed to lean against her rescuer. As Darcy's arms wrapped around her, the feeling of safe homecoming melted her insides to a puddle. Boldly, her hands reached around his waist—to hold herself up, she justified.

Darcy swept her off her feet. "Pray, place your arms around my neck."

Gratefully, she did as she was instructed, her icy nose burrowing into the crook of his neck. She was chilled through and through. She was tired—oh, so tired! She feared she could not have walked had he asked.

As Darcy began moving toward the cottage, he whispered, "The woman of the house hates the British, so Jonah has kindly shared with her that we are all from the Carolinas and I am mute."

"I see." Her mind spun. "He is a clever lad. However, I cannot believe that it would not stretch the bounds of incredulity if I pretended that I was unable to speak as well. Perhaps you wed an educated tradesman's daughter while you were in London?"

He nodded as the woman stepped outside her home. She was short and stocky, her graying hair springing from a bun askew at the top of her head. Her lips were pinched together in disapproval. Her fisted hands rested upon each hip. Looking them up and down, she approached Darcy, rudely felt the inside of his palm, spat on the ground as she called him a lazy rich man in an insulting tone, shook her head, then went back inside, leaving the front door open in as much of a welcome as the three were likely to get.

Elizabeth was shocked at the mistreatment. Who was this woman who had sat as judge and jury, finding them inadequate without a word? In truth, it mattered not. If her hospitality had been reluctantly given, it still provided them a place of respite, she hoped.

The inside of the cabin was completely opposite to the starkness of the outside. Every surface was covered with pots of dried flowers and intricately crocheted doilies. Shiny-bottomed pots hung on each side of the fire. The hearth was bordered by baskets filled with stalks of long sea grasses. It was far more welcoming than their hostess.

Their hostess offered, "We will first warm your insides. Then you will have the strength to change out of your wet clothing."

The soup smelled divine. As Darcy and Jonah appeared to inhale theirs, Elizabeth kept bringing the spoon to her mouth, only to lower it back to the bowl. The salted broth on her abused throat would not do.

"You will not eat my food?" The woman, Madame Vartan as she had identified herself, was as sparse with her words as she was with tender care.

Elizabeth called upon the multitude of French lessons she had obtained at the hands of her mother's claim to fame, a French chef. "Pardon me, Madame. I believe that I swallowed enough salt water for a lifetime."

*"Mon Dieu!"* The woman pushed aside her bowl. She rounded the table, wiping her hands on the cloth hanging from her waist. Feeling Elizabeth's forehead with remarkably beefy hands for a female, she asked, "You were under the water?"

Without hesitating, Jonah spoke for her, his sentences a quaint mixture of a variety of languages. "Mrs. Darcy was out like a candle under a basket, madame. Why, I think the Channel be a mite lower for all the drinkin' she did."

The elderly woman moved with a quickness that was deceptive for her age. Within minutes, both Darcy and Jonah were hauling water from a distant well. Elizabeth had been pulled from the table to a small room filled with a wardrobe, a bed, and a wooden chair. Madame Vartan swiped the faded cushion to the floor then helped Elizabeth to be seated. Departing the room, she returned with a heavy mug in one hand and a worn cotton nightgown draped over her arm.

In the interim, Elizabeth's gaze could not help but linger on the blanket covering the bed. The quilt was of no particular pattern. Rather, it looked like someone had taken scraps from every sort of exquisitely made garment fashioned from the finest materials worn over a period of years to be pieced together with various patterns of stitches. A deep purple velvet was joined to a piece of sky-blue silk with a neat row of daisies sewn with yellow thread. Embroidered green leaves wound around each flower. A playful red with white dots adjoined a yellow silk with white stitches in the shape of small hearts.

"Mrs. Darcy, the boys will have enough water warmed for a bath in but a moment. We shall clean you up before we put you to bed. Until then, you might want to sip this cup of cool water. It will help ease the pain in your throat and begin to wash the extra salt from your insides."

By the time an hour had passed, Elizabeth had been scrubbed from head to toe. She rubbed her feet together under the blankets, her eyes struggling to remain open. From the noises outside of the room, Darcy and Jonah had been sent outside to bathe themselves. Thus, it took a long time of standing in front of the warming fire before either of them joined her. Jonah pulled the covers up to slide in on her right side. Darcy did the same to her left. The three huddled together for warmth.

Elizabeth was concerned for their hostess. "Where will Madame Vartan sleep? Have we taken her bed?"

Because the door remained open, Jonah answered instead of Darcy. "No, she says she always sleeps in the chair in front o' the fire for warmth and in case Christophe and Alex comes back home. I wonder who they is?"

"I wonder too." Darcy softly whispered. "Are you well, Elizabeth?"

"I am unused to the weakness I feel. My throat is raw. My stomach still moves to the motion of the sea. Nonetheless, I am well. And you, Mr. Darcy? How are you faring?"

Jonah piped in. "Nobody asked me yet, but I wanna tell ye that

I be fairly pleased we landed here. She may be a bit of a grouch like Boone when someone crosses him, but Madame Vartan can cook." His pleasurable sigh made her chuckle.

Darcy was finally able to reply. "I, too, am pleased, Jonah. You did well."

"I can tell she's the sort who'll make us work, so we better sleep when we can." Jonah yawned. "Mrs. D, ye sure do smell better 'an the salts below decks."

She chuckled. "I thank you for the compliment, Jonah."

Darcy turned on his side and pulled her to him. Elizabeth felt the rumble in his chest, though he made no sound.

"I believe we all smell better now than when we arrived." he spoke into her ear, his breath melting knees that were already weak.

She was eternally grateful that they were together. Snuggling closer, she was pleased to seek the heat radiating from him and his strong presence. Their day had gone from one level of fear on top of the other to comfort. She had no idea what the morrow would bring. Elizabeth decided to ponder the matter later. Her eyelids drooped once, then twice, then she could hold them open no longer.

## 13

Faint light drifted through the only window in the room. Nevertheless, it was not this that woke Darcy; it was the clatter of pots and pans. If he listened carefully, he thought he could hear the creaking of Madame Vartan's joints as she moved around the kitchen area of her tiny home.

He stretched his legs while rolling onto his back. Elizabeth followed, her head resting on his shoulder, her arm across his middle. Peeking across the bed, he discovered that Jonah had most of the space for himself. The lad slept flat on his belly with his arms and legs splayed out.

The night had been rough for Elizabeth. Twice, her sleep had been disrupted by nightmares. He discovered that speaking to her calmly while running his fingers through her hair from her scalp to the curls at the ends settled her back into a deep sleep.

Easing himself out from underneath her, Darcy rubbed his hands over the whiskers on his jaw and smoothed his hair as best as he could before joining their hostess in the kitchen. The wood and water that he and Jonah had hauled in the evening before was gone. Without a word of greeting or welcome, Madame Vartan tilted her head towards the axe and an empty bucket that rested by the only door in and out of the dwelling. Then, she pointed to the table.

There, draped across the surface, was a heavy wool coat, matching wool socks, and a knitted hat. On the floor rested well-worn leather boots of the sort worn by Pemberley's tenant farmers. He was so appreciative that he had to stop himself from thanking her out loud. Catching himself in time, he patted his heart and smiled.

The socks, hat, and coat fit him like a second skin. The boots pinched his toes. He knew they would be sore and numb by the time he brought in enough timber to satisfy the hungry fireplace.

Outside, the air was brisk. A frosty sheen coated the coarse grass clumped at the front of the house. This morning, he took his time to survey their surroundings as he walked the narrow path to the back of the cottage and beyond. Behind the building was a small kitchen garden with sparse patches of leafy greens, tall shoots of one sort of vegetable, and a few wispy fronds of another.

Pemberley had massive gardens he rarely noticed. They had always been there and always would be there. He knew the exact quantity of the plants, when they needed to go into the ground, and when they needed harvesting. He knew their yield. He knew their location in relation to the rest of the estate's crops. He knew that if his gardeners and tenants planted them, God would make them grow. What he did not know was how exactly all of that was done. It was the same with the laundry, the cooking, the baking, the cleaning, and the various other tasks with assigned personnel who quietly went about seeing their job completed with no inter-ference from the master and his immediate family.

Every Darcy born to Pemberley had cut his milk teeth on the task list handed down from father to son. The lot that fell to him was mountains of correspondence along with investment research and consideration as to the sort of diversity that would make his estate viable for decades to come. He had a responsibility to his family name to know the rules of propriety and society until he represented and maintained a sterling reputation to bring honor to future generations.

Therefore, in his twenty-eight years he had never chopped wood. In his arrogance, Darcy had assumed he would perform well at the task if ever needed. Despite his imagination never conjuring a situation where it would actually happen, surely, a man of well-developed muscles from hours spent at gentlemen's sports of rowing, boxing, and fencing would do well. After all, an uneducated man could cut timber. Even a growing boy could fashion a pile of kindling in no time at all. How hard could it be?

When he reached the area of a sparse forest where limbs had fallen to the ground, he raised his axe like he had observed other men do and swung. The wedged end hit the thick branch with a thud, bounced back off the hardwood stinging his hands, barely missing his chin.

Immediately, he looked around to see if anyone had noted his ineptitude. As his racing heart calmed, he stepped back to consider what had happened. Then, he remembered. He needed a block of wood as a base. Sure enough, about six feet from where he stood was a semi-round chunk from the base of a tree with a surface that was well-weathered and hard. Dragging the limb over, he rested the smallest end on the stump. He hefted the axe over his head, putting the full force of his strength into the swing.

*Oh, good grief!* The stinging from the first swing combined with the freezing temperatures had served to practically paralyze his hands. The axe slipped from his grip to fly between two narrow trees, landing in a puddle a dozen feet from where he stood.

He wanted to kick the stump—hard. *Could he be any more of a failure?* It had been the same on the *Peregrine*. While others scampered across the tilting decks, Darcy had clung to the railing of the ship, his feet sliding first one way then the other. Others spliced

lines and tied intricate knots. His looked like a mangled fist or the
ball of yarn Georgiana made the first time she attempted knitting.
His fingers were blistered from the rough ropes and his shins were
bruised from trying to stand upright on a rocking vessel. He was
not a sailor. Apparently, he was not much of a farm hand either.

Last evening had been another first in the life of Fitzwilliam
Darcy. After Madame Vartan had helped Elizabeth to bathe, she
indicated to him that he was next. Never had he used bath water
that was not fresh. Inside he was slightly repulsed, even though it
was salt from Elizabeth's body in the tub. Nonetheless, he had
gone about his business, changing into the man's night gown that
had been left out to protect his modesty—and that of the others.

Without hesitation, Jonah had gone third into the lukewarm
water.

Pushing back a limb, so it would not poke out his eye, Darcy
retrieved the axe, determined to not let it win. He was the master
of Pemberley. He *would* conquer this!

Rubbing his palms against his thighs, he gripped the axe
firmly. Then, he stepped back. Remembering the servants who
chopped the wood at Pemberley, he pulled the limb from the
stump. Instead, he searched for a piece showing the grain on the
end. Setting it firmly on the block, he estimated the length of his
arms and the handle of the axe. Imitating the stance he remembered from Pemberley's staff, he pulled the axe straight back over
his head, then swung it straight forward, building up speed as it
went.

The sound of the wood cracking was a satisfying thunk.
Making the wood do exactly what Darcy wanted was powerful.
Determined to do it again until the chunk split completely in two,
he lifted the axe, only to have the whole piece of wood come with
it. The axe was stuck. That was nothing more than a nuisance.
Wrestling it out was nearly as fulfilling as the original blow. With a
few gentle hits into the crack, the piece split in two. Gripping the

handle, he raised the axe into the air, celebrating his victory. He could do this. Those big obstinate pieces of wood would be at his mercy from this point on. Bending at the waist, he grabbed another victim. Then another.

"Hey, Mr. D," Jonah called from behind him. "Madame Vartan wants ta know if ye are planning to chop down the whole forest 'fore she can make tea?"

Darcy came to a complete stop, surveying the pile of wood he had tossed to the side of the stump. Sweat dripped from his brow. His hands burned from the wooden handle rubbing against his skin. He would have more blisters where dark red patches were already appearing. The warmth from his exertion was fading until a chill settled around his face and arms. Time had flown by.

Darcy sighed in satisfaction. Gathering an armload of the heavier wood, he signaled to Jonah to pick up some kindling. It might take all day but once the wood was transported to the house and stacked against the outer wall, Madame Vartan would have enough fuel to warm her hearth and home for days.

His mind turned to the one occupant who warmed his heart. Would she be proud of him, appreciative of his effort in seeing to her comfort? "How is Elizabeth?"

Jonah shrugged. "Madame Vartan has her cookin'. I think she's just about as good at it as you were when you first started swinging that axe. She'll get the hang o' it soon enough."

Red heat covered Darcy's cheeks. He had not gone unobserved as he had hoped. *Blast!* Darcy had to know, "Have you ever chopped wood before?"

Again, Jonah shrugged. "I'm just a kid. Most assume I'm too little to wield an axe, an' they's probably right. Boone's always tellin' me that everyone is a beginner at some point, so they's no shame in not knowin' something. Where the shame comes, he says, is in knowin' an' not doin.' Me? I'm a doer sorta kid, I guess. No one expects much from me, so I work an' work an' practice an' practice until I get me some skills. I want 'em to be surprised ta see how much I know'd an' can do."

Darcy pondered Boone's outlook. "Boone is correct and so are you. With that in mind, I intend to practice and practice until I can cut wood with the best of men and see that Madame will stay warm for the winter."

"Are ye thinkin' then that we'll be here a while?" Jonah appeared unhappy with the thought. "Shouldn't we see about you gettin' back ta England and me ta my ship?"

Darcy stopped. "Jonah, I will not pretend that being back amongst my home and friends is not my greatest wish. It is. Nevertheless, I cannot in good conscience expose Elizabeth to the danger of trying to escape until we know for certain that she is well. In addition, your health and welfare is important to me."

"Aw, thanks, Mr. D." Jonah blushed.

"We cannot forget that we are on enemy shores. We have no money to purchase passage on a smuggler's vessel, which would likely be our only means across the Channel. We have no connections here, so we do not know whom to trust. We, the two of us men, must care for Elizabeth and Madame Vartan. Should it become known that she is harboring us, I fear what would happen to her, and to us."

The lad wore his pride well at being called a man. "Then, I be lookin' out for Madame while you keep an eye on Mrs. D. We will keep 'em safe."

Had his arms not been full, he would have patted the boy's shoulder. As it was, Madame had stepped out of the house looking for them. They hurried to the cottage. They stepped inside to discover Elizabeth seated at the table, her eyes red and puffy, her cheeks damp from tears.

Darcy could no more stop himself from speaking than to reach up and halt the sun from its orbit. "What have you done to her?" He glared at the French woman. Dropping the wood by the stove, he hurried to Elizabeth's side, kneeling beside her. "Are you well?"

"You are a Brit?" The old woman demanded, raising the wooden spoon she held like a weapon. "You can talk?"

"I can." Darcy removed the knife from Elizabeth's hands. She immediately lifted a towel resting on her lap to cover her eyes. Turning to their hostess, he howled, "How dare you hurt her."

"I have done nothing! You, on the other hand, have pretended to be something you are not."

"The decisions I made about revealing our identity were done to protect those under my care. You may have superior knowledge of how to run your farm, but I know where I came from and who I am. What I also know is that my French is not nearly as good as yours because it is not the language that I was born with." At her nod, he boldly added, "I am aware that you, too, were not born to speak French. You have a subtle accent you endeavor to hide but I hear it."

"You know nothing!" The woman turned her back on him.

Darcy ignored their hostess. "Elizabeth, what has she done? Whatever it is, I will make her pay before we leave this place." His righteous indignation knew no limits. Before they walked out the door, Madame Vartan would feel the full force of his ire.

Pushing the small knife away from her, his beloved wiped her face with the back of her sleeve before bursting into ... laughter?

EVERYTHING ABOUT ELIZABETH'S morning had been a learning experience. Madame Vartan had rinsed the salt and smoothed the wrinkles from her clothing the night prior for her comfort. Dressing herself in the empty room, Elizabeth's appreciation for the garments and the effort it took to see to their care pricked her conscience. Recalling the years of her insisting on strolling the muddy paths around Longbourn must have caused their maid an unending and unnecessary amount of work. Shame on her! Why had she never considered other's efforts on her behalf before? Had she been asked, she would have insisted without qualms that she was the most considerate of all of her sisters.

*Goodness!* And she had thought Mr. Darcy was arrogant!

Joining Madame in her kitchen, she had quickly learned something else about herself. All the years Mrs. Bennet had insisted that her daughters act like accomplished young ladies had been a waste. What good were netted purses or painted tables when your hostess directed you to a pile of vegetables, six eggs still in their shells, a bowl with a yellow blob in it, a crusty loaf of bread, and a small knife?

Elizabeth was not ignorant. She recognized potatoes, carrots, something that sort of looked like a carrot though bulkier in shape with a paler hue, onions and other gray bulbs with long green-ish stems with soil-coated tentacles growing from the bottoms. Next to them were green ... somethings that looked like Madame had stripped all of the local plants of their leaves. Some were delicate and small. Others broad and firm. She knew that at Longbourn, a maid took an empty basket into the hen house and returned with eggs daily. She had witnessed Cook with her hands covered in flour as she kneaded bread dough. Had Elizabeth ever done it herself? Never! Her mother would not allow it nor had Elizabeth been inclined to give it a try.

She had barely kept from slicing off the end of her finger as the pile of carrots, what she learned were parsnips, potatoes, and garlic grew. The greens were identified as parsley, chard, and kale. What tortured her beyond measure were the onions. The first one made her sniff with only a drop of fluid pooling in the corner of her eyes. However, the next onion made tears stream down her cheeks. By the third onion, she was ready to cry foul and offer to empty chamber pots rather than cut another slice. How humbling to admit that she, who had long prided herself on being bold and brave, could be felled by a mere vegetable. It was then that Darcy and Jonah came through the door.

The ridiculousness of the situation lit her fancy until all she could do was laugh—at their situation, at the silly look on Jonah's face, at Darcy in all of his rustic finery, unknowingly wanting to slay the wrong culprit, and at herself.

## 14

Darcy's final humiliation was when Madame sent him to milk her lone cow. Normally the task was done by a milkmaid. Their hostess had Elizabeth busy at the table, so Darcy had been elected. He knew it was part of his punishment for being dishonest with Madame Vartan. Jonah had been correct. She was the praying and preaching sort who muttered threats, under her breath, of eternal damnation for telling a lie while he tended Elizabeth. As was her way, Elizabeth calmed the woman with a reminder that the three needed to use caution because they did not know her. Bless Elizabeth!

The bovine refused to cooperate in spite of his best attempts. Why had he not learned basic farm skills while growing up at Pemberley? Why had not Eton or Cambridge provided practical knowledge by preparing their pampered students for the reality of life beyond the boundary of his office as master? Why had his own father deemed it improper for a Darcy to soil his hands with common labor? His uncle, Lord Matlock, who had two sons of his own, had felt the same. All three boys were exactly like their peers. Their families spent the majority of their time in London with a few visits to the country in the late summer and early autumn for the harvest. Well-trained stewards and housekeepers cared for the properties in the interim.

Darcy genuinely loved his country home. Many of his fondest memories were when his cousins visited, especially the younger of the two boys. How long had it been since the three of them had been together in Derbyshire? Darcy could not even remember.

When the cow bawled loud enough to stir Madame from her cottage, she deftly pulled the stool closer, rested her brow against the side of the cow's hide, and proceeded to generate white streams into the bucket. After a few moments, she stood, gesturing for him to take her place.

He heard her whisper under her breath as she guided his hands to their task. "Lazy rich man."

In perfect French he replied, "Madame, in fairness, I will admit that I was wrong to accuse you of hurting Elizabeth. For this error in judgment, I apologize." He added, "Your accusation of me being a 'lazy rich man' is also wrong. It is true that I am untrained in the daily activities of a parcel this small. However, I will have you know that I oversee many properties, a staff of hundreds, investments that you could never imagine, and a sister of whom I am guardian. I take pride in being a fair master, a loyal servant of my King, and a good husband to the best woman on this earth." The last was said with an honest heart. Until they married and beyond, he would do everything within his power to see her cared for as mistress of his home and keeper of his heart.

She harrumphed.

"Madame Vartan, our path to knowledge may be different, but I will share what I know. For example, I can see by the milk already in the pail that it has little cream in it. This cow will dry up before long unless she is bred. I also see that your garden plot is practically empty. Where the eggs came from this morning, I do not know. There are no chickens clucking in your yard. You have kindly shared your resources with three strangers. For this you deserve praise." He paused to see her reaction. The woman barely breathed.

Her spine stiffened. "What do you want?"

Darcy thought the cow might have sighed when he quit trying to force liquid from a dry well.

"Madame, I want safety for Elizabeth and Jonah. I want to return to England to set to rest those who fear what has happened to us. I want to be home."

She nodded once.

Moving the bucket out from under the cow's hooves, he stood. Extending his hands towards her, he turned his battered palms up, so her view was clear. "I do not know how long it will be until we can return to England. In exchange for a warm place to stay away from the French military, I promise you that I will work as hard as I am able to make your situation more secure. The lad, Jonah, is industrious. He is also likely smarter than I am when it comes to surviving with nothing. Together we will do our best."

"You will, will you?" she taunted. "Monsieur Darcy, I know things as well, and that is all I will say. I need no one to survive. I can do for myself easier than train a fop who is better with a quill than an axe. I do this work in my sleep." She left him standing in the middle of the shed without a word of goodbye.

Like a bad card player, Darcy wondered if he had overplayed his hand.

HAVING Jonah underfoot was worse than a three-month old puppy. With each ingredient Madame added to a large round metal plate suspended over a rack in the middle of the coals that she called a sadj, the lad licked his lips and rubbed his middle. First onto the disc came that small yellow blob that Elizabeth now understood was butter. Next came her thinly sliced onions. When Madame added a pile of diced potatoes with a bit of salt, Jonah began salivating. It was not until the widow began chopping beets and greens that the boy balked.

"Madame, you might believe those weeds ta be good fer what ails ye, but I got a belly ache from eatin' too healthy once an' that's not good fer a young body like mine."

Elizabeth looked at him closely to find he was entirely serious. She had to chuckle, despite the scratch in her throat.

"You remind me of my younger sister, Mary." Elizabeth encouraged him away from hovering over the food cooking on the fire. "She is all things righteous. Each day she spends exactly ninety minutes practicing the pianoforte, twenty minutes walking circles around the rose garden in rain or shine for her constitution, and forty minutes reading aloud from *Fordyce's* sermons. No matter what day it is or what else anyone has planned, she sticks to her routine."

Jonah lifted a quizzical brow. "How in the world am I like her?"

"Mary loathes kale, chard, spinach, lettuce, parsley, and anything else that is green. To carry her point, she will not wear a gown with green in it nor will she soil her walking boots by stepping on grass." Elizabeth smiled. "As a matter of fact, in our family, when my sister was much younger, she was caught praying to the Almighty, questioning him about why he had to make so much of our corner of the earth green."

With each word, Jonah's head shook back and forth. "Nope! I'm not like her at all. I love ta run through a grassy field with me feet bare. And I don't mind the grass stainin' me knees neither." He wiggled his toes as Darcy stepped into the room. "Say, Mr. D, I've been wonderin' if yer any good at sharpenin' knives. Might be we could take that small stone I found in the wood bin and earn us some coin or table scraps by workin' fer Madame's neighbors. I'm a pretty fair hand at it me self but I wouldn't mind having ye fer company."

"No!" Madame Vartan blurted. "He will not go where he can be seen by others. The clothes do not hide the man. One look at the way he carries himself and my neighbors will know he is the very sort of man they despise."

Elizabeth volunteered, "Then perhaps I shall go with Jonah."

"And do what?" the French woman snorted. "Teach a farm woman how to cry when they chop onions, how to spill flour on the floor instead of baking it into bread? I do not think so, Madame Darcy. The only one in this room besides myself who has marketable skills is the lad. For his safety, he too will remain here."

Elizabeth rose to her full height. "I have worked in the still room at Longbourn for a full decade. I know the plants and flowers with which you have filled your home. Your hands are stronger than mine, but mine have a stamina to mix tinctures and a delicacy of touch that I believe you may lack. Pray, let us not work against each other. Let us take what abilities we have to see how we can make the best of our situation. Already we can easily discern that you have an abundance of generosity, for you have shared your produce with us without skimping on the portions. Jonah can perform any of his sea-faring tasks much more easily on land and my ... my husband, he is not ashamed to apply his hand at tasks he routinely assigns to others." Elizabeth swept her hands to encompass them all. "You see before you three individuals who will work together. Let us find whatever advantage we may, please."

After a long pause, the woman nodded. "I trade ointments for what I have in my larder. The local hens are almost done laying so eggs will be rare. Due to the war, many of the properties have only the women and children at home. Few have money so we trade or barter. We are a strong, independent people who are used to making do with what we can grow or build."

Darcy offered, "We are willing to do whatever it takes so you do not suffer for our presence, Madame."

Jonah quickly volunteered, "Madame, I will kindly offer ta test out any o' yer cookin'. I remember me ma fixin' me what she had, but nothin' she cooked was like those potatoes, even with the green parts an' the beets. I would eat it every mornin' if I could fer the rest o' me life." He rubbed his belly, then yawned. "Me watch has ended. It be time fer me ta hit me bunk."

As the sun dipped under the horizon, Darcy's eyelids drooped. Just as he had promised, he and Jonah had chopped and hauled wood most of the day. Inside the cottage, the two women had ground petals and leaves with a mortar and pestle until the air was thick with a sweet, earthy fragrance.

Before banking the fire for the night, Madame Vartan placed several rosehips in a pot with herbs and what looked like strips of bark she pulled from one of her baskets. Simmering it over the coals, she shared the steaming liquid with each of them.

"I suspect each of your bodies will be complaining before too long. This tea will ease the ache in your muscles." Brushing off their thanks, she reluctantly admitted, "I thank you for gathering fuel for my fire."

With that, she went to the chair in front of the fire, pulled a knitted blanket over her legs, and closed her eyes.

Elizabeth was the first to go to the bed chamber. As they had done the night prior, Jonah and Darcy stepped outside, changing into their nightwear in the dusky light. By the time they returned, Elizabeth was sound asleep.

Lifting the heavy quilt, Darcy slid in alongside her. Jonah did the same from the other side of the bed. Madame was correct. His muscles in his legs, back, and shoulders screamed at him each time he moved or flexed. When Elizabeth immediately sought his warmth, turning in her sleep towards him and resting her head on his upper arm, he felt no pain. Instead, his heart filled with appreciation for her kindness to their hostess, to the boy who was attached to them, and to him. Shaking his head at himself at the depth of the changes less than a week had made to his life, it would have been impossible for him to have imagined these events should someone have asked.

He would never have conceived of being kidnapped, smuggled aboard a ship destined for the Americas. He never would have guessed that he would be stranded on French soil. He would not deliberately have assigned himself the task of farm work. Most of all, in his wildest dreams he would not have pictured himself sharing a bed with Elizabeth Bennet and a gangly lad from the Carolinas. Nonetheless, where he thought he loved Elizabeth before, he loved her now with a depth he had never felt for another person. Additionally, his life would have been less rich not coming to know Jonah Hackett. Even the cantankerous Madame Vartan was wiggling her way into a corner of his heart. Grinning to himself, upon reflection, he had no reason to repine.

## 15

He wanted to die.

If Madame Vartan had a gun in the cabin, Darcy would have begged her to load it, aim it, and pull the trigger to end his suffering. She likely would have done it with glee. As it was, he had seen no evidence of a weapon in the cottage. *Drat it all!*

Every single muscle ached to the point that it hurt to even think about getting out of bed. When Elizabeth rolled away from him to rise and join their hostess in the kitchen, he had thought to follow her. Then he moved. One infinitesimal motion, less than an inch, was all it took to change his mind.

He had suspected that he might be a little sore after his physical exertions of the day before. The reality dramatically exceeded his imagination. Nevertheless, he could not remain in bed all day, having two women and a child bring in the wood, the milk, and the water. Tentatively he lifted both arms to the ceiling. The muscles and tendons of his shoulders and neck resisted each fraction of movement, insisting that he put his arms back down. It took him three tries before his elbows straightened and his fingers could point straight up.

Elizabeth tapped on the door before reentering the room. In her delicate hands was a mug with steam rising from the top.

"Madame Vartan has prepared the same tea as last evening in hopes it will ease your pain and relax your muscles," she whispered to keep from waking Jonah.

"Bless her." His dilemma hit him square in the face. Did he pretend he was unaffected? Was he even able to sit up without groaning? Or would he bawl like a baby as soon as he attempted the feat. Fortunately, Elizabeth sat the beverage on the small table next to the bed before departing the room. Thus, it was only a sleeping Jonah who would have witnessed his agony had his eyes been open.

Swinging his legs over the side of the bed, Darcy grabbed the post next to his pillow, pulling himself erect. He gulped, restraining himself through sheer force of will not to utter every curse word he had ever heard or made up when under duress. Inhaling deeply, he grasped the back of his upper arm with his other hand and pulled it toward him, crossing his chest. Agony! Doing the same with the other arm, he was able to determine he could pick up the mug without dropping it on the floor.

The brew was hot and pungent. Madame must have let it steep a long time since it was stronger than she had given them the night before. Within moments, he was able to tilt his head from side to side with a measure of freedom. By the time he swallowed the final drop, he stood and walked to the corner of the room and back on steady legs. Two steps forward. Two steps back. He wanted to crow his victory like a proud rooster.

Changing into his rustic garments quickly, he marveled at Madame. At some point during the night, she had entered their room, gathered their clothing, and brushed it out. Her care of strangers was exemplary. If only she had fewer nettles to her personality. She was like a hedgehog Georgiana called Rosebud that resided in Pemberley's garden. Soft underneath but prickly on the surface.

Reaching over the bed, he gave Jonah a gentle shake. Immediately, the lad's eyes shot open.

"I smell me some food," were the first words out of the boy's mouth. "Do ye smell food, Mr. D? I'm thinkin' I dreamed about those potatoes we had yesterday. Do ye think Madame has made more fer today? If she weren't so old I think I would marry her. 'Cept I'd grow fat an' lazy eatin' all day long so I'd better not."

Jonah leaped out of bed and changed without looking at Darcy. He was out the door like a cannon shot. When Darcy followed, it was a disgruntled, disappointed lad who turned his back from the pot hanging from the fire,

"Mush!" He spit out the word. "Here I was thinkin' ye were the finest lady on the planet besides Mrs. D, an' then ye gone an' fixed gruel. Ye are a cruel, cruel woman, Madame Vartan. I wouldn't have thought it, but the proof is in the kettle."

Jonah likely missed the woman's grin since he plopped into the chair with his back to the table. Sympathy at the boy's plight surged inside him. Darcy, too, hated gruel.

"Come to the table and eat," Elizabeth offered an order cloaked in the velvet of her tone.

Darcy knew he needed to step in. "Come, Jonah. We have hours of work to do. The gruel will help us to get it done. Once our tasks are complete, I suggest the two of us go back to the beach to see what sort of seafood we can gather." He turned his attention to their hostess. "Do you have tackle we might use for fishing?"

"My husband's gear is in the basket by the door. You are welcome to it. Only take care. The sea is volatile this time of year and cannot be trusted. Do not turn your back on it or lose track of each other while you are on the shore. Look out for boats and ships. If you see one, get out of sight and stay hidden until they pass."

"This we will do." Darcy promised.

By then, Elizabeth had loaded the table with bowls, spoons, and small cloths for use as a napkin. Each place had a mug of fragrant tea.

Darcy knew they were in for something unexpected when the scoop Madame served him was dotted with what looked like dried currants. Both Elizabeth and the French woman waited until the males took their first bite. Jonah's eyes rolled back until it looked like he was swooning.

"Well, bless me soul!" The lad immediately dug his spoon back into the bowl and took another bite. "This be the best awful gruel I ever had, Madame V."

Darcy could not help but agree, although he hoped that he would have had a more polite response. The taste of apples, currants, and cinnamon was on his tongue. Milk and honey had been stirred into the pot.

After two more bites, he placed his spoon next to his bowl.

"I agree with Jonah. This has the most welcoming flavor that I have ever tasted." At the woman's nod, he began eating again, gratefully filling his stomach with the warm grains. Both he and Jonah accepted the offer of a second serving with glee.

Elizabeth's throat must have improved; she emptied her bowl. Once the pot was left without a bit of food inside, Elizabeth broached a subject that had been on Darcy's mind.

"Madame, how long has your husband been gone?" Elizabeth's tone was gentle.

"It will be five weeks tomorrow since I last laid my eyes on Alex."

"Five weeks!" All three of them blurted, looking back and forth to each other.

Darcy spoke, "Pray accept our sincerest condolences on your

suffering such a fresh wound to your heart. Had we known, we would have sought refuge elsewhere."

"Condolences? Of what are you speaking?" The widow looked puzzled. "Alex did not die—or at least I do not believe him to be dead. He went to *Ouistreham* to look for work. He is an adept hand at any task. And he is humble enough to earn money doing tasks no one else is willing to undertake. I begged him not to go. Nevertheless, all but one of our cattle and pigs had been confiscated by the army. Had our remaining cow been of sturdier stock, she would have gone too. They took our grain and hay that Alex had gathered not two months past. I expect his return at any time."

"Pardon me for not fully understanding you, but we had assumed you were a widow alone. In addition, there are no storehouses nor evidence of any livestock that have roamed the area between here and the shoreline or from your house to the trees."

Standing, the woman swept all of the used dishes into a pot and poured a pitcher of heated water over them to soak.

"Come with me."

Gathering as much warm outerwear as they could find, they followed Madame Vartan out the door along a pathway Darcy had not noticed. Running parallel to the beach, it was not long before they entered a glen surrounded by tall trees with their tops leaning sideways from the direct wind. The whole area was fenced, perfect pasture for farm animals. A low-topped barn was well-situated at the far end. Its doors were wide open, revealing the inside to be bare.

Continuing through tall grass that circled the field, Madame stopped at an open hole in the side of an embankment that had been boarded shut. Someone had draped sheaves of tall grasses in front of the wood to hide its location. Darcy would have walked right past it without knowing it was there. After pulling away the covering, Madame bent almost double and disappeared inside.

Jonah shook his head. "I don't like dark, tight spaces that ain't below-decks on a movin' ship."

Elizabeth volunteered to keep the boy company.

Darcy knelt down and peered inside. Just then, Madame lit a candle.

"Come inside for here lies the Vartan treasure." Her voice echoed loudly.

Jonah heard it all. Before the word 'treasure' left her mouth, the boy darted past Darcy into the mouth of the cavern. Within seconds, Darcy heard his exclamation, "Aw, nuts! Madame V, that ain't no kinda treasure. I thought ye meant gold."

"No, young man. Gold has no value when you are hungry and there is no food. It cannot keep you alive when there is nothing to buy. This is life-sustaining and pure. It is also a miracle to have it on our parcel so close to the open sea."

Darcy and Elizabeth looked at each other in confusion. Before they could join the others, Jonah popped back out of the cave.

"It's only water an' some stores in a big old cave. Nothin' more." The lad sat himself on a tuft of grass. He pulled a blade from the ground and proceeded to crumple it in his palm.

Elizabeth, with her soft heart, approached and sat next to him. Clasping his small hand in hers, she told him, "Do you want to know about my family's great treasure?"

He instantly looked up. "You've got gold?"

"I am sorry to disappoint, Jonah Hackett. No, I do not have one gold piece to my name."

The boy shrugged, wearing his disappointment like a shirt. "Then you have no treasure at all."

"There you would be wrong. I discovered my treasure when I was five years old and have kept it with me since. In fact, I have it with me right now."

"Where? Show me, please?" He demanded.

"In one moment, I will. First, I need to tell you how I found it and where."

"I guess, if ye have to." Jonah looked up at her, his curiosity piqued.

"It was a dark and stormy night," Elizabeth began. "The winter winds were harsh. Rain had pounded the windows from daylight until dark. My father told all of us that we would have a surprise by morning. I knew in my mind there would be ice and snow. Can you feel the cold that seeped through the casing on my window as I peered outside hoping for even a small break in the weather?"

Jonah shivered.

Elizabeth smiled, then continued. "I was miserable. When the first bolt of lightning struck, followed by thunder, I was frightened to my toes. My older sister, Jane, was already asleep. Mary was still in the nursery. My mother was heavy with child. We discovered the very next day that babe would be my sister, Catherine, or Kitty as we call her. That was my father's surprise. I was completely unimpressed; I will tell you."

"But when do we get to the treasure part?" Jonah asked.

"Be patient and I will tell you." Elizabeth leaned into the boy with her shoulder. "My father knew that I hated storms. That night, he came to me with a story about a man named Jonah. Are you familiar with the tale?"

Jonah hung his head. "Yeah. Me Ma told me when I was little. Other kids teased me about being named for a coward. I wanted to be called Richard the Lionhearted or Hercules. Instead, she called me Jonah."

"Jonah Hackett, you have the story wrong. You see, the Jonah who was swallowed by a fish as told in the Bible, was a valiant man. At first, he was foolish, forgetting when he calculated his odds that he had help. After he was cast out of the belly of the fish, what did he do?"

"I guess he did what he shoulda done in the first place."

"That is correct. It was a hard assignment he was given to speak to God's enemies. However, when under test, Jonah showed bold courage. When my father told me this particular story, he had me place myself in the tale. He helped me to ponder what choice I would have made. Do you know what I told him?"

"I don't," the boy replied, scooting closer to Elizabeth.

"I reminded him that I was only five years old. I would stay home and play with my doll." Elizabeth laughed. "However, I was yet to discover the treasure. When I finally did, it changed everything for me."

The boy bounced. "What is it? What is it?"

Darcy was distracted from her tale by the camaraderie between the two. Jonah looked at her with eager anticipation and awe. In his heart, he felt the same as the boy. She was a wonder. Madame Vartan came from inside the cave to listen.

"Very well. I will come to the good part." Elizabeth inhaled, then slowly released the air. "My father gave me the task of explaining to him in full detail all that I would feel, all of the emotions I would expect, in facing a daunting task like Jonah. Despite my young age, I knew fear, especially with the wind and rain pounding at my window. First, my father reminded me of the other storms I had lived through that winter with no damage to myself and others. Jonah must have done the same, recalling times in the past when others had survived harrowing situations. Then, my father reasoned with me that each little drop of rain and each puff of wind were tiny in comparison to our big house. He explained how Jonah could ease his fears by thinking of taking his message to only one person at a time rather than to the city as a whole. Jonah did this and was a huge success. Then he gave me my treasure."

"What?" Jonah whispered.

"He referred to another Bible account when he told me that young David had no fear of the giant Goliath, not because he saw how much bigger the giant was than himself, but because he realized how much smaller Goliath was than God."

"Oh! I know that story. Boone told me that one." He pondered a bit. "So yer treasure was knowin' ye got some powerful help like Jonah had."

"Exactly. I also learned the value of a good imagination. And I learned to step back from my fears to break down whatever scared me into small pieces or portions. For example, instead of thinking of the storm, I pictured one tiny raindrop sitting in my palm. There was nothing fearsome in that, was there? Or, facing one person at a time who was much smaller than God. Then, I was taught the value of seeking help from a beloved family member, a close friend, or God above. This fills me with courage. Since then, I probably have more boldness than is good for me. Yet, I am able to work things out in my mind so I can move forward instead of being paralyzed by terror. It was a tremendous gift my father gave me that night, one I hope never to forget."

"I kinda see it is sorta a treasure." Jonah jumped up. "Though I much prefer gold."

It was a merry group who wandered in the direction of the cottage. Darcy's delight with Elizabeth filled his chest. Even Madame Vartan might have chuckled a mite.

They were less than twenty yards from the house when they heard voices carried on the breeze—demanding male voices speaking French.

Without hesitation, all four of them turned and ran back to the cave. Even Madame moved quickly. It was a harsh reminder that their lives were in danger. The penalty for Madame harboring enemies would be severe.

Darcy yearned for a weapon or a group of well-armed friends to come to their rescue. He wondered who the interlopers were and how many of them had invaded Madame's property. Turning to ask her if she had recognized any of the voices or what they said, it was then he noted that Jonah was gone.

## 16

E lizabeth's heart plunged to her toes. Jonah was not inside the cave. "Jonah!" she whispered, though her inclination was to yell his name with the full force of her lungs.

When Darcy just sat there and Madame did the same, Elizabeth's anger ignited a fire under her. Standing, she stepped in the direction of the entrance. She would save the boy if no one else would. How could they do nothing? He was so young and defenseless. He needed someone to rely upon who would look out for his best interest. How dare Fitzwilliam Darcy claim to be a gentleman! He was nothing but a...

"No, Elizabeth. We cannot risk the safety of three in the hopes of recovering one." Darcy tugged on her arm until she sat roughly upon the stone.

*Of all the cowardly things to do!*

She challenged, "You may not care about Jonah," she poked his chest with her finger. "But I do. Release my arm, sir! The lad has no chance on his own. He is frightfully young and too bold for his own good."

Darcy shook his head. His stubbornness served to increase her ire. His grip on her arm tightened. "I do care, more than you could possibly know. Nevertheless, I will not risk your life for anyone or any reason. Nor will I willingly bring harm to our hostess. Jonah knew what he was doing when he turned back to the cottage."

"He is a boy!" she hissed.

"Yes, he is." Darcy ran his hand through his hair. "A boy who has lived on his own for two years, Elizabeth, surviving circumstances that we could never know. I cannot take the chance of leaving two women defenseless against who knows how many men. I will not do it."

"I see," she sneered. "Your intention is to sit here and do nothing, completely unconcerned about the future of a lad you have known for mere days." Crossing her arms, she wanted to cry out in frustration. "What if it were one of my sisters? I could never live with myself if one of them were in danger and I did nothing. Please? Please let me see if I can help him?"

"No."

"No? You truly are telling me no?" She wanted to put her hands over her ears to contain the steam she knew had to be pouring from inside them. "I should have known after the poor way you treated poor Mr. Wickham that you cared only for yourself. Your empathy and compassion stretch to no one other than your precious sister." She threw her hands into the air. "I cannot abide doing nothing. I need to find him."

"Elizabeth," he shook his head, closing his eyes. "Have I proved nothing to you over the past few days? Do you not know my character by now?"

His plaintive tone caught her attention. She looked at the man, truly looked at him.

His hair was a mess. Around his eye and his cheek, he still wore a deep purple-ish bruise. His upper lip was less swollen than it had been, but the signs of abuse were still there. The shirt he wore displayed his neck and forearms. His pants were of a rough fabric the color of old bricks. The hem, which reached mid-calf, was frayed. The leather boots were well-worn and scuffed. Puffy clouds of white vapor appeared each time he exhaled. For a certainty, he was as cold as she.

Dipping her head, a trickle of shame budded in her stomach. Had she learned nothing from their trials? Was she so deficient in character that she could not see, or rather, allow herself to see the man in front of her? The real man?

She was wretched. Had she learned nothing?

She softly admitted, "Indeed. You are not the man I stood up with at the Netherfield ball. That man was full of arrogance and pride. His prejudices against my family and neighbors made him abhorrent to me. His actions towards a gentleman whom I admire, sealed my opinion of him as being unworthy of my respect."

She sighed, her words hard to admit to herself and harder to say aloud. "You have put my needs and care ahead of your own. You have protected me without one word of complaint from you. You have adapted to our circumstances far easier than I have. I do know that you care for Jonah. You tease him as you two go about your tasks. I see that your eyes rarely stray from him when he strolls away from you." She slowed her breathing until she was calm. "I was wrong to imply you did not care. Very wrong."

Darcy nodded, but kept silent.

"What about you?" Madame asked. "What about what he has done for you? The boy told me how he saved the lives of all three of you. How can you not be grateful? Your husband, he is a good man like my Alex." She pointed her bony finger at Elizabeth.

Darcy spoke first, looking away from her at the wall. "It is not necessary for Elizabeth to speak of what I have done or not done. My actions should stand on their own."

Elizabeth pleaded, "Then, tell me about Mr. Wickham, I pray you. You have judged him harshly and I need to understand why. For us to have true peace, I believe that this disagreement needs to end today." Elizabeth touched his arm. "I need to keep my mind from being overcome with worry over the child. If any time is the right time, it is now."

His chin dropped to his chest as he considered her request. Nodding once, he began, "Madame Vartan, Elizabeth and I argued vehemently the night of a ball over the character of my old friend and companion, George Wickham. We took the disagreement to a small balcony where we were so engaged in our battle that we failed to see men approaching. They kidnapped us by force. It was a case of mistaken identity since the men thought the two of us were others. We woke the next day on a ship bound for America. Jonah served as ship's boy to Captain Lucien Bartholomew, the master of the *Peregrine*. At first appearances, the captain and his crew were merchantmen. However, at dinner the first evening we were there, there were gaps in the captain's story that were explained the next day when his vessel was threatened by a ship. They were pirates."

"What do you mean by gaps?" Elizabeth challenged. At that same meal, she had been reassured of Captain Bartholomew's good character. It was only later that she discerned they were rogues.

Darcy shook his head. "How could you not see? I do not know whether he was trying to convince himself or us that he was an honest businessman. He made certain that we knew from the moment he appeared that he was in charge of everything that happened on his ship. Then, he too easily passed blame onto Silas Bingley when we explained that we had been kidnapped. At first, he pretended to be shocked at having two captives rather than one. In the next breath, he appeared to shrug it off. Then, he decided to make use of the fact that he had a female on board. Everything about his character was as criminal as his actions proved to be."

Madame shook her head. "How dreadful!"

"Yes." Darcy again ran his hand through his hair. "The greatest danger was to Elizabeth. The captain immediately showed his interest. The crew watched her every movement, eavesdropping on every word. All they had to do was toss me overboard and she would have been fair game for their heinous intentions."

He swallowed before continuing, "When her stomach rebelled at the movement of the ship, I was distressed to see her so overcome. However, since that same illness caused the three of us to be tossed into the sea and we ended up in the safety of your cottage, I am now grateful." He harrumphed. "Would that I could have protected her from the beginning. She would not have been exposed to vile characters who meant her harm."

Madame asked, "This Wickham. This man who was the subject of your argument. He is not a good man?"

Elizabeth watched Darcy carefully as he spoke. His honest countenance erased all doubt.

"No!" Darcy replied before Elizabeth could open her mouth. "He is the sort who always seeks his own advantage. For him, even if the truth is good enough, he plays with lies like they are toys. He uses women in atrocious ways then tosses them away like refuse. He wants what he will not work for. In basic terms, he is lazy and immoral. He desires what I have with no care to the amount of effort it takes to sustain my estate. At one time, he was a friend. Now, he speaks of me and my sister with disrespect. I want nothing to do with him."

"What of Madame Darcy? How does he speak of her?" Madame asked.

Darcy looked at Elizabeth, lifting his brow before answering. "This summer, Wickham imposed himself upon my young sister. In her innocence, she agreed to an elopement. When I arrived and stopped her from stepping into the coach he had rented, Wickham, in front of her, proclaimed his only affection for Georgiana was for her dowry of thirty thousand. When he arrived in Hertfordshire, he must have seen my interest in Elizabeth. His new goal was to destroy any hope of affection in her heart for me."

"What?" Madame was puzzled. "Hope of affection? Was there no love when you wed?" She directed her gaze at Elizabeth, frustration pounding out with each syllable. "How do you not know of this attempted elopement? She would be your sister too. As well, why would you take the side of a stranger over that of your husband? What is wrong with you young people? Do you not know that the only way to make a marriage work is to be joined together in everything?"

Each question to her was valid. Why would she believe Mr. Wickham, a man she had spent less time with than the man seated next to her? Had she completely lost her senses, or were her prejudices blinding her to what was real and honest?

She was struggling to come up with something clever to say to diffuse the tension. Darcy offered her no help, allowing her to take the lead. No, now was not the time for wit. Rather, an honest look at herself was needed.

Did she know anything? How was it that she had been blind to both Captain Bartholomew and Mr. Wickham's true selves? Worse yet, she had accused Fitzwilliam Darcy of lacking in the very areas where those two other men were completely bereft. Compounding her error, Elizabeth had completely misjudged Darcy. In practically every way, she had been far more wrong than right. As Thomas Gray's poem, *Ode on a Distant Prospect of Eton College* aptly stated, "Where ignorance is bliss, 'tis folly to be wise."

Knowing there was no other way to set matters straight, she told the truth, which was always better than a lie. She blurted, "We had these misunderstandings because I am a fool, and we are not married."

"Yet," Darcy added. "We are not married—yet."

Sparks flew from Madame's eyes. "You sleep together in my bed and you are not wed?"

Darcy scoffed. "We sleep together fully clothed with a ten-year-old boy, Madame Vartan. There has been no inappropriate behavior between us, nor will there be until we are united in a marriage recognized by the church and the law."

The older woman sat back, leaning against the rock wall. "This explains much."

Darcy and Elizabeth had yet to speak of marriage. Certainly, both of them knew the danger to their reputations if they remained unwed. Any hint at an elopement would forever tarnish their good name and that of their close families. Should he not offer marriage, her shame would be complete.

Her relief at hearing him state his purpose allowed her mind to travel back to where the discussion began. Drawing on her courage, she admitted, "I thank you for your patience. I admit that my opinions are daily undergoing drastic changes. Mr. Wickham and the captain are both undeserving of my admiration, whereas you, are a worthy man."

His blush touched her heart.

"Ah," Madame's eyes darted between the two of them. "You two will do well," she pronounced as if she were a prophetess.

"Where could Jonah be?" Elizabeth asked no one in particular, her heart racing in fear. She swallowed, closed her eyes briefly and inhaled. Relaxing her shoulders, she admitted, "I now comprehend that your decision was the course of wisdom, but not knowing or doing anything is torturing me."

"It tortures me as well, Elizabeth." Darcy uttered softly.

He took her hand in his, immediately extending comfort. Madame crossed herself in a move Elizabeth had seen other Catholic worshippers do.

Amidst her deep concern, she noticed how rough the palm of his hand was against her own. Madame was correct. The man had exhausted himself cutting and hauling wood the day before, without one word of complaint. He was a good man. He willingly sacrificed for the benefit of others. To Jonah, he had been a valuable friend.

Distant male voices that seemed to be drawing closer, captured their focus.

Darcy asked, "Did either of you happen to note how many men there were?"

"I did not," Madame replied.

Elizabeth agreed. "Neither did I."

"I did not see how many there were as well." Darcy moved to the entrance, placing himself in front of the ladies.

Madame's gaze went over Darcy's form inch by inch. He had positioned himself to spring up quickly in defense.

"If you are not Mrs. Darcy, then who are you?" Madame demanded quietly.

"I am Elizabeth Bennet, the second daughter of Mr. and Mrs. Bennet of Longbourn in Hertfordshire, north of London."

The voice of one of the approaching men rang clear in the winter air. All three of them pressed their lips together in silence.

"Where are they?" The tone was brusque.

The three leaned forward to catch the reply.

The sheaves covering the cave rustled as they were pulled away from the opening and tossed aside. Next, the wooden planks were violently jerked from their snug position.

Without thinking, Elizabeth grabbed Darcy's right arm as Madame did the same to his left.

When the final slat was tossed aside, they saw the faces of two angry men and one scared boy.

## 17

"What have you done to him?" Darcy yelled in perfect French as he burst from the cave. "If you have harmed him..."

"Wait!" The older man of the two threw up his arms. The younger one was not nearly as quick, although he too catapulted his hands high into the air.

Without any warning, Jonah flung himself into Elizabeth's waiting arms. The lad's eyes were closed as he shivered. She knew immediately it was not from the cold. He was afraid.

Elizabeth was soon joined by Madame, who fussed over the boy.

"Madame Vartan, I have news of Alex." The eldest stranger said after removing his hat, his Norman French Cauchois identifying him as a local. Elizabeth recognized it as the same accent as Longbourn's chef.

"*Mon Dieu!*" Madame appeared to shrink in size at the expression on the men's faces. Her own reflected her fear. "What has happened, Jean Paul?"

The burly man who was standing to the side replied,

"Madame, I am relieved to see you are safe. There are dangerous men about. Early this morning, a group of runaway soldiers wearing their tattered uniforms, raided a farm a short distance from town."

"Who was it?" Madame demanded. "Who is it that needs help?"

Elizabeth secretly applauded the woman. While she was a blunt sort, her hospitality and concern for others was unequaled.

"The victims were Madame Latour and her children." Disgusted, the man slapped his hat against his leg. "They were locked inside the bedroom while the thieves ransacked the house. They took what little the family had of value, leaving a path of destruction behind them. As you are aware, her husband was killed soon after the war began. Without the help of the townspeople, they would have starved long ago. They had nothing before. Now, they have less than that."

"*Mon Dieu!*" Madame exclaimed. "At least they are alive."

Elizabeth pulled Jonah closer, wanting to cover his ears. This sort of news was chilling to the soul. He wiggled himself loose, though he did not completely seek his freedom.

"They got to yer cottage," Jonah cried. "They took yer cow an' yer perty blanket an' yer flowers is smashed to bits. The crashin' an' bangin' inside yer place went on forever. Then," he sobbed. "Those bad men lit it afire."

Madame reeled. Darcy clamped his arms around her, a silent offer of support.

The one addressed as Jean Paul spoke, "The five of them did their nasty deed, then left. The three of us, including the lad, poured water on the fire until it was out. I will not lie to you, Madame. The destruction to the outside is minimal. The damage to the inside is extensive. We can only be grateful that you and your guests were away from your home."

"How could they?" Elizabeth asked, ire moving her to express her indignation. "How could they harm defenseless women and children with no regret?"

Jean Paul glanced at her before his attention became fixed on their hostess. "That question leads us to the reason we were coming to see you, Madame Vartan." He sighed. "Trouble has been brewing in town for the whole of the two months since the men first arrived. At first, they told stories of their heroic actions of how they were injured, gaining sympathy and free food from the inns. When there was more drinking than eating, the innkeepers requested that they move along. Their response violated everything proper. Settling in with the vagrants down by the docks, it was not long before they were involved in the traffic crossing the Channel."

The other man added, "It was them who introduced our neighbors to ether. Somehow or somewhere, they obtained a large measure of sweet oil of vitriol. Mixed with alcohol, it renders a man senseless. After claiming that Napoleon partook of the mixture for his personal entertainment in court, which may be true or not, they easily convinced good hard-working fishermen that the pleasures would give them freedom. Instead, it made them dependent and under their control. I've not seen the like since I learned of opium dens in the *Toulon* region."

Madame perched her fisted hands on her ample hips. "What does this have to do with my Alex? You know as well as I that he would not have associated with that vermin. No, when he left here, he told me he would be gone a month to six weeks. Neither of us were happy at the separation, but it was necessary. He has been gone five full weeks seeking what work he could. He would not go close to the docks. He knew it would destroy me if he met the same fate as Christophe. The sea is a thirsty maiden who sucks the life out of those who dare to enter her domain."

"Madame, I saw your husband when he first came to town. When I did not see him again, I did not worry because I knew his purpose. The two of us assumed he had found work. How wrong we were. I am sorry about it, Madame." Jean Paul rubbed his whiskers. "I regret to inform you that your husband was taken captive by those men all of those weeks ago. He is very much alive —or at least he was when my son and his crew returned from Cornwall early this morning. They took advantage of some friendly merchants who appreciated the price of the goods to make enquiries of two men who had gone missing over a month ago. That is when they discovered Alex. It was told that all three were captured by the tax men and are waiting for transportation to Launceston for the assizes."

Darcy, who had been listening to the men closely, noted, "I was under the impression that smugglers are welcomed at the English coast, that they carry on their job in open defiance of the law. Why was it that Madame's husband and the others were arrested?"

"Sir, you are in the right. Most revenue men appreciate the value they get for very little money, far more than the duty levied against the goods. As for our French sailors, they are fully aware that shipping products to England pays more than fishing ever would. In these hard times, even honest men bend the law to feed and house their families and friends." He shrugged. "None of them knew the tax man would be in town that night. Along with him were a new set of law men who decided to flex their muscles to let everyone know who was in control."

"How could that be?" Madame asked. "We know more of what takes place at Steeple Brink than the people who live there do. How could this have happened?"

Jean Paul answered, "I regret to inform you, Madame, that word is that Alex, who had been unable to find work, was convinced by one of those phony soldiers of the riches to be had smug... no, shipping goods to the Brits on that particular night. No one else would man their boat. The gossip is that Alex joined with the wrong people at the wrong time. They were an ill-prepared lot, I am afraid."

"No!" Madame Vartan insisted. "My Alex has always been a cautious man. He would never have willingly put himself in a dangerous situation, no matter how badly we needed the coin."

Both men shook their heads. "This we know. We are merely telling you the gossip that is to be heard. While we do not know for certain, we suspect that your Alex and the others were put upon by these men who used that vile ether substance, rendering them unconscious."

Elizabeth glanced at Darcy to see his reaction. His eyes immediately met hers.

He said, "We, too, were the victims of a sweet-smelling fluid soaking a cloth that was pressed over our mouths. The two of us woke the next day on board the *Peregrine*." Darcy gave his full attention to their hostess. "Madame, if what happened to Elizabeth and me was the same as happened to your husband, he had no choice."

The words spouting from Madame's mouth burned Elizabeth's ears. Jonah grinned up at her. "I knows those words. They's the first French I learnt from the Jamaican fella."

It was a none too gentle reminder of the background of the lad.

Even as her protective instincts rose to shelter Jonah, her worry over their situation churned her insides. The loss at Madame's cottage was devastating, causing damage that could not easily be undone. Thinking of others, she asked, "Cannot something be done to stop these rogues? Surely, enough men could be gathered to see they are put away from society."

Madame pinched her jaw. "The cow will slow them down for I am thoroughly convinced she would not move quickly even if a fire was lit under her. We have no neighbor to the west; they will run into the estuary if they go that direction. North is the sea. East would bring them right back to us. Their only option is south. If they mean to do mischief, they will get a rude awakening. Monsieur Robinette has more guns and knives than sense. The criminals will not fare well if they attempt to steal from him."

Jean Paul offered, "We have done our duty in telling you about Alex. What can be done about him, I do not know." He shuffled his feet on the trail. "If we could beg your pardon, we will seek help to go after these men. To do so means we leave you to your own repairs and to see about your husband."

Madame patted the muscle on Jonah's upper arm. "We have two strong men who are willing hard workers. We will make do."

Jonah grinned his cheekiest grin to date. Dropping his arms from around Elizabeth, he flexed his muscles for all to see. Elizabeth wanted to kiss the older woman. Despite the hardships and uncertainties Jean Paul had poured at her feet, she cared enough about the dignity of a mere boy to set aside her painful fears to see to his comfort. She must have been a wonderful mother.

THE MEN HAD BEEN accurate in their description. Wisps of steam and smoke rose from the charred exterior. The smell burned Elizabeth's nostrils and the back of her throat.

Ignoring the damage, Madame charged through the doorway. Jonah moved to follow, but Darcy held him back.

"I do not believe Madame would want witnesses to the grief she feels at her loss." Darcy reasoned.

Jonah nodded. "Boone had ta do the same when we were in New York. I offered to go with him to see his family, thinkin' he'd appreciate the company. Cap'n said a man needs to face they's problems on their own. I guess ladies needs ta do the same."

Elizabeth wanted to hug the boy. His insight was far beyond his years.

Before they could gather themselves to see how best to help their hostess, she surged back through the door, a small metal box held tightly in her hands. Moving quickly, Madame walked away from the house to where Darcy had been cutting wood.

Curious what she was up to, the three followed.

Wiping the surface of the container with her skirt, she carefully placed it on top of the splitting block. Stepping back, she lifted the heavy axe in one hand. Elizabeth was impressed at the ease with which she handled the tool. From the looks on Darcy's and Jonah's faces, they were too.

The cold air carried Madame's words, "Alex and I promised not to open this until Christophe walked through the door and we could hold him in our arms. It has been twenty-one years since I last saw my boy. He and another lad had to go fishing despite the incoming storm. I have lived with my regret at not stopping him all of these years. I will not regret breaking my promise to Alex, nor do I doubt that he would do the same if I were in trouble."

The side of the metal box facing Elizabeth had a set of small hinges set in the seam separating the body from the lid. Walking around it, she was unsurprised to find a lock fastening them together. Madame's intention was not to smash the container. With one well-aimed blow, the padlock's arm should break.

"Monsieur Darcy, let us see if you have enough skill to release the lock without damaging what the box contains." She thrust the handle at him, allowing him no opportunity to refuse.

He wiped his palms on the side of his pants, his breathing quickening. Inhaling deeply, he asked that the three of them move away from the chopping block.

Jonah whispered loudly to himself, "Whatcha think be inside? Treasure? Gold? Diamonds and pearls? Green emeralds and rubies?"

Elizabeth doubted it contained that much in value, although it appeared to be priceless in their hostess's eyes.

With one mighty swing, the axe arched from high over Darcy's head to the box below. The ring of metal on metal preceded a thwack as the wedge embedded itself deeply into the block.

Madame slowly approached, hesitant to touch the box. Darcy's grin at his success was fleeting, but Elizabeth caught a glimpse of it before it disappeared. Jonah was on the verge of dancing, begging their hostess to hurry. Instead, she picked up the container, asked Darcy to remove the axe, then sat on the wooden stump. Carefully, she pried off the lid.

It took every bit of Elizabeth's strength to keep the boy from hovering.

The first item out of the box was a handful of coins. It was the next item, a small packet wrapped in soft cotton that affected Madame. Her eyes closed as she threw her head back, pain filling every cell of her body. Her agony robbed Elizabeth of her breath and Jonah of his speech.

When Darcy silently approached Madame, dropped to his knee in front of her, then reached out to gently touch the back of her hand, Elizabeth's heart melted into a puddle at her feet.

"Madame," Darcy covered her fist where she clasped the tiny bundle. "We will step away so you can have your privacy.

"Aw... do we have ta?" Jonah whined.

Darcy stood and pressed the lad's shoulder with a firm hand. "We do this for her."

His tone brooked no argument.

Jonah allowed himself to be led a few steps away but could not resist looking back. At his gasp, Elizabeth turned her head slightly before forcing herself to look away. It had been enough.

Her heart pounded as her mind flooded with possibilities and questions that demanded answers. Where on earth and how had Monsieur and Madame Vartan obtained something like that?

## 18

He heard Elizabeth's gasp and saw Jonah's mouth gaping wide open. Whatever Madame held in her hand must be of shockingly high value. Nevertheless, Darcy refused to allow himself to look. He would not disturb the woman whose range of emotions pained him to read the expressions on her face.

When the lad looked up at him, a question in his eyes, Darcy quietly explained. "Those items in the box tell a story, Jonah. The coins represent the work that she and her husband have done together to save for their future or an emergency such as this. She wed a man she cherishes only to believe him lost as well. While the news that Monsieur Vartan was apparently still alive was positive, the simple fact is that an unscrupulous or overzealous lawman could justify seeing him hang for merely being French or for crimes committed by association. Her home has been damaged. Her possessions are destroyed. She was burdened with three strangers who appeared on her property without invitation." He rubbed the boy's shoulder where his grip had been firm.

"Strong men have been brought to their knees by far less than what she has faced. Thus, we will give her the time she needs to draw herself together."

After a short pause, the lad nodded his agreement.

Looking directly at Elizabeth, Darcy was stunned at the warm softness in her eyes, towards him. Quite unexpectedly, she reached over and inserted the fingers of her hand between his, completely robbing him of his ability to breathe.

*What did she mean by this? Had he inadvertently stumbled upon an action or a word that allowed her to see inside the secret place of his heart? Did she finally return, even in small measure, his love for her?*

Completely oblivious to the emotions swirling around him, Jonah's stomach gave a loud rumble, followed by Darcy's own middle gurgling so loudly that Madame heard.

"Come, let us cook."

By the time Darcy turned around, the items had been placed back inside the box.

"Thank ye, Madame fer yer kindness an' fer thinkin' bout me poor stomach. It be so empty that I could eat some a those green things you been wantin' me ta eat." Jonah bounced over to help her up from the block. "I don't suppose ye got any eggs hidden away like ye did that box." He danced in circles around her. "Say, where'd ye have it stashed away so they couldn't find it? I didn't spy no hiding place inside yer cabin. Me? I never had a place ta hide nothin'. Course, I never had nothin' ta hide, neither."

Madame paused before heading to the cottage. "Who taught you French, young man? It is worse than my English. In fact, who taught you English? I see Monsieur Darcy grimace each time you go on and on."

Unfazed by her questions, Jonah raced to the cottage. He yelled from inside, "Don't ye worry none, Madame. Those thieves stole yer knives, but they must notta had manners 'cause they left behind yer forks an' spoons. Course, all yer plates an' cups be broken. But, look here. Why, they left yer green stuff just like I thought they would." He exited the house with a handful of chard and kale, "yeah, they musta not knowed what was good fer 'em."

Madame handed Darcy her treasure box. Without a word, she approached Jonah and took him into her arms, greens and all. Kissing him on the forehead, she looped his skinny arm in hers before walking to the kitchen garden. "Those fools do not know the value of a little work." She gestured where the straw covering the plants had been crushed beneath booted feet. "Bring me my heavy fork, young Jonah. I will show you what was right under their noses."

Within moments, she pushed aside the hay with her boot. Bending over one of the green tops, she pulled, digging the fork into the soil at the same time. One mud-covered potato followed another until there was a small pile in the dirt. Next, Madame moved to an area with tall light green fronds. Before long, a bunch of carrots joined the potatoes. As Jonah praised and encouraged, she gathered leeks, a well-weathered onion, and garlic.

As much as he regretted letting go of Elizabeth, Darcy needed to help. Handing her the box, he returned to the stump for the axe. Next, the cow shed contained a rustic wooden handle with a narrow shovel strapped to the end. Grabbing a well-used cloth bag on his way out of the door, he returned to the kitchen garden.

Elizabeth called him to assist her inside the cottage. Together, they brought a small table that had been tipped on its side to the back of the house. There Madame set the box. Returning inside, Elizabeth retrieved whatever unbroken pieces she could find. By the time Darcy had helped Madame to dig up the rest of the potatoes, a small pile of utensils, various tins, and one crock with the edge chipped off dotted the end of the table.

Madame selected the largest bowl available, then sent Jonah for water.

As he continued to harvest the garden, Darcy surveyed the familiar area to see what else could be scavenged. The water bucket was gone, most likely used to carry off what the men had stolen. The pitchfork used to spread the straw that had leaned against the shed was missing. The fabric covering the inside of one of the windows had vanished.

Shaking his head at such blatant thievery, Darcy bent his back to the work. When Elizabeth and Madame came out of the cottage with the chamber pot that had graced the bedroom full of coals, he set aside the shovel to help.

Leaving the women to scrub the vegetables, he and Jonah gathered branches and chopped pieces of wood.

In a clear spot in the yard, Darcy had earlier noted a ring of stones where fires had burned in the past. Over the circle was an iron stand that was hollow in the middle. There were no hooks or handles. He had wondered about its purpose.

Madame scooted the table closer to the fire pit after the coals were dumped inside. Handing Jonah the now empty pot, she sent him for more water. From the cottage she brought out the large metal disc she had used to cook on the day prior. Setting it on top of the iron rack, the water she poured inside soon began to bubble.

Darcy returned to his task of clearing the garden, stuffing the produce inside the feed bag. Elizabeth was at the table cleaning vegetables. Jonah raced to bring her bowl after bowl of water.

With regret on her face, Madame went inside and ripped the other curtain from the window frame. The edges were singed. The fabric was damp. Nevertheless, she wadded it up and grabbed the edges of the round pan, dumping the water out. Placing it back on the fire, she wiped the surface with the edge of the cloth. Then she brought the chipped crock close.

Sniffing the inside, she used one of the spoons that Elizabeth had washed to scoop the contents into the pan.

"Monsieur Darcy," she asked. "Pray clean the blunt end of the axe, if you please?"

As soon as the task was performed, Madame used that end to smash several of the largest potatoes. Next came the rest of the vegetables. Scooping them into a bowl, she poured them over the butter sizzling on the fire.

The smell wafting up from the pan went straight to Darcy's taste buds, making his mouth water.

Moving quickly, their hostess stirred the mixture from the middle to the edges and back, not allowing the vegetables to rest in one place too long. Within seconds the pleasing aroma battled with the smoke from the charred surfaces of the cottage.

Under Madame's direction, Elizabeth tore pieces of the greens from their stalks to drop into the pan.

Darcy noticed that she moved with the same calm efficiency as their hostess. Every minute it seemed his admiration for her grew.

When the edges of the potatoes were a deep golden brown, Darcy, using the folded curtain to protect his hands, carried the pan to the table.

Their *alfresco* meal was rustic and the best that Darcy could recall consuming. Never in his lifetime had he eaten directly from a cooking vessel. He doubted that Elizabeth had either. However, young Hackett was in his version of heaven, even eating the kale and chard like they were manna.

Once their appetites were satisfied, Madame handed out tasks like she was a Rear Admiral of the fleet. Elizabeth started sweeping up the mess in the bedroom before moving to the main room. Madame sifted through the debris left by the robbers, handing anything worth saving to Jonah.

As Darcy hauled the heavier pieces out into the yard, he considered the growing pile on the table. Lifting a small tin containing a fragment of precious tea, he considered the difference in his life at Pemberley to the one he was living that day.

He felt Elizabeth's presence at his side.

"Longbourn is a small estate compared to Netherfield Park. From Miss Bingley's conversation, I deduce that your Pemberley is much larger."

He nodded, still gazing at the table. Despite being pleased that her thinking was apparently in line with his, his heart was in his throat, keeping him from giving word to his troubled thoughts.

"Should Longbourn suffer the loss that Madame did today, the parade of servants it would take to empty our buildings of what would be considered worthy of being rescued would stretch across the yard. My father would crumple at the loss of his books, my mother's nerves would shatter, Mary would weep at any damage to the pianoforte, Kitty and Lydia would sob if their ribbons and lace could not be saved, and Jane would rush from one to another offering comfort."

Darcy swallowed. "What of you, Elizabeth?"

Without hesitation, she replied, "I would work."

His chest filled with love for this woman. Taking her hand as she had done his earlier, he decided that the time was right to be forthcoming.

Gently caressing her fingers, he opened his heart to her, leaving him more vulnerable than ever. Yet, he trusted her like none other. The streak of soot and ash on her cheek and the tip of her nose failed to mar her loveliness. Seeing the depth of her concern in her beautiful eyes, he began, "Elizabeth, it has been a mere four days since we were taken from Netherfield Park, though it seems we have lived a lifetime since the ball."

Without breaking her gaze from him, she nodded.

"From the moment we stepped onto the balcony at Netherfield Park, we have repeatedly faced danger at the risk of our lives. We were thrust together in horrifying circumstances entirely foreign from anything either of us has ever known. Yet, through it all, it was made bearable to me because of you." He paused to consider how best to formulate his words. He wanted her to be left with no doubts how he felt. His mind failed him. Nothing poetic or romantic came to mind. Finally, he blurted, "I love you, Elizabeth. I admired your beauty and wit before we were kidnapped, but my love for you has been forged and shaped by fiery trials. I cherish you now and will love you as long as I live."

Her eyes filled with tears, liquid pools shining brilliantly. When the corners of her mouth lifted, he dropped to his knee.

"Elizabeth Bennet, will you do me the honor of becoming, not my pretend sister, nor my pretend bride, but my wife in actuality? Will you marry me?"

Before she could utter a word, Jonah burst from the cottage.

"Marry her? Ain't she yer sister or yer wife already? Well, I guess not or ye wouldn't be on yer knee. So, what are ye gonna say, Mrs. D? Surely, yer gonna say yes since Mr. D be a fine man who can chop wood to keep ye warm in the wintertime. He can't tie a sailer's knot worth beans, but he can swim like a fish. What are ye gonna say? Tell him yes. The poor man looks miserable down on his knee."

Elizabeth's smile had grown with each word out of the boy's mouth. On the other hand, Darcy felt like pieces of lead were being dropped inside his gut with every sentence. He wanted to strike himself. His proposal should not have been the work of a moment. He should have considered the setting *and* the company. *Blast!*

Jonah was not yet finished. "Go ahead, Mrs. D, ye can pretend I'm not even here. Just tell him yes, an' we can get back ta work."

Elizabeth tugged on Darcy's hand. He stood, unable to keep his shoulders from drooping at his failure. When she gave his hand a firm squeeze, he looked at her, truly looked at her. What he found lifted the weight from his middle,

Grinning at Darcy, Elizabeth finally replied, "In the words of the most eloquent ten-year-old that I know, yes, I will marry you, Mr. D."

"Kiss 'er, Mr. D." Jonah bounced with joy like it was he, and he alone, who had brought the two of them together. "Ye got to kiss 'er now. Me? I don't understand all this kissing and hand holdin' business, but the fellas on the ship seem to like it when we is in port. I'm not ever gonna kiss no girl." He made the silliest face, wrinkling his nose. "What if she ate an onion? Or what if I did? That would be the worst kiss in history in my..."

"Jonah!" Madame stopped his rant. "Come inside. Leave them alone. Do not meddle in business that is not yours."

"Aw, Madame. Do I have ta?" The lad shuffled his feet.

"Come now. This is not your concern."

"But... he might not get it done right proper without my help." Jonah whined.

"Not another word." Madame hooked her hand at the back of the boy's neck like a shepherd with a staff would do an errant sheep, leading him back through the doorway into the cottage.

Relief at having privacy filled Darcy from his head to his toe.

Elizabeth studied his face, her eyes moving from one surface to the next. He knew he was not at his best. Far from it, in fact. He had not bathed properly since the day of the ball. His growing stubble itched. His wavy hair was completely out of control. His clothing was rough, ill-fitting, and borrowed. His feet were pinched in worn boots, and he had not a farthing to his name. Jonah had a valid point. He had not washed his teeth in days. Neither had Elizabeth. Yet, she was stunning, like a ray of the sun bringing light to his world. He loved her so much.

He had to ask. "Could you ever see yourself loving me in return?"

It was the boldest of questions. She inhaled sharply. Her pause nearly crushed his heart. However, he should have known better.

She had proven in their days together that she knew when to speak and knew when to act.

Stepping forward, she placed one hand on his chest, the other on his cheek. Just before her eyes closed and her lips touched his, she softly whispered for him alone, "I already do."

## 19

E lizabeth's toes curled as heat rushed from the soles of her feet to the tips of her hair. She feared lightning would shoot from her fingertips. His lips barely brushed hers, stirring a hunger inside her for something unrecognizable that she did not know she possessed. Her lips ached to feel his again. He was delicious!

Had she been honest with him and with herself when she declared her love? For a certainty! Nothing in her lifetime had prepared her for how good it felt to be in this man's arms. The warmth and security flowing through her paled when compared to how cherished she felt. The simple truth was that her heart yearned to make him feel the same. She would love and honor him for her entire life.

Nevertheless, how had she gone from despising the ground he walked on to eager anticipation of being joined to him forever? Was she insane? Not at all. She now knew the man behind the mask. She loved and admired that man. More than that, with each word and action confirming the depth of his character, she trusted him.

Jonah shouted from the doorway, "He kissed her! I knew he would an' she liked it. I can tell 'cause her foot lifted off the ground like the ladies on the docks when the sailors come in with a purse full o' gold."

"Jonah!" Madame barked. "Come, I will show you my hiding place."

The boy vanished in an instant.

Elizabeth felt Darcy's smile as he kissed her forehead. Then, she felt his sigh.

"Elizabeth, we need to talk." Darcy hugged her to him. Holding her hand in his own, he led her to where he had earlier moved four large blocks of wood to each side of the table. "We must get back to England. Only then can we set matters right between us to secure our future. Our loved ones need reassurance of our safety, and we need to discover why Bingley is in such a mess and what can be done to keep his uncle from making another attempt to force him to America." Assisting her to be seated, he went to retrieve the others.

Smoothing the fabric of her skirt, she pondered how much her life had changed. Had it truly been only four days since she readied for the ball? How was that possible? Considering the events of each day separately, he was correct. They woke aboard ship the first day. They were swept overboard the day following. They had been in France for parts of two days. Less than one hundred hours had altered the course of her life and that of Darcy's.

"I extend my sincere congratulations to the both of you," Madame offered. "It is my hope you are blessed with joy in your marriage like I have been with my Alex." Once seated, she looked up at Darcy. "Now, how do you mean to get us to England to begin your life together and rescue my Alex?"

"What about me?" Jonah asked, crushed at having not been included.

Madame answered immediately. "You, young man, have a choice. Once Monsieur Darcy rescues my husband, you can come with me and Alex or you can stay in England with the Darcys. My preference is to keep you with me. It has been too long since we had a boy of our own to look after and feed. However, your shipmates, should they be looking for you, will know where to find you in England if you remain with them."

Jonah replied, "I sure would like ta stay here fer ye to cook fer me, Madame. I could help ye find another cow. But I wanna go back ta the sea. That be the life I'm happiest at. Besides, Mr. D already tried ta teach me my letters and numbers when we were aboard the *Peregrine*. He would likely see me in school if I stayed with him an' the soon-ta-be Mrs. D. I won't be havin' it, I tell ye."

Madame nodded in mock solemnity as Darcy winked at Elizabeth. The lad was correct. Should he stay with them, a priority would be to hire a tutor as quickly as possible.

Their hostess continued, "My land lies three miles from *Caen*. We can take the produce from the garden to sell at the market. It will not bring much, I am afraid. Yet, each franc will help."

"What about yer ring? You know, the one in the box?" Jonah asked.

Madame sighed before heaving herself up from the stump. Moments later, she returned with the box. Carefully opening it and unwrapping the piece of fabric as she had done earlier, she placed the ring on the table. The muted winter sunlight bounced off the rose-cut diamonds set in silver against a background of cobalt blue guilloché enamel. On the surface was a crown shaped from diamonds and filigree like that worn by Catherine the Great, Russia's ruler during the last century.

Only one time had Elizabeth seen something similar. It was an Imperial presentation piece worn by one of her uncle's customers at his import/export business. The older woman had been fashionably dressed with ropes of heavy pearls around her neck, dangling sapphire drop earrings, and a magnificent diamond brooch. However, it was her ring that had captured young Elizabeth's attention. Similar in style and materials to Madame's, it differed only in that there was a lovely curved "E" below the crown on the surface. The design was elegant, the stones flawlessly cut. The filigree work on the band was exquisite. Elizabeth had always wondered what the "E" stood for. Possibly, Elizabeth? Immediately, she knew there was a story attached to the piece of jewelry on the table.

"Madame, how did you come by this ring?" Elizabeth kindly asked before Jonah could bluntly insist on the information. "Is your heritage Russian?"

"Da," Madame nodded. "My parents were what you would call landed gentry. My mother had known Catherine II prior to her marriage. Once her *coup d'état* was a success and she came to power, the empress remembered my mother's kindness and gave her the ring. My mother cherished the friendship far more than the jewelry."

Looking toward the horizon, she continued. "For decades, the empress listened to the common people, or serfs. Then, for reasons only she knows, she stopped. Rebellion followed. There were millions of the lower class. Catherine had a half million serfs of her own. During one of the bloodiest of the conflicts, my father decided to pack up all that he and mother held dear to head toward the Western borders. Having those goods piled in wagon after wagon was an invitation for trouble. We should have been more cautious and taken little with us. Shortly after our departure, we were attacked. My parents died defending what was rightly theirs. I ran into the woods and hid until the next day."

"How did ye get away? Did ye have a gun or a blade hidden in yer boot?"

Madame smirked. "I had been an indulged little girl who had others do all of the things that I should have known how to do.

The only thing I was good at in that forest was shedding tears. We were foolish in our privilege." She patted Jonah's hand. "Young man, I learned quickly that just because I had been raised to believe I was superior, it was not true."

Elizabeth asked, "How did you escape?"

Madame smiled. "Alex."

"Yer husband saved ye?" Jonah finally paid attention to something other than that ring.

Madame ruffled his hair. "He did save me though he was not my husband at the time. He was a stranger who first scoffed at the ignorance of a silly girl." Her eyes looked at the distant horizon, though Elizabeth knew it was not the view at the forefront of her mind. "We were fortunate that the weather held and that strangers were generous with their food and protection. By the end of the first day, I had shed my fine gown for peasant's clothing. I hid the ring in a small pocket I stitched in the waistband. It was not until we left Russia for the Kingdom of Sweden that I finally felt the first hint of freedom. However, by that time, my heart was no longer my own. On the day we wed, I showed Alex the ring. He vowed that only the direst of circumstances would force us to sell the gem." She focused back on her visitors. "Because he is a man of many skills, we have been able to live simply with little distraction. I learned that wealth created pretentions in me that my husband found unattractive. I, too, have learned to value genuine qualities in a person." Reaching over, she grabbed Darcy's wrist. "You do what you need to, Monsieur Darcy, to bring my Alex home. Use the ring if needed. It means nothing against the value of my man."

When there was a lengthy pause before Darcy responded, Elizabeth's heart fluttered at the seriousness by which he attended Madame's request. Here before her was evidence of finally having read his character correctly. He was not disinterested. He was a careful thinker.

"Madame," he began. "I desire nothing more than to have your home restored to what it was only this morning. No, that is incorrect. I long to have it five weeks and one day ago when we could have met your husband here." He gave his attention to the boy. "I invite all of us to freely express ideas or suggestions even if they appear outlandish at first thought. Jonah, with your experience at sea being far superior to mine, pray join in our planning for we cannot avoid a crossing of the Channel." To all he said, "Any movement away from this property will place all of our lives in peril. We cannot afford to be incautious."

"Agreed." Madame nodded.

Jonah was the first to speak. "I'd noticed ye said 'we' when ye was talkin' 'bout goin' ta England, Madame Vartan. Ye be goin' with us then?"

"I will." Her arms crossed as she nodded once.

"Then we can sell the ring an' buy a ship, hire a crew, an' be across the Channel by tonight, I 'spect. Perty simple if'n ye ask me." Jonah grinned. "Or I could offer me services and work my way across. Madame could cook fer the crew an' they'd love her fer it. So, we'd only need ta figure out what to do with Mr. an' Mrs. D."

"Thank you, Jonah. You have offered a fine idea." Darcy grinned at the lad, indicating he had taken no offense to the innocently given insult.

Then he directed his full attention towards their hostess. "I will not attempt to dissuade you from your course, Madame. Your opinion of the sea being dangerous is justified. That you are willing to venture forth to attempt a rescue shows your devotion to your mate, which is admirable. With that said, there is a risk to you once you reach the shore. As we would be most unwelcome by the French army here, you would face the burden of the same there."

"I will go."

He dipped his head in agreement. Then, he gave his full attention to Elizabeth. "My dearest, after your ordeal at sea, I would do anything to prevent you from ever needing to enter the Channel again. Yet, I am powerless against the water that separates us from home. Will you..." his eyes pleaded. "Will you fare well?" He rushed to add, "Pray understand that I do not doubt your courage, my dear. I only worry that it is too soon."

If she did not love him before, she would have lost her heart to him at that second in time.

His concern was valid. The thought of being at the mercy of the powerful, tumultuous wind and waves made her hands shake, her heart race, and her stomach churn. Nevertheless, there was no other way home. She would have to cross the Channel.

Lifting her hand to his mouth, his lips brushed over her knuckles. "Elizabeth, if it proves to be too much, Jean Paul said they have oil of vitriol at the port. Perhaps it would ease your way if you soundly slept while we crossed." Darcy gently squeezed her fingers.

Before she could reply, Madame spoke, "She will be fine. Her desire to be back on familiar land, hearing familiar language, and eating terrible British food will keep her eyes focused on where we are headed. Do not worry about your Elizabeth. A woman knows how to focus her heart on where it needs to be, despite the hardship it takes to get there."

Darcy glanced at her, his brows up by his hairline.

"Madame is correct," Elizabeth said. "I will do whatever it takes to make a successful crossing without drugging me. I will need to be alert when we arrive on the shore."

Darcy smiled with approval.

"Very well, then. I propose that we take a page from Madame's book and present ourselves as we want others to see us, or how they would expect to see us." He paused. When no one objected, he continued, "Jonah is correct when he suggested that he has much to offer during the crossing. My plan is that he offers his skill sailing and my muscles in helping to load and unload the cargo. I will again pretend to be mute. As payment, we would ask for a one-way passage for our two ladies, one who is Jonah's grandmother and the other my wife. Do you see anything in this idea where a smuggler would object?"

"Why not just give 'em the ring? Then we'd pay for ourselves to go across."

Darcy responded, "That may appear at first glance to be the course of wisdom. Pray recall the sort of men we would be dealing with, Jonah. They are willing to break the law to earn money. What would stop them from taking the ring and throwing us overboard once we were away from the shore? Additionally, the value of the ring far exceeds passage for four. No, until I can prove my identity once we are on British soil, we might need a grand sum to buy Monsieur Vartan's freedom. Therefore, I suggest we approach Jean Paul to put us in contact with the men who returned from Cornwall this morning. Due to the fact that the sailors, including his son, attempted to locate the missing men, I would be more inclined to trust them to see us to safety. As well, if they knew our purpose was the rescue of all three men, they might welcome us aboard."

"I see," Jonah's head bobbed up and down. "Yeah, it sounds like a good enough plan ta me."

Madame Vartan agreed.

Elizabeth squeezed the hand that Darcy still held. "I will stand by you."

Madame picked up a spoon that had been left on the table. She studied it like it held the secrets of the universe. Then, she tossed it back on the small pile they had recovered from the cottage. It was then that she uttered words that would change her life forever.

"We will not be coming back."

## 20

D arcy inquired of their hostess one last time, "Are you certain there is nothing else you wish to bring?"

"I have everything I need."

Hours had passed while they cleaned the inside of the cottage to Madame's satisfaction. When Jonah inquired why they were going to so much effort if she was not planning to return, their hostess merely shook her head and replied, "We do not know what tomorrow will bring. I know what I want but Alex may have something else in mind. I will follow where he leads, even if it is back to France."

Darcy carried the sack of vegetables. Madame had in her hands a small cloth bag with the metal box and several items she had gathered from the cottage. She had not looked back once since they left.

The trek to *Caen* went fairly quickly since they only stopped once on the way. Rather than selling the vegetables as she had earlier stated, Madame gave them to the Latour family who had been robbed that morning. When the lady of the house had attempted to express her sincere thanks, Madame brushed off the words. Instead, she insisted that Madame Latour busy herself feeding her children. When the younger woman glanced down at the child at her feet, Madame used the momentary distraction to walk away.

As she marched by him, Darcy lifted the small bag from her hands. Surprisingly, she gave it up with no struggle, only the command to be on their way.

"But I'd a thought we was goin' ta sell the potatoes fer francs," Jonah puzzled.

Madame grabbed his hand, pulling the boy along. "They need the food more than we need a few coins. Let us go."

Not far from the Latours, a farmer with a cart gave them a ride for the remainder of their journey. Thus, there was about an hour of daylight remaining when they arrived.

The sun setting on the buildings in *Caen* showed the city at its best. On one of the hills the *Château de Caen* was flanked by the Romanesque abbeys of *Saint-Étienne* and *Sainte-Trinité*. Their substantial stone structures gave the whole area a feeling of solidity and permanence. Under other circumstances, Darcy would have spent hours learning of their history—in Elizabeth's company, of course.

Without a word, they moved through the crowds to the river *Orne*. Fishermen were offloading their meager catch from the day. Boys ran from berth to berth to help them tie up their vessels in hopes of a few francs. Businessmen made loud demands on the men's time and their income. Emaciated females lurked in the dark doorways, desperate to ply their ancient trade. Napoleon's war had been harsher on his own people than it had been on their enemies. Darcy clasped Elizabeth's hand tighter, pulling her closer to him. Danger hovered over the whole area like the foggy mist rising from the water. Even Jonah was unusually subdued.

Worldly weariness settled on Darcy's shoulders. He had observed this life many times in London, though he had never been as much a part of the scenery as he was on that day. His cousin had shared few details from the conflicts he had endured during his tenure on the continent. None of it was pleasant. Mentally shaking off the thought, Darcy knew that their safety rested on his staying alert.

He watched Madame as she wandered amidst the docks. In spite of the slowness of her gait, she gave every appearance of having a purpose to her movements.

Stopping at the beginning of one of the piers, she whispered an inquiry into the ear of one of the boys. When he pointed further down the row of vessels, Madame walked off without checking to see if they followed.

Elizabeth looped her other arm through Jonah's. The three of them were able to walk abreast on the crowded pier with Madame clearing the way. She was small but fierce. When Madame stopped by a rickety-looking ship, Darcy shuddered. *Not this one!*

Elizabeth's steps slowed. "Pray let us find a ship that can provide us a safe crossing," she whispered under her breath.

"Well, look-ee there. She's not a perty ship but she appears sleek and fast. Now, don't be lookin' at the mess on the deck and the chipped paint on her wheelhouse. Instead, see how her hull is sound, an' her riggin' is tip top." Jonah relaxed. "I tell ye somethin', Mrs. D. There's many an old salt who'd like people ta think they're having tough times. But that's to get their customers ta relax they's purse strings. I would bet ye good money that the man captaining that there clipper is as smart as Cap'n Bartholomew or even Boone."

Elizabeth released the breath she had been holding. "Then we will see who is the wiliest, the old captain or Madame."

Jonah piped up, "My money's on Madame."

Darcy's was too.

They did not have long to wait to discover their fate.

As they moved to where their hostess was waving to them,

Darcy's attention was caught between the difference of the ships closer to the center of the city than those at this end of the port. Those were offloading fish, their crew was departing for home. These were beginning their workday (or night) preparing to depart. Smugglers. Madame had done well.

THE CAPTAIN WAS APPROXIMATELY the same age as Darcy, he guessed. His hair was whipped by the chill wind, his skin was as weathered as his ship, and he was dressed far differently from the crew of the *Peregrine*. This captain wore a heavy dark wool coat and long trousers. A knitted cap was in his hands from having taken it off when he spotted Madame. The attention he gave the older woman was respectful—possibly a mite fearful. As the two discussed the terms of the transport, Darcy observed the stance of the combatants. First, the captain would vigorously shake his head 'no'. Then Madame would do the same. After going back and forth in this manner several times, the captain threw his hands into the air, the universal signal that he capitulated to the force that was Madame Vartan. Moments later, their hostess rejoined them on the dock.

"We are to go aboard now. The rest of his crew will arrive shortly. They will be stopping before we reach *Ouistreham* to load their cargo. From there we sail directly to Cornwall."

Jonah ran down the pier, hopped aboard, saluted the officer, and immediately settled himself next to the man in charge. The captain assisted Madame. Darcy turned to help Elizabeth step down into the vessel.

Her eyes were tightly closed. Her lips were pressed together. Her face was pasty white. Fear rested upon her like a heavy cloak.

Darcy kissed her.

Her eyes popped open. "What? Why did you do that?"

"It was the only thing I could think of to gain your attention quickly," he admitted, hoping that he had not turned her away from him with his brash actions in a very public setting.

When the corner of her lips tilted up, he knew his impulse had worked.

"Mr. Darcy, please know that I shall remember that move for the rest of our lives. Should I ever need an immediate response from you, I will not hesitate to follow your example no matter what you are doing and whose company you are keeping," she teased.

"*Je t'aime,*" Those were not the words he had intended to utter, but he felt his devotion so strongly at that moment that nothing else came to his mind.

"I love you too." The melody of her voice harmonized with his heart. Smiling, she took a deep breath, blinked twice, then stepped down to where Jonah and Madame were waiting.

Her courage humbled him. He could not wait to have Elizabeth be his Mrs. Darcy.

Before they could settle, three men dressed in the same dark clothing as the captain came aboard. Making little noise, they slipped away from the dock to ride the tide down the river. During the whole of the nearly ten-mile journey to the mouth of the *Orne,* not one word was spoken. When they pulled into a cove down river, the crew and Darcy went about loading the cargo with quiet efficiency.

*Ouistreham* had been a trading port since the Middle Ages. Few lights were visible as the vessel passed along the riverbanks. Once the lights were left behind, the movement of the water changed. So did the activity of the crew.

The captain informed them, "You might want to go below and remain there until we cross the bar into the sea. It will be rough going for a bit. We will catch quite a bit of spray until we are away from land. Right now, the flood tide is about to end. We will be in slack water where it should be calmer for a few minutes. The ebb will see us to our destination. The Channel likes to have its own way, as do I. It takes anywhere from eight to twelve hours, depending on the winter winds, which can howl fiercely." The captain directed one of his crew to show them to a small cabin.

The quarters were tight, exactly as it had been on the *Peregrine*. This time, there were four beings squeezed inside instead of two. Madame settled at one end of the bunk at the first hint of the ship rolling up a wave then splashing down. Elizabeth quickly joined her, as did Darcy. It was only Jonah, who remained standing, his feet planted firmly on the deck.

"I don't know why the cap'n wanted me down here. I coulda helped with the crossin'. I told him that I is a trained ship's boy with two years a service, but he just told me to get below. I tell ye, Captain Bartholomew woulda had me workin' before the lines dropped from the dock." Crossing his arms, he harrumphed.

"Come, *mon garçon*," Madame patted the bunk next to her. "I have known Jean Paul's son since he was younger than you. He is a good man who does not hesitate to sacrifice and risk his life for his wife and the little boys he has at home. Where your Captain Bartholomew knew the sort of young man you are, my friend does not. You will have your chance on another journey on a future day. Be patient. Learn to wait. It is a skill that will serve you well for your lifetime."

Elizabeth added, "Wise words, Madame." She shifted closer to Darcy, then patted the narrow strip between her and their hostess. "Pray be seated, Jonah, for I have a grand favor to ask of you."

The boy practically bounced in his eagerness to please Elizabeth. "What is it? Do ye need me ta tell ye about me sea-faring days? Do you need me ta tie a knot fer ye? Do ye need me ta stitch a sail or get ye a drink or somethin'?"

She smiled despite the ship climbing another wave. "I need you to sing for me. This will assist me to get my mind away from where we are and how long it will take to get back on solid ground."

"Ye want me ta sing? Like a sea shanty? I don't know if ye really would like one o' them, as they's not the sort a song fer a real lady."

Chuckling, Elizabeth bumped his arm with her elbow. "Do you know any appropriate for my ears?"

"Hey, I got one 'propriate fer Mr. Darcy's ears too. We sing it when we do heavy work to count off the time. An' it helped me learn me letters when I first went ta sea. Now I can read just fine, mostly 'cause o' this shanty."

What Jonah lacked in tune, he made up for in volume as he sang:

*A's for the anchor that lies at our bow*
*B's for the bowsprit and the jibs all lie low*
*C's for the capstan we all run around*
*D's for the davits to lower the boat down*

He stopped and asked, "Do ye know what a davit be?"

Madame replied, "It sounds like something a Christian woman would not want to know, Jonah Hackett."

The boy giggled, then continued.

*E's for the ensign that at our mast flew*
*F's for the forecastle, where lives our crew*
*G's for the galley where the salt junk smells strong*
*And H is the halyards, we hoist with a song*
*I's for the eyebolts, good for the feet*
*J's for the jibs hoist, stands by the lead sheet*
*K's for the knightheads where the petty officer stands*
*L's for the leeside, hard found by new hands*
*Merrily, merrily, so merry sail we*
*No mortal on earth like a sailor at sea*
*Heave away, haul away, the ship rolls along*
*Give a sailor his grog and there's nothing goes wrong*

Again, he paused. "Just so you know, I'm not a grog drinker."

Very seriously, Darcy replied, "I am pleased to know I do not need to worry about you over-indulging in front of the women, Jonah."

Holding in their laughter, all of them asked him to continue.

*M's for the mainmast, it's stout and it's strong*
*N's for the needle that never points wrong*
*O's for the oars of our old jolly boats*
*And P's for the pinnace that lively do float*
*Q's for the quarterdeck where our officers stand*
*And R's for the rudder that keeps the ship in command*
*S is for the stuns'ls that drive her along*
*T's for the tops'ls, to get there takes long*

This time, it was Elizabeth who lifted her hand so he stopped. "I believe I know what most of the letters represent. However, what on earth is a pinnace?"

"Why, that be an old boat with eight oars. Remember, Mrs. D, this be an old song. Old boat, old song."

"Thank you, Jonah. I do believe we are nearly to the end of the alphabet."

"Just a few letters ta go."

*U's for the uniform, mostly worn aft*
*V's for the vangs running from the main gap*
*W's for water, we're on a pint and a pound*
*And X marks the spot where old Stormy was drowned*
*Y's for yardarm, needs a good sailor man*
*Z is for Zoë, I'm her fancy man*
*Z's also for zero in the cold winter time*
*And now we have brought all the letters in rhyme*
*Merrily, merrily, so merry sail we*
*No mortal on earth like a sailor at sea*
*Heave away, haul away, the ship rolls along*
*Give a sailor his grog and there's nothing goes wrong.*

By the time Jonah finished, Darcy wanted to cover his ears. No, that was not accurate. He had wanted to cover his ears when the lad began the tune. Nonetheless, the joy on the boy's face at having sung the shanty in full was delightful.

"Thank you, Jonah," Elizabeth was quick with her praise. "You certainly sang with enthusiasm."

"That he did," agreed Madame, her eyes rolling up to the ceiling, possibly in gratitude for the shanty's ending.

Darcy nodded, suddenly overwhelmed—not from the song, which he had heard before. No, it was the people in the quarters; the three particular individuals sharing the room had become precious to him, so precious that he never wanted harm to come to any of them, ever. The volume of emotion flooding his chest was painful.

He not only loved Elizabeth with his whole heart, both Jonah and even Madame had wiggled their way inside his thumping chest as well. Yet, they belonged in different parts of the world from him. Whatever was he going to do when he needed to tell them goodbye?

## 21

To Elizabeth, the crossing was exactly as she feared it would be. Having Jonah distract her worked, but only temporarily. The first time the stern of the ship was carried portside by the ebbing tide, her stomach dropped to her toes. When the bow rose high to the top of a wave then plunged down the other side, her insides gave up every ounce of the precious meal that she had consumed earlier.

Once the trauma stopped, Jonah grabbed the pot and disappeared outside of the quarters.

She felt wretched. Darcy was a man above all men. He had held her hair back from her face and kept his arm around her, so that she did not lose her balance with the movement of the ship while she heaved. She was far too miserable to be mortified.

The smell inside the tiny room was horrid. Within moments, Madame joined Jonah on the upper deck.

"Elizabeth," Darcy spoke softly. "I would do anything to ease your suffering. I love you, Dearest." He kissed her temple.

"Thank you." She smiled despite her misery. "Fitzwilliam, I need you to speak of our plans once we reach shore. The diversion will help to calm my fears, for it is not only the movement that has my stomach unsettled. The memory of going over the side is still too fresh."

"*Blast!* I should have found someone with ether. I beg your pardon."

"Whatever for? For respecting my opinion when I told you I did not want to make the crossing while unconscious or for something else entirely?"

"I hate to see you suffer. It is that simple."

"Then please speak of a subject I am most interested in, our future."

He was quick to comply. Elizabeth could not help but think of the many times her father withheld information that her mother yearned to know simply for the sake of stirring her nerves. She realized that it was a mean art. Darcy was not like that at all. Although he was a man of few words when amongst a large crowd or people whom he did not know well, he held nothing back from her and had not once during this whole journey.

"My dear, our first concern is identifying ourselves to the authorities. This way, I will be able to access the funds we need to pay whatever fine has been imposed upon Madame's husband and the others captured with him." His confidence was reassuring. "After, I will send a message to your father and Bingley to meet us in London." He ran the hand not holding hers through his hair. "I only wish that we knew what story your father has created to explain our absence from the ball. If he and Bingley put it out that they suspected criminal intent, they might have sent out a cry throughout the land that we were abducted. If so, I suspect that the law in every port will be on the lookout for a well-dressed gentleman and a lady, not common laborers sneaking clandestinely into port from France."

When the ship took another roll, Elizabeth lay down on the

bunk, her head on Darcy's leg, desperately wishing the sea would calm.

She considered the dilemma. "If they, on the other hand, proclaimed that we ran off to Scotland, then our appearing in Cornwall unwed would leave our reputations in worse condition than if we had actually eloped."

"Exactly. It would be much harder to convince anyone to believe we are who we really are." Darcy kissed the knuckles of her hand. "Another option we must consider is that they were able to contain any rumors, not start them."

She scoffed. "You truly believe that of my mother? You are a generous man, Fitzwilliam. No, I rather suspect that once it was determined that we were missing, her hue and cry would have been loud enough to inform the dead that we were Scotland bound. It would not have mattered if the kidnappers had dropped the ether-covered rag on the balcony, left behind their pistol, or wrote a note stating their intent. She would convince herself and anyone who would listen that we were off to be wed."

"I do not know whether to agree or not. If I do, will you accuse me of disdain for others in thinking poorly of your mother? If I do not agree, will you consider me arrogant to believe my viewpoint superior to yours?"

In the darkness, Elizabeth heard the teasing in his tone, "My dear man, I have learned a thing or two about you since waking next to you on the *Peregrine*. While I might have accused you of being small-minded before we were kidnapped, you have revealed to me that you are far less prejudiced and prideful than myself. Pray, feel free to agree with me any time you are inclined."

He chuckled. "I will keep that in mind, especially after we are wed."

The vessel took another wave to the side, tilting it precariously. The memory of the last time this happened to her evoked a fear in Elizabeth that paralyzed every fiber of her being. "No!" she squeaked, so taut were the muscles in her throat. "I will not allow fear to consume me. I will not!"

"Come!" Darcy jumped up, banging his head on the low roof. The sound of the thud barely penetrated Elizabeth's consciousness. "Blast!" Grabbing Elizabeth in his arms, he pulled her out the door.

When he headed for the stairs leading to the upper deck, her body rebelled against her traitorous mind, her heels attempting to dig in on the smooth wooden surface. Her heart knew he would not endanger her on purpose. Summoning every ounce of courage she possessed, she followed.

The cold air coupled with her fear shook her to her core.

He attempted to help her along. "Please, we will only stand at the top of the stairs. I will hold you tightly so we will not go overboard. I promise. I will never let you go."

"I will be well. I will. I trust you. I do." she repeated over and over as tears stream down her cheeks. Her body shivered. Her stomach roiled. Yet, her courage rose with the wind. The ship traveled up each high wave. Hovering at the crest, the vessel plunged safely down the other side. They were not swallowed by the sea. After tracking their movements, each wave became a small victory.

Jonah had sailed for two years in good weather and in bad with no harm to him. Madame told her while they were slicing vegetables how she had traveled by ship from Viapori, Sweden to *Calais* when she and Monsieur Vartan escaped Russia. According to her, the hazardous trip took fifteen days through the violent North Sea. If they could survive those journeys, Elizabeth Rose Bennet would survive this one.

Blinking rapidly, she wrapped her arms tightly around Darcy. Gulping down her rising bile, from the ship's movement, not from fear, she stated with complete honesty, "I will be well."

Jonah appeared at the top of the stairs. "Can ye feel it, Mrs. D?

We are across the bar so we should have smooth sailin' fer a mite. Come on up. Why, we be close enough we can see the lights o' England, almost."

Remaining where she was, Elizabeth rested her temple against Darcy's cheek. "You would not have let me fall, would you?"

"I would do anything within my power to keep you safe," he vowed, as his hand rubbed up and down her back. "Do you not yet know that you are my life? From now on, anything we do will be done together. I plan to live a long life with you, my Elizabeth. I have every intention of standing alongside you, at whatever chapel you choose, to marry you for better or worse, in sickness and in health, until death do us part, which will *not* be today."

"You are a remarkable man." Relaxing her grip, she said, "I will follow you wherever you lead." Leaning back, she caught his eye. "Or I will lead you a merry chase and you may follow, should you choose."

"Oh, I will choose, Elizabeth Bennet, my future Mrs. Darcy. Have no doubt that I will," he grinned. "Come. Let us see those lights welcoming us back to England."

By the time they reached the upper deck, the clouds parted. Light streaming from the full moon gleamed on the surface of the water. The waves were slight causing the ship to rock like a cradle with a baby. Joining Madame and Jonah by the wheel at the stern, Elizabeth gratefully hung onto the railing when Darcy moved away from her to avoid bumping into a stack of kegs tied to the side. It was these same wooden containers that had been quickly stowed aboard in that dark cove before *Ouistreham*.

The captain approached. "Sound carries over water. I ask that you keep your voices low or do not speak at all. When we near shore, do not be surprised if we do not steer towards the fires. Often, they are lit by wreckers who would love nothing better than to have us run onto rocks so they can scavenge our valuables to sell to the same buyers we use. There is little loyalty in this business. As well, we run the risk that the same tax men who captured Monsieur Vartan will show up on the beach. If that happens, we will rush back to the ship to seek another cove. This might mean the night would be longer than we hoped. Our goal is to leave for *Caen* before light."

"Thank you, Captain. We are grateful for the information." Darcy paused before he added, "Since the three of us will be arriving on this vessel with this cargo, do you have an opinion as to how best we could present ourselves for our safety?"

The captain considered for a good length of time before he answered the very question that Elizabeth had been wondering. "The second you and the lady open your mouths they will know you are British. Whether they believe you to be a smuggler or not will be up to how clever you are at convincing them. The boy will have no trouble as they are used to wharf rats. My concern is Madame." He looked directly at the older woman, whose chin lifted, her eyes glaring him down. "Madame, pray do not be a stubborn French woman. This lot would have no qualms about tossing you into the brig with your husband."

What came out of Madame Vartan's mouth was a spate of words in a language unknown to Elizabeth. With one brow lifted in arrogant disdain, this was no French country maid on board. Instead, aboard the smuggler's vessel was a czarina from Imperial Russia.

"Very good," the captain chuckled. "I now no longer doubt that you had the authority to see our transaction completed, Madame. *Alex est un homme chanceux*."

"He is lucky, indeed." Madame replied. "Now, we will all be quiet. Let us hurry to my man."

Elizabeth needed to discuss the particulars of what might or might not happen. However, the captain had been clear. The need for silence protected them all. She would do nothing to endanger any of them.

Darcy lightly tapped her chin then pointed up. Their ship appeared to be sailing along a mystical path in the water, lit by a glowing moon. She met his gaze, admiring the light reflected in his eyes and thinking he was the handsomest of men—even with bruises and whiskers. What a privilege to have a lifetime to share sights like this with him.

Smiling, Darcy pointed upriver. There the stars twinkled magically, reflecting their sparkles on the water. It was a sight unlike anything she had ever seen.

From beside her, Jonah whispered, "It's a sight I never tire o'lookin' at. When at sea, there's nothin' but glassy water in the summer time, so's it seems like we'd be sailin' inside a tunnel o' stars. I tell ye, Mrs. D. There's nothin' like the beauty of the ocean on nights like that or when we's in the West Indies. There the water is the color of light blueish green stones on a lady's necklace. Ye can peek over the side an' see fish an' rays an' sharks. Ye can even see the sand on the bottom. It's a sight to behold."

"I do imagine it is." Her mind simply could not fathom what he described. There were many wonders in the world she had dreamed of seeing, always hoping that travel would be possible at some time in the future. Until she could lose her fear of the ocean and her misery from the motion of the waves, they would forever remain undiscovered. She sighed her disappointment.

Darcy leaned in close and softly spoke for her ears alone, "Each wave is bringing us closer to England, my love. We are going home."

Home! The word itself invoked comfort and warmth, filling Elizabeth's heart with good cheer. For home, she would endure anything.

## 22

The night was still dark when they reached the British coast. The few lights that were visible beckoned the ship toward the shore. The captain sailed past them. When one of the lanterns started flashing twice then pausing, repeating the pattern over and over, the captain steered the ship toward them. Once they were anchored in a narrow cove, Darcy helped Elizabeth and Madame to the beach. Jonah made it just fine on his own.

There were still a few hours until daylight when Darcy hefted the last barrel in the cargo hold onto his shoulder. His body protested the hours of hard labor. The cave where the brandy was stored was guarded by four men bearing arms. Once that final barrel was stacked with the others, Jean Paul's son conferred with a man who had walked out of the darkness.

When a lantern was lit and swung in an arch, the sound of harnesses and the huffing of hard-worked horses filled the air. Into the light, approached a team pulling a large wagon.

"Get her unloaded men," the newcomer barked.

Darcy went to the back of the wagon to discover a pile of metal intended for the French army to make into weapons. The irony of British smugglers equipping their enemy turned his stomach. Nonetheless, this was not Darcy's battle to fight on this particular night. Grabbing heavy pieces in his hands, he carried them along with the four other men to the ship in which they had crossed the channel. By the time the cargo area was full enough to weigh the vessel down, Darcy was past exhaustion. He needed to rest with the others of his party.

Jonah sat with Elizabeth and Madame in a clump of tall grasses. All of them were tired, cold, and hungry. The potatoes Madame had prepared for them the morning before had served their purpose hours prior. They needed shelter and sustenance.

As suddenly as the five men had appeared, they vanished into the darkness. The captain approached Darcy.

"You need to get your women away from the beach. The guards have not gone far. The delivery men will be here as soon as day breaks for the kegs. They will not treat any of you well if they see you since their first assumption would be that you are poachers wanting what's in the cave. With this lot, it is each man for himself. They are likely to shoot first and ask questions later."

"Thank you, I am grateful for the information. Is there anything else?"

"Yes. The town where Monsieur Vartan is held is four miles from here. I was told that the transport for the prisoners will arrive this afternoon. It is about a full day's travel or more to Launceston from Fowey, so you ought to try to get them free before they are tossed in with the rest of the prisoners being held. Monsieur Vartan will appear before the judge during the next quarter session. It will not go well for him, despite his innocence. Do not linger, sir, or your travels on this night will be in vain."

"How do we find this town?"

"Follow the cart tracks then head east." The captain stuck his hand in his pocket. "Here is your pay for the work you did hauling kegs and loading iron."

Darcy was surprised at the offer. "I was given to understand that my labors helped to pay for our passage."

"No, Madame took care of that. These are your wages along with a flask of water. It isn't much but it should help."

The moonlight glinted on one of the coins. In his palm were three silver crowns.

Closing his fists around the precious resource, Darcy thanked the man. Never before had he received so little for so much hard work. Yet, he was grateful he had something he could put in his pocket.

He hated disturbing the others, but the captain's advice was sound. They needed to leave. Darcy worried most about Elizabeth. The ocean had taken its toll on her. When added to the amount of walking they had already done, the upcoming four miles would seem like an ancient marathon.

"Come," he said to the others, urgency sharpening his tone. "The walk will warm us."

"What did he say?" Madame demanded.

Darcy held nothing back.

"My Alex!" Madame took off like a bullet from a gun. "Let us go now. We need to hurry."

As they rushed to catch up with her, Darcy told Elizabeth and Jonah, "Pray think, please, of how best we should use these coins. The ring is gone since the captain said that Madame had paid for our passage. We cannot afford to waste a farthing."

"Food," Jonah suggested. "I don't think I'll ever be full."

"Then, we have four miles between us and something for you to eat. For now, we need to be silent and listen for approaching men. As the captain said, they will not treat us well."

"I'll keep a look out, Mr. D, don't ye worry none."

Clasping Elizabeth's hand in his, they climbed the sandy trail.

THE RISING sun gleamed off of the droplets of frost melting on the tops of the grass. It had not taken long to be away from the rocks and sand. Following the cart trail had been fairly easy. There had only been one time that they had to shelter off to the side of the road. The jangle of the harnesses and the creaking of the wheels had alerted them enough in advance that they were able to protect themselves.

Madame's initial boost of energy waned after the first mile. She, too, had no food or rest since the day before. They were each of them weary to their souls.

Elizabeth knew that she was in trouble when the next step she took felt unstable; her right leg seemed to wiggle at the knees. When she moved her left leg, the same thing happened. Holding tighter to Darcy's hand, she forced herself to move one more step. Weakness coursed through her whole body.

"Fitzwilliam, I fear I cannot continue." As soon as she stopped, her legs quivered, then gave out underneath her. Darcy caught her before she collapsed to the ground.

"Elizabeth!" He searched the surroundings before carrying her to a small stand of trees. Helping her to lie gently on the ground, he called for Madame, who immediately left the road to come to their side.

"We will rest here until you can continue," Darcy insisted.

How her heart warmed with his tenderness.

"You cannot risk being too late for Madame's husband. She has done so much for us, Fitzwilliam. We need to do all that we possibly can for her."

Madame approached. "I feared this would happen. She lost too much of her insides to bear up under this sort of trek. Do not worry about me, Monsieur Darcy. I shall continue on alone."

Elizabeth recognized when Darcy was faced with weighty

indecision. He rubbed his chin with his hand. She knew it would be up to her to provide direction and reassurance.

"Madame, without Monsieur Darcy's help, you might be able to see your husband, but you would not be able to rescue him."

"I cannot leave you alone," Darcy stated. "I will not."

Elizabeth thanked him, then said, "We are far enough away from the coast that we must be out of danger from smugglers. Would you not be confident of Jonah's protection should you leave him with me? I trust him with my life. Would you not do the same?"

The lad's chest nearly burst from being puffed up. Then, it deflated.

"I was hopin' ta help break Monsieur Vartan outta jail, then we could eat an' maybe sleep in a bed before eatin' again. 'Course, I'd want Mrs. D. there too." His foot scuffed the grass.

Elizabeth looked to Darcy, her eyes pleading with him to agree. When his pause seemed to go on for a length of time, she began to worry. Finally, he nodded.

"Jonah, as the captain of this ship, I assign you and only you the task of protecting Elizabeth. As acting quartermaster, there is no greater service you can do for the ship and the crew. I will take Cook into town to care for necessary business before returning with supplies and the rest of our crew. Do I have your loyalty, Jonah Hackett?"

"Aye aye, Cap'n." With a smart salute, Jonah moved to stand in front of Elizabeth, arms crossed, and feet shoulder-width apart.

Before leaving, Darcy bent to kiss her temple. "If there were any other way..." he began.

"There is not. Pray be safe and return quickly. We will not move from here until we see you."

"I love you, Elizabeth soon-to-be Darcy."

"As I love you, Fitzwilliam, soon-to-be my husband." Her fingers brushed over his lips. "Be safe."

Pressing the tips of her fingers against his mouth, Darcy kissed each one. Standing, he patted Jonah on the back before walking away with Madame.

NEVER HAD Darcy yearned to be in two different places at the same time. For a certainty, his heart was back with Elizabeth. It almost broke him the first time he looked behind to where they were hidden. Quickly studying each rock, each tree, each tuft of grass, he cemented it into his memory so he would easily find them again. He would be back as soon as was humanly possible, he had no doubt.

Madame interrupted his intentions. "Do you have a plan?"

"Our first order will be to find your husband. I will speak to whomever is in charge to see if any arrangements can be made to release the men before they are taken away."

"Oh, how I long to see Alex." Her eyes twinkled up at him. "You will know soon enough how eager anticipation to see the other half of you will fill you with a joy you cannot find elsewhere. I will be whole once I am reunited with my man."

Worry settled upon Darcy's shoulders. Madame gave him the impression that it would be an easy task to set Monsieur Vartan free. Jean Paul had revealed that this group of tax men were bent on making an example of Alex and the two others. It would be anything but easy.

He scoffed, if only to himself. How in the world was he to defend a man against a crime that Darcy knew little about? The laws of land ownership, deeds, and variances were as familiar to him as the back of his hand. But smuggling? Taxes and duties on imported goods? Being an unwelcome foreigner on British soil? He knew nothing other than the basics.

The coins in his pocket would not allow him through the door to a skilled attorney's office. Nor would he have enough time to send an express to his personal man of business to obtain what he needed by the afternoon. He looked like a vagrant. He smelled like someone who needed a good scrubbing, and he was as poor as a pauper.

Yet, he had an asset that none could steal from him. Others may not recognize him, but he was Fitzwilliam George Darcy, Esq, master of Pemberley, grandson of an earl, and nephew to the Archbishop. He was Cambridge educated with five years of single-handedly overseeing hundreds of staff and a fortune in investments.

Pushing his shoulders back, he walked alongside a fiercely determined female. Her steps had become smaller until she began lagging behind him. As soon as the town came into view, her energy reserves gave her what she needed to make it the rest of the way.

Darcy's admiration for her grew with each stride. Before Elizabeth, he would not have comprehended what could move a person to outstanding feats of strength. Now, he knew that he would pour out his life's blood if needed to protect his future wife.

He shook his head at himself. He had been a fool, thinking that Bingley's constant pursuit of the perfect angel for a wife was a ridiculous result of youthful impetuosity. Now that he was assured of Elizabeth's love and devotion, Darcy had to humbly admit that Bingley knew what he was about. He would do whatever it took to finish their business on this day.

He stood tall as they strolled into the small village of Fowey. He was Fitzwilliam Darcy, Esquire.

## 23

He was Fitzwilliam Darcy, prisoner.

Sitting on the grimy bench in a small room at the back of the stable, Darcy fretted about Elizabeth. She would be expecting his return at any time. With his current incarceration, he was afraid for her and Jonah. He was afraid for himself.

Madame had been insistent that their first order of business was to find Alex. Darcy had to dig in his heels against the force that was her to use a portion of one of his precious coins to purchase a sheet of paper and borrow a quill from the first inn they approached on the west end of town. Quickly sending a message to his butler at Darcy House in London, he used another coin and the promise of much more if the Harbormaster arranged delivery for the missive on the next vessel leaving for London. Weather permitting and the tides cooperating, it would be two days before his letter reached his house and days before he would receive a response. Once they left the port office, they inquired of the innkeeper where the gaol was to be found.

The blacksmith was a huge man with arms the size of most

men's thighs. His shoulders were broad; his hands made Darcy's look like a child's. Surprisingly, bold as ever, Madame Vartan took one look at the giant and stepped behind Darcy, pushing him forward. Darcy had no reason to hesitate.

"Sir, this lady is looking for her husband. He was kidnapped five weeks ago while attempting to find work in *Caen, France,* by evil men seeking a scapegoat in case they were caught smuggling. We heard reports that he and his two companions might be here. Are we at the correct location?"

"They're in the back." The man lifted his heavy hammer and struck the metal on the anvil without taking his eyes off Darcy. "You best hurry since they will be leaving here in an hour or two."

Madame took off like a bolt of lightning. Within moments, they could hear her exclamations of welcoming relief.

Thinking quickly, Darcy attempted to reason with the blacksmith. "Sir, might there be any possibility of returning to their homeland for those three innocent men? They were not personally involved in illegal activities. They are as much a victim as anyone."

The man looked Darcy up and down. "You speak like an educated gentleman, though you do not look like one."

"I, too, was kidnapped by those who used the same oil of vitriol. It is how I came to be in these dire circumstances."

The man nodded, his hammer finally ceasing to move. Placing his tool on the bench behind him, he said, "I tell you what. Someone needs to go to Launceston today to stand trial before the judge. If you're so convinced of their innocence, feel free to take their place."

"You do not understand," Darcy pleaded. "My intended and a young boy with us were too weak to make it all the way to Fowey. They are hidden alongside of the road. If I do not return before dark, they will be defenseless. I cannot do this to them. As well, we have family who are searching for us as we speak. My betrothed's father is very ill. My own sister is young." Darcy would use any tool possible to evoke empathy in the man. "We lost our dear mother twelve years ago and my father five. We are orphaned. Please, sir. Have mercy on myself and the others."

"Mister, that is not my concern." He picked up his hammer and started pounding the metal, ignoring Darcy completely.

"If you could wait several days for them to depart, my man of business will be here to vouch for my identity and pay whatever fine has been incurred for all three men."

"I don't care if you are the King of England or as rich as Croesus. I am to send a prisoner to Launceston this afternoon, so a prisoner will get into the wagon when it arrives. Whether it's you or them, I don't care. My mind will not be changed."

*Blast!* What was he supposed to do now? His attempt having failed, Darcy joined Madame in front of the stall, hoping to come up with another plan.

The whole front had been boarded up with thick timbers. A four-inch gap was left in the wood to provide prisoners their daily rations, Darcy suspected. It was through this window that Madame conversed quietly with her husband. When Darcy approached, they both became silent.

"Well?" Madame straightened and put one fist on her hip, her other hand gripped the window where a man's hand covered hers. "What did he say? Will he let my Alex go free?"

Failure was an uncomfortable fit for Darcy. He considered his options, then recalled Elizabeth telling Jonah about her treasure when they were back in Madame's cave. The lesson he had taken from the exchange was that setting aside emotions to do the right thing was usually the right course. If Elizabeth or Jonah were standing here instead of him, he had no doubt that either of them would hold their head high as they climbed inside the prisoner's wagon, waving cheerfully at the others until they were out of sight. What a woman! What a lad!

With this clearly in his mind, he made the only decision that he could.

"Monsieur Vartan and the others will go free as soon as someone takes their place."

His heart was crumpling into a million pieces, most falling into the pit of his stomach while others clogged his throat. Doing the right thing did not make him suddenly feel better. He was wretched. Would Elizabeth ever understand him not putting her ahead of near strangers? Except they were not strangers. Elizabeth cared for Madame as much as he did.

"Take their place? What is this?" Madame demanded. "If they need someone for the assizes, I will stay," she readily volunteered.

Her husband cleared his throat from the other side of the door.

"*Pardonnez-moi*, Monsieur Darcy. It is my pleasure to introduce you to my husband, Alex Dimitri Vartan. I have briefly explained to him how we have arrived here and who you are."

Darcy addressed the hole in the door where the light barely penetrated. He could see the man's eyes and his cheekbones.

"Monsieur, I fear for the safety of your wife and yourself should you remain on British soil. The sooner that we can get you back to France, the better you will be."

The timbre of Monsieur Vartan's voice was rich and low.

"Monsieur Darcy, my sweet wife told me that you are a clever man. I have never had reason to doubt her word before, and I will not start now. Therefore, if she chooses to remain here with me to face our future together, then so be it!"

*Sweet?* Any human who would refer to Madame Vartan as sweet was either overly generous or blind and deaf to her stubbornness.

"I pray you, the both of you. You will need to make your way back to your home in France. Only then will you be safe."

"Harumph!" Madame blurted. "Safety in a country at war? No, sir."

"Madame." His frustration almost getting the better of him, he sucked in a deep breath. "You cannot do this."

"Oh, do not tell me you would not do the same for your Elizabeth, Monsieur Darcy. In a heartbeat, you would give up everything you own for her. I see it in your eyes and the way you are drawn to her. Sacrifice for the sake of togetherness is worth more than gold; even the boy knows this."

While his mind rebelled at her comments, his heart agreed.

"I will stay, Madame Vartan." Once the words were said aloud, it was as good as done.

"Monsieur Darcy, you are the best of men." She pulled her hand away from the window to offer it to him. Gripping his fingers tightly, she promised, "We will hurry back down the road to the boy and lady. We will find this Launceston and we will find you. Do not fear. We will care for your woman like she is our own."

Her words were no sooner uttered than the blacksmith rounded the corner with his hammer in one hand and a ring of keys in the other. In silence, he unlocked the makeshift cell, stepping back to allow the three inside to leave, and Darcy to enter. Slamming the door shut, the padlock closed with a deafening click. Darcy's future was sealed.

Elizabeth had no idea how long she slept. When her eyes opened, her first thought was worry over Darcy and Madame. Her first sight was Jonah tearing grass from the ground to fling each piece as far as possible.

"Jonah," she whispered.

He spun around. "Good. Yer awake."

"I am." Struggling to sit upright, she reached for the flask.

Thankfully, the water sloshed inside when she lifted it from the ground. Taking a sip to see how it landed in her stomach, she drank fully, saving enough for later.

"Pray help me to stand, kind sir. We have far to go. We do not have all day."

"We are leavin' here?" He glanced around their little oasis. "Well, Mr. D told me ta look after ye, but he never said I had ta do it exactly here. An' I confess that I'd rather be in town with Mr. D and Madame. I'd love ta help break her man outta jail."

As they stepped out onto the road, she reminded him of the need for caution. They knew no one in the area and there were criminals about.

"Maybe we'll get arrested by the same lawmen who throwed Monsieur into the gaol. Then we'd all be together. I bet it's cramped inside there. We'd be seven people in tight quarters."

Jonah continued chattering as they walked until Elizabeth needed to sit and rest. By then, the lad was picking up small stones from the road to throw them as hard as possible. After a short time, they were back on the road again.

The two of them needed to stop twice more before they walked over a rise to see a village in the distance. It comforted Elizabeth that Darcy had walked the same path. Perhaps she even unknowingly walked in his footsteps. It warmed her heart to believe that she had.

They made it to the bottom of the next small valley when they heard voices coming towards them. Before they could find shelter, Madame and three others crested the hill. The one closest to Madame who held her hand in his must have been Monsieur Vartan. He was a tall man, though not as tall as Darcy. His dark hair was streaked with gray, as was his beard. His cheeks were hollowed, his skin a pasty sort of beige. He had the same determined chin as Madame. As well, his eyes sparkled with life.

Many times over the course of the two days they spent in

France, Elizabeth had heard their hostess boast of the strength and accomplishments of her husband. He could chop wood and plant crops for hours at a time without the need to take a break. He could carry heavy loads, even his wife, if necessary. These were not taunts to make Darcy feel less of a man. Rather, they were absolute truths as seen by a wife who held her husband in deep respect.

It took less than a second for Elizabeth to realize that they were short one person.

Madame said, "It is good you made your way here."

"Where is Darcy?" she demanded.

In as few words as possible, Madame explained the situation, then made introductions. Digging into the cloth bag with the metal tin inside, she handed the two Frenchmen the francs she had hidden, telling them they would need to make their own way home.

"Now, we go back to get Monsieur Darcy from the gaol."

"Yay! I get ta break someone outta jail." Jonah pumped his fists into the air.

"Come," Elizabeth grabbed his hand. "We need to hurry."

Her heart was in her throat, making it difficult to draw in the next breath. Of everything the gentleman had suffered, this humiliation had to be the worst for Darcy.

"Your man is truly a man among men." Madame stated, her hand pressed over her heart. "When the blacksmith explained the terms of Alex's release, I had barely given myself reason to hope. Monsieur Darcy did not hesitate to volunteer himself, though it was obvious he ached at not being able to come for you. You both were his first concern."

As Elizabeth processed this information, her steps quickened. Her desperation to see him rose with each step towards Fowey. Glancing at the others, she saw the need to moderate her pace. Her own body was still attempting to recover from the crossing. They had been without food for over twenty-four hours.

Madame's spirit was resolute, forcing her to put one foot in front of the other. Her husband, *Oh Lord!* Upon closer inspection, Elizabeth saw his hand shake uncontrollably. *What had they done to him in the gaol?*

She wanted to run, to rush to Darcy's side. No, she needed to run.

"I am aware that you are ready to drop from exhaustion, Madame, but I cannot linger. Pray give me directions where I might find Monsieur."

The older woman nodded.

By then, they had crested the hill.

"Jonah, let us run." The momentum they gained going down the hill aided her to make it most of the way up the side of the next rise. Fortunately, the road flattened as it neared town.

Fowey was a lovely seaport city situated on the banks of the Fowey River. It was considerably larger than Meryton with the same feel where families grew old together with little change. Ruins of a large castle dotted one of the hills. Church steeples guided weary travelers into town.

They made one wrong turn, finding themselves approaching a dark, deserted alleyway.

Stopping in place, they asked a woman who had stepped out from her house where the blacksmith was located.

"Hurry, Jonah."

The need to be in Darcy's presence grew inside Elizabeth until the first tendrils of panic wrapped around her heart and lungs. A desperate sense that something was wrong drove her legs to keep moving when her weary body wanted to lay down on the street and rest.

Finally, they found the market that Madame had described. Three buildings beyond was their destination. Elizabeth's heart dropped to her toes. There was a carriage with a crude sort of box in the back with bars across each window. It was painted stark black, evoking doom. The driver was already seated at his perch in the front, ready to start his horse on the way. A large man was inserting a padlock on the door at the back.

"Wait!" Elizabeth yelled.

Grabbing Jonah, she pulled him off of his feet.

"Wait! Do not leave, I beg you," she wailed as her feet pounded on the packed dirt. "Open the door."

Unexpectedly, the man did as she bid.

Without hesitation, she leaped up onto the step, dragging Jonah behind her.

There sat the man of her dreams, his chin dropped to his chest.

## 24

---

In her eyes, he was the most beautiful sight she could have imagined. When his face lit up at seeing her, her heart sang.

"Elizabeth," he said in hushed awe as he attempted to stand inside the tight confines of the wagon. "You are here. How? No! You cannot be here. Step outside, I beg of you."

Ignoring his plea, she seated herself next to him before the wagon began to move. He wrapped his arms around her, squeezing tightly. The feeling of being at home, the rightness of being in his arms, soothed her battered soul.

Her hand sought the roughness of his cheek, seeking reassurance that he was really there, not some flighty figment of her active imagination.

The blacksmith cleared his throat. He held the door a moment, giving her an opportunity to change her mind. "This be good. The magistrate is expectin' three. He'll get three," he muttered.

She squeezed Darcy tighter, burrowing her nose in his throat as she felt him dropping kisses on her forehead, hair, and cheek. She was going nowhere without him.

Shaking his head, the blacksmith locked the three inside. Signaling the driver, they were practically jerked from their seats when the wagon started to move.

They had rounded several corners before Jonah spoke. "Ah, man! We're too late to break ye out, Mr. D. Mrs. D hurried as fast as she could, I know'd she did." Jonah's young voice filled the box. "Are ye gonna kiss her? Are ye?"

Elizabeth felt his sigh.

"Elizabeth, Jonah, how and why are you here?" Darcy begged. "Oh, do not mistake me. I am pleased beyond measure to see you both. However, do you not understand our circumstances? Our journey will be long and uncomfortable. Our destination could be deadly. I cannot have you..."

Elizabeth held onto him tighter. "Where you go, we will go."

He released the breath he had been holding. "Did you walk all of the way here on your own? Were you safe? Did you meet any strangers? Pray, where are Monsieur and Madame Vartan?"

Elizabeth had not the energy left to utter a single word. Jonah loved to talk. He could fill Darcy in on all the details. Before he was finished, any fragments of energy left in her muscles seemed to drain from her entire body. Closing her eyes, she slept.

"We be goin' back the same way we came, Mr. D. I bet we will be seein' Madame and her man before too long."

Darcy considered his course of action. Digging in his pocket, he produced the two remaining crowns. Handing them to Jonah, he assigned him the task of getting the Vartan's attention, so they could catch them when they were tossed from the transport.

"But that be all the money we have." Jonah closely examined the silver coins. "If we give it to them, which is a mighty fine thing ta do I must say, then we will have nothin'."

He understood the boy's confusion. Settling Elizabeth more comfortably in his arms, he sought to clarify, saying, "They have only a few coins with which she and her husband will start anew."

"No, she gave those francs to the men captured with her man. She has nothin'."

"Then, it is only fitting that we repay her for her hospitality with what we have, do you not agree?"

The lad's chin lowered, as his eyes rested everywhere but on Darcy. "I guess."

"Jonah, pray look at me." Darcy waited until the lad complied. "I understand that it must have been frightening to you to find yourself alone in Charleston with no funds to pay for your next meal. That is a memory that will likely haunt you for your lifetime."

The boy nodded.

"In spite of your being quite young, you considered your options and chose to join Captain Bartholomew, working rather than begging. I praise you for being so wise at that tender age. But think, in the two years you were at sea, were you ever without provisions?"

"Nah, if I worked, then I ate like the rest o' the crew."

"Was it not the same at Madame's? If we worked, which we did, did we not have food to eat and a warm place to stay?"

"Yes, we did." The boy's face brightened. "So, if we are still willin' ta work, then we shouldn't need to worry about fillin' our middle?"

Darcy grinned. "I believe you are correct. It might not be exactly what we would wish on our plate, but it will be enough to be able to work another day."

The boy considered. "I surely didn't think you gentlemen-like men put so much stock in workin' as you do. But I don't doubt yer word, Mr. D. I'm willin' ta make do until our circumstances change. I 'spect ye and Mrs. D ta do the same, huh?"

He peered out the side window, his head small enough that he could stick it through the bars.

"I see 'em," he hissed. "They's walkin' towards us."

"What?" Darcy strained to see out of the window behind him. His view was of the hind end of the horse and the back of the driver's legs. Sure enough, Monsieur and Madame Vartan were marching rapidly in their direction. "I assumed they would be heading toward the sea."

"Nope! I bet they's comin' after ye, Mr. D. Madame would never leave someone she loved in trouble, same as you."

Darcy sat back, stunned. Jonah was right. Every inch of Madame was loyal. Look how long she had remained by the sea in hopes of their son returning home. Twenty-one years of keeping a fragment of hope alive. He should have expected this from her and her husband.

Tossing the coins to them, Jonah yelled, "See ye in..." He looked to Darcy. "Where we goin'?"

"Launceston."

"See ye in Launceston, Madame and Monsieur." He waved, his small hand sticking through the bars.

From the bars in the back, Darcy could see Alex Vartan bending to retrieve the coins as Madame returned Jonah's wave.

"*Faites bien attention à vous*," Madame yelled.

"We will try to be as safe as possible," Darcy replied so only Jonah could hear.

ELIZABETH WOKE to the noise of the wagon in one ear and the regular beating of Darcy's heart in the other. Warmth on both sides indicated that Jonah had fallen asleep against her back, his thin arms at her middle.

Their situation was dire. Even so, she could not help but

believe that with the three of them together, there was nothing they could not endure with equanimity.

Unable to resist, she tilted her face just so until her lips brushed Darcy's jaw. His eyes shot open. A broad grin appeared, delighting her.

"Thank you for sharing your warmth, my dear man."

"My pleasure," he whispered, hugging her to him. "I see you have a youngster taking advantage of the comfort you provide."

"Fitzwilliam," she sighed. "In an unexplainable way, I am perfectly contented at this moment. Oh, I am well aware that we are headed into a horrible situation with little hope of immediate relief. Nevertheless, it will be one more adventure we can share with our grandchildren when they believe their grandparents are staid in their countenance and exceedingly boring."

He chuckled. "Do you believe that our children will think the same of us?"

"Most likely." She smirked. "I do think, my dear man, that the both of us will never be the same if and when we are able to return home."

His smile disappeared. "Elizabeth, I cannot help but look back on my actions prior to the Netherfield ball with abhorrence. I was exactly as you accused me of being, arrogant and prideful. The events since then have been harrowing. They forced me to see myself in a whole new light. What I discovered was not pleasing." He rubbed his chin, scratching his whiskers with the roughness of his palm. "My love, I had always thought myself to be cleverer than most of my peers, that I held myself to a higher standard, and that I was…I do not know, different, I suppose. Now, after seeing how others live their lives and the reasons behind the choices they made, I understand that, in truth, I was more like my peers than I could have guessed. This realization, while not condemning those I grew up with, has thoroughly demonstrated massive flaws that I can no longer ignore."

"I think you are wonderful," Elizabeth quickly reassured him, stating what was the truth in her heart.

He kissed her cheek.

"I thank you for that, Elizabeth. Yet is it the man you knew then whom you love or the one in front of you now?"

Leaning back, she looked him square in the face. "You are a brave man, Fitzwilliam Darcy."

"How so, for I do not believe that of myself."

"Then listen to each word, I pray you." Elizabeth stroked his jaw and chin before resting her hand on his shoulder. "Change seems to come hard to some people. It is a giant obstacle few men are willing to challenge, in my limited experience. Thus, when I watched you adapt to each situation you were confronted with, I began to admire you. As I watched you slough off the accoutrements of a wealthy man for the simpler garments of a laborer, I noted that your dignity and moral principles remained intact. It was then that I glimpsed your true character, Fitzwilliam. Where before I had seen pride in abundance, now I recognized your deep abiding sense of loyalty and self-sacrifice. I love the man you are inside. I cherish knowing that your constancy can be relied upon when you are under trial. Mostly, I love how you now see others with eyes of appreciation for their finer qualities."

"Like Madame and Jonah."

"Exactly." Elizabeth kissed the tip of his chin. "Your wealth is what you carry in your heart. It is your having a fine mind that you willingly use to make the lives of others better. It is your sense of improving yourself for that same purpose." She heaved a great sigh. "In actuality, I do not believe that I am the same person as before the ball. My intentions that night were to forge new acquaintances and have a delightful time. Now, I discern how shallow were my expectations. When I discovered who shared the bunk on the *Peregrine,* I thought you would be a burden to myself and the crew, one who insisted on his own way to the detriment of others. How wrong I was. Instead, you became my hero. You are a hero to Madame for finding and arranging for the release of her husband at tremendous cost to you. You are a hero to Jonah for being a man he could look up to with confidence. You, Fitzwilliam Darcy, will always be my hero."

The depths of his eyes pulled her in until her lips met his in a kiss so tender, she wanted to sob.

"I love you, Elizabeth almost Darcy," he whispered against her lips. "You own my heart and my soul."

"As you own mine."

His next kiss melted her insides to a puddle until she felt as bound to him as if the blacksmith had joined them together like iron to iron.  When he tilted his head back and chuckled, Elizabeth's curiosity got the best of her.

Darcy explained, "I cannot believe young Jonah did not wake in the middle of that kiss to tease us both for expressing our love for each other. He is a scamp who, one day far in the future, will meet his match, lose his heart, then want to challenge anyone who would torment him like he does us."

Elizabeth appreciated his humor. The lad still lay quietly at her back, the purr of his steady breathing telling her without seeing that he was sound asleep.

"Elizabeth, will you still marry me, Fitzwilliam Darcy, criminal?"

She snorted. "Hah! The question is, my good man, will you still marry me, Elizabeth Rose Bennet, criminal?"

Elizabeth discovered that it was possible to kiss and smile at the same time, something she looked forward to repeating for the next six or seven decades.

---

## 25

The journey to Launceston was traversed in miserable weather. A heavy freezing rain began falling soon after they left Fowey. When the wind picked up, it blew sideways in through the barred windows—open holes containing no glass. Darcy and Elizabeth placed Jonah between them to keep him as warm as possible. That night, they were again locked in a stall behind the blacksmith's shop. The straw had not been changed, it reeked of refuse and waste. With only one damp blanket for the three of them, the worn and weary trio chose to place it on the straw instead of covering themselves.

Their meal was a thin soup with a chunk of bread. No spoons were provided so they each drank out of the bowl. A small pitcher of water was provided to wash down the crumbs.

All three of them woke the next morning with scratchy throats and stuffed up noses. Even Jonah felt the need for a warm bath. The same soup as the night before was barely warm when they received it, providing little comfort and satisfaction to their bellies.

Fortunately, the driver allowed them the use of the blanket when they returned to the wagon. The rain had ceased during the night. A thick layer of heavy fog settled on the village, soaking everything it touched. The inside of the wagon was still damp from the rain. A small puddle was in a low spot in front of the bench where they sat.

Darcy's concern for Elizabeth was a living, breathing thing. From almost the moment he first came to know her, he knew she enjoyed lengthy outdoor walks. When her sister became ill at Netherfield Park, Elizabeth made the three-mile journey from Longbourn on foot to verify that her sister was being cared for properly with no adverse effects. Her skin and hair glowed with good health, attracting his eye. Now, no matter how much he rubbed them with his own, her hands remained cold. Her skin was pale. Her hair dull in the early morning light.

He wrapped the blanket around her and Jonah before pulling them close to him. It was not enough.

"Ah-choo!"

From the corner of his eye, Darcy could see through the window behind him. Their driver sneezed and snuffled several times in a row, cursing the bad weather and the muddy roads. When he muttered under his breath, Darcy strained to listen. What he heard was far from reassuring.

"This oughta do it. Them smugglers gotta be good fer somethin'."

Likely, it was not coffee or tea in the jug the driver placed at his feet after taking a lengthy swig. Within moments, he lifted the jug for another drink. Depending on the quality of the barrels shipped from France, the man could be inebriated well before the next town.

"Whatcha watchin', Mr. D?" Jonah had plucked a piece of straw from Elizabeth's skirt and was tying and untying a variety of knots until the straw fell apart. "Ye lookin' fer somethin' I need ta help ye with?"

Lowering his voice, Darcy said, "I am counting to see how

much of that jug of brandy our driver is drinking, attempting to calculate at what point he will tip over, hoping he will not fall to the ground."

"If he lands on his head and knocks hisself clean out, we will be locked in here with no way out, huh?"

"I was thinking that very thing, Jonah."

"Well, that'll give Madame and Monsieur 'nuf time ta catch up ta us." The lad grinned. "I sure could use some a her cookin' 'bout now." He rubbed his stomach.

He hated to disappoint the lad. The Vartans had already done more than their share of good for the three of them. "Jonah, we have no guarantee they will follow. I know that you believe they will, but do recall that they have a home to repair. As well, Monsieur Vartan has been gone from his property for over five weeks. He must be desperate to return to set matters right."

"Would you gentlemen like my opinion?" Elizabeth smiled. "I think...oh, there goes the jug."

Sure enough, the driver drank greedily from the vessel.

"Pardon me," Darcy dropped his arm from around the two of them and spun to look out the window. The grassy knolls lining both sides of the road were reassuring. However, up ahead the bank to the west dropped off steeply. From his angle, he could not see how deep the ravine went. He could not take a chance on the safety of Elizabeth or Jonah."

"Driver!" he yelled. "Driver! We need to stop immediately, I beg you. Pray, stop!"

The man belched before pulling on the reins. "Whoa!" When he bent to peer at his cargo, he said, "This had best be good. I can't be affordin' ta stop. The rain'll be startin' any minute, and I wanna get as far as we can before I's soaked."

"I beg of you. Pray open the door." Darcy knew that to insist would be to their detriment. The man would likely balk at being ordered by a prisoner.

In his stupor, the driver failed to tie off the reins. Turning to let himself down the side of the wagon, his foot must have met with air. The next thing they heard was a thud and a groan before they heard nothing but the howling of the wind through the trees.

"Now whatta we do?" Jonah asked.

"We wait." Darcy mused. "Either the coming rain will wake the driver, or the next transport will stop. We can hope for the second rather than the first."

Jonah glanced out the side window. "Look! He be asleep on his back with his mouth wide open. He's likely to drink more rain than brandy in that pose."

They heard a snort from the ground before the snoring commenced.

"Boone didn't snore, but the cap'n could wake the dead."

Elizabeth chuckled, then asked Darcy, "Would you stop for a prisoner wagon? I cannot believe help will come to us easily."

She was correct.

The road was well traveled. In the hours they sat there, other carts and carriages slowed to creep around them with most of the passengers and drivers staring at them from the comfort of their seats, but not one stopped.

To pass the time, Elizabeth tasked Jonah with guessing which direction the next travelers would come from, north or south. Darcy guessed the mode of transport. Any sound from the approaching vehicles was drowned out by the wind, evening the odds of him being right or wrong.

Elizabeth teased, "I am convinced that the next one will be an elegant barouche with the gold-embossed seal of nobility on the door. The occupant could only be an elderly lady dressed in rich satins and silks layered with a string of pearls a mile long and a diamond brooch bigger than my hand. Her spoiled daughter, who believes the sun and moon circle around her, insists her maid lick the sugar from her fingers and brush the crumbs from her skirt after eating her fifth pastry. She will need a wealthy suitor to satisfy her sweet tooth."

"Nah, the next one be a hackney with a load o' pirates who scuttled their ship on the rocks. They rescued two kegs o' the finest rum from the West Indies to sell, so's they can buy 'em a bigger ship. They heard the drinkin' men in...where are we going?"

"Launceston," Darcy and Elizabeth said in union.

"Yeah, Launceston," Jonah continued. "They heard they like their rum more'n brandy from France there, so's they's heading in that direction to get 'nuf money ta fund their pirating ways."

Darcy laughed. "I am sad to tell you that you are both incorrect. The next person to drive by us will be a family with a frustrated husband, a crying wife, and six screaming children under the age of five. Their nurse and maid gratefully abandoned them in Fowey not ten feet from where they had departed. The parents are exhausted. The driver wants to quit, and the horses refuse to move until one of the children shares his apple. All in all, they are a miserable lot."

Soon, a family coach came into view. They could hear a squalling baby through the pounding of the rain on the roof of the wagon.

"You win!" Elizabeth declared.

"An' they lose," Jonah added, covering his ears as they passed on by.

The three of them huddled together until the next coach slowed. It was a post chaise approaching from the south. For the first time, upon passing by the wagon, it came to a complete stop.

Their faces pressed to the window bars, Darcy, Elizabeth, and Jonah were surprised when two passengers alighted from the coach. The coach immediately departed, barely allowing time for their safe descent to the ground.

"Madame!" Jonah shrieked, bouncing on the hard bench. "I knew you'd come."

Elizabeth hugged him.

Darcy hugged them both.

Monsieur Vartan riffled through the driver's pockets for the keys, quickly unlocking the back door. Madame had stood hunched over until her husband handed her inside the wagon. Jonah launched himself at her, barely keeping from knocking her down. Madame pulled him to the bench, rocking him back and forth.

A tear welled up in the corner of the boy's eye as he looked at the woman he had missed.

"Ye brought food." He grinned. "I told ye they'd come fer us, didn't I?" Jonah spoke between stuffing the yeasty bread in his mouth.

~

"YOU DID, INDEED," Darcy admitted. Looking at Madame, he asked, "Why did you follow us?"

She shrugged.

Her husband replied, his accent thicker than his wife's. "We are not here for you or your bride, Monsieur."

"Me?" Jonah was incredulous. "Ye came fer me?"

Madame took his small hand in hers. "Yes, young one. You see, the others will be starting a new life together. They both are strong-willed and stubborn like me and Alex were many years ago. They will have many adjustments to make as they settle into whatever their future will be. For the two of us, our marriage is as solid as a piece of iron. We lack only one thing for our happiness."

"Me?" The lad's voice quivered.

"Yes, you." Madame rested her temple on the top of Jonah's head. "We need a boy to keep us young, to love and to feed, to teach and to train. If we had all of the lads in the whole world lined up for us to choose from, we would pick you."

"The other stuff sounds kinda nice, but I would've said yes at the feeding part." Jonah leaned into her. "Are we goin' back ta France then? To yer cottage? Do ye need me ta find ye a new cow?"

Monsieur Vartan answered, "No, we will not be returning to France. Madame and I have always dreamed of one day sailing to Nova Scotia. It is farm and timber rich, perfect for a couple willing to work hard with their hands."

The boy excitedly sat up straight. "I've been there. Why, there be ships going' in and outta there both day an' night. There be whalers an' fishermen a plenty. I'd have an easy time findin' work ta help ye both if ye need."

"I thank you, Jonah Hackett." Madame pulled at the waistband of her skirt. "However, did you forget I had this?"

Jonah's mouth gaped open. "The ring."

"How?" Darcy sputtered. "You bartered for our passage from France, did you not?"

She appeared offended. "Of course, I did. Jean Paul's son would never have taken us on his ship until payment was provided in advance."

"Then, if you did not use the ring, how...?"

Madame's grin was sly. "I offered him our land and what was left of the cottage. At first, he had no interest. However, when I told him of the natural spring and what we had stored inside, he immediately agreed to my terms."

Darcy's smile lit his face. "You are a skilled negotiator, Madame. And you are a fortunate man, Monsieur Vartan to have such a wife."

From outside, the driver snorted and snuffled before his snoring settled again into a regular rhythm.

"We are flirting with danger the longer we remain. We cannot be seen escaping by other travelers." Darcy reminded them of the precariousness of their situation. "The rain could start again any second, which could wake the driver."

Elizabeth asked the Vartans. "What are your plans?"

Monsieur Vartan replied, "My wife would give me no peace unless we see you on your way to your people before we board a ship for Canada."

Grateful that the parting was not immediate, Darcy stepped from the wagon, turning back to assist Elizabeth. "Let us go."

The walk was brutal. The road was littered with ruts filled with muddy water, making it impossible to determine how deep they were. The shoulders of the road were narrow in places where they needed to walk single file.

Darcy fretted about the toll the arduous trek would have on Elizabeth and Monsieur Vartan. Neither looked well. Neither complained nor asked for rest.

With relief, they entered the valley surrounding a small farming community where the main road crossed in all four directions. The soil was rich and dark, the air heavy and gray. A steady mist had been falling since departing the wagon. The five of them were soaked through.

Rather than stopping at the first inn they approached, the group headed through town toward the Plymouth road. Seeing a busy inn where the front was filled with an assortment of transports in various stages of unhitching and harnessing, they decided this was the place to stop. The stables were busy. Grooms and drivers were loudly jockeying for position so their teams would be next in line.

By the time they stepped inside, he could see that Elizabeth was close to collapsing.

Bringing Elizabeth with him, Darcy pushed through the crowd surrounding the fireplace until he could feel the warmth of the fire on his face. He cared nothing for those who sought to halt his approach. His move was bold as brass since they had no money or no way to obtain any. They could not pay for any services the inn had to offer. He would go back outside to offer his help in hopes of earning some coins.

Madame approached the busy innkeeper. Darcy could not hear the exchange. However, he knew the value of a French cook who made tasty meals with basic ingredients to an inn this size. There would be no questions asked about why and how she had arrived in the small village.

Within moments, the innkeeper's wife approached with two hot cups of tea. Darcy was so appreciative that his inclination was to embrace the poor woman.

Glancing back, he noticed Madame disappearing behind the bar to the kitchen area. His heart landing in his stomach, Darcy realized their tea came at the price of Madame's labors despite her being as exhausted as the rest of them.

Jonah approached, dropping down at Elizabeth's feet. Monsieur Vartan soon followed.

They were a weary lot who had escaped one terrible situation for another. There seemed no hope of relief. Frustration gnawed at his gut. He needed to work, but he could not leave his loved ones on their own. Who would help Elizabeth if she needed it? Or Jonah or the Vartans?

He would do anything to improve their situation. They needed warm baths and beds. Each of them deserved to have their bellies filled with good food and drink. They needed comfortable transport to Plymouth, then on to their eventual destinations.

When Elizabeth's fingers intertwined with his, he knew any hope for bettering their situation rested with him.

Kissing Elizabeth's temple, he told her that he needed to stand.

His palms were sweaty. He had to fist his hands to keep them from shaking. His father, if he were still alive, would castigate him, perhaps even disowning him for what he was about to do. The humiliation of begging for help practically choked him. That his efforts might not meet with success was unpalatable. Once he started, any hopes of salvaging his reputation or Elizabeth's would be at an end.

Inhaling deeply, he closed his eyes until he gathered his fortitude. Before he could lose his courage, he opened his mouth to speak. Immediately, Darcy was bumped from behind by a gentleman attempting to avoid a small child playing on the floor.

"Pardon me," the gent mumbled before moving toward the door. The man was dressed in fine clothing with a walking stick in one hand and his beaver hat in the other.

As he passed, Jonah reached down to pluck a gold watch fob from the floor that must have fallen when the two men collided.

"Look here, Mr. D. We're saved." Jonah whispered, cupping his hands over the fob, so only Darcy could see.

Not for a moment did Darcy hesitate. "It does not belong to us."

"But I found it fair and square," the lad's pride in being their salvation had him pocketing the treasure. "Finder's keepers."

"No, Jonah." Darcy stretched out his hand. "The fob does not belong to us."

The lad balked. Crossing his arms, he thrust out his chin. "It will feed us, Mr. D."

Darcy stooped down until his eyes were level with the boy's. "Jonah, your motives are the best in the world. I am sincerely pleased that your first thought was not to selfishly keep this for yourself but to trade it to benefit all of us. However, we did nothing to earn this piece. We paid no price for it that would make us feel good inside about having it."

"But food makes me feel good inside."

"It does me too. But the better, lasting feeling is a good conscience at doing what is right."

"Ah, Mr. D." Jonah stuffed his hand in his pocket, pulling out the fob. "This don't feel right to me right now. But I'll trust ye ta look after the ladies an' me."

When the boy went to hand the fob to Darcy, he said, "No, please keep fast hold of it, Jonah, and come with me."

Checking to verify that Elizabeth was resting as comfortably as possible, they quickly approached the door where the man stood waiting for his carriage.

"Pardon me," Darcy bowed. "You dropped something of value, sir. The lad found it and wants to return it."

The man looked at them both before holding out his hand. When he saw the item, his eyes blinked rapidly, dispelling tears.

"I thank you for its return." He swallowed. "My wife, who had little money, gave me this fob as a wedding present forty-one years ago. The gold is of little value. The diamond is paste. But it is worth more to me than had it been real."

"Then we are pleased to return it to you, are we not, Jonah?" Darcy asked.

After a pause, the boy nodded.

"I lost my beloved wife two years ago. I would have been devastated to have found this missing." Placing the fob in the small pocket of his waistcoat, he insisted, "Pray accept my thanks along with a gift for your honesty."

Jonah's face lit up.

Darcy's pride resurfaced. Tamping it down, he said, "We thank you."

A mixture of intense relief and victory warred with the indignity of receiving assistance. Before his arrival in Hertfordshire, had anyone suggested he would have willingly lowered himself to accept a stranger's help, Darcy would have sneered. Never! Darcys were the benefactors, not the recipients.

Before an hour had passed, the five of them were bathed and fed. Elizabeth and the Vartans were resting in a comfortable room. Jonah stood next to Darcy in the sitting room attached to Elizabeth's bed chamber. Due to the lack of rooms, the three of them would again be sharing a bed.

"That had to be hard to give that back even for you, Mr. D." Jonah observed.

"In actuality, it never occurred to me to keep it to use for our care. What was challenging to me was accepting his reward. None-theless, when the health and happiness of people you cherish is at stake, there is nothing I would not do for all of you."

The boy nodded. "Do ye remember I told ye about me mother an' how I had to ask the cap'n for money to buy her medicine?"

"I do."

"Well, I was more scared that no one would listen and help her than I was embarrassed to ask. I bet ye felt the same today, huh?"

"I did."

"Mr. D," Jonah looked up at him. "I wanna love Monsieur and Madame that same way. I wanna do anything ta make their lives easier."

Squeezing his shoulder, Darcy reassured him, "I have no doubt that you will do well, Jonah Hackett."

They stood in silence until they heard Elizabeth moving in the next room.

"Will ye name yer first boy after me?"

Darcy's heart brimmed with admiration for the lad. "Name my son Jonah, you ask? Nah, I best name 'em Hercules or Richard the Lionhearted, don't ye think?"

The boy flung his arms around Darcy's waist, squeezing hard.

"I love ye, Mr. D. With all of me heart I wanna be a man just like you when I grows up."

He looked up to see Elizabeth standing in the doorway, her eyes brimming with tears. She had been witness to one of the greatest moments in his life. He would never forget this boy—ever.

## 26

The sky was pitch black when they arrived in Plymouth. The twenty-mile journey had been fraught with disruptions ranging from the mail coach stopping at all of the inns they passed to the large carriage constantly being stuck in the muddy ruts.

Darcy was familiar with Plymouth since the ship from London to Ireland often stopped at that port. He immediately steered his group to the White Stag Inn. The gift from the gentleman allowed them to improve their lodgings from the night before.

The hushed tones of the patrons were music to Darcy's ears. A young couple sat by the fireplace. He was reading. The wife's loving eyes rested upon her husband as he turned each page. Would Elizabeth and he be like that in the future? He hoped they would be.

A short and stocky man stood as they entered. The man was a few feet from them when Darcy exclaimed, "Mr. Stanton. You cannot begin to imagine how pleased I am to see you."

The man stood taller with the recognition.

Darcy was elated. Here was a man who knew him well and was

in a position to offer exactly what they needed. Bernard Stanton was the Darcy family's man of business.

"I am quite surprised to see you here, sir. I expected to meet you in Fowey once the ship's mast is repaired. It is quite providential that we are both in Plymouth."

When they were seated in a private room, Darcy asked what he knew of their circumstances.

"Before a full six hours had passed since you and one Miss Elizabeth Bennet were reported missing from Netherfield Park in Hertfordshire, word arrived in London at Darcy House of your absence. Many, including your host, Mr. Charles Bingley, who I might add is a horrible correspondent, concluded that the two of you were on your way to Scotland for a quick wedding over the anvil. However, knowing you, none of your staff believed this to be true." He glanced at Elizabeth. "I beg your pardon if I have offended you, Miss Bennet. It was not the prospective bride that stopped us. Rather, Mr. Darcy's character is well-known to all of us as one who would not act on impulse on any serious decision. What could be more serious than marriage?"

She nodded, "You know him well."

"Therefore, your cousin Colonel Richard Fitzwilliam was contacted to aid in the search. With no leads and little to go on, we felt as if we were spinning our wheels until your signet ring turned up at a London pawn shop close to the docks." He reached inside his satchel to retrieve a box with the ring inside. "Unfortunately, the shop owner had no idea who he purchased the ring from, clearly stating that he had not seen the man before or since. Nor had he made the effort to determine to whom it had belonged."

He cleared his throat. "Sir, your note was received yesterday. I gathered what I felt would be needed and sailed for Fowey as soon as the tide was favorable. Your cousin set off from London in your coach along with Mr. Bennet and Mr. Bingley, who insisted on coming. I will send a series of messengers to intercept them so they can be diverted south. I expect them to arrive by tomorrow if they drive as hard as I believe they will."

"I thank you for your service and your support, Stanton."

"Sir, your valet, Parker, accompanied me. I suspect that he is currently above stairs folding and refolding your garments as well as sharpening his razors in preparation for our arrival tomorrow in Fowey. We are, each of us, staying on the third floor. If I might, I would be pleased to secure rooms appropriate for all of you."

Darcy agreed.

"My father is coming?" Elizabeth asked in wonder. "I cannot imagine his distress at making a lengthy trip in the winter months. My joy at seeing him will know no bounds."

Mr. Stanton bowed. "Miss Bennet, your father sent items for your use. They, too, are above stairs."

Her smile lit the room.

"It is well that he will be here, my dear. There is much we will need to discuss before our return to town."

"A WORD, MR. DARCY." Monsieur Vartan walked from the room, Darcy followed.

Once they were outside, the Frenchman said, "My wife, the boy, and I will be leaving you as soon as passage can be arranged."

His response was immediate. "Please, let us have this night to rest and be refreshed. Allow us to say a proper goodbye in the morning."

The man considered Darcy's request. Finally, he nodded his consent.

"Allow me to be your host tonight, Monsieur Vartan. Elizabeth will need time with Jonah before you take your leave. Your wife, she took us in as strangers, then cared for our needs without a word of complaint."

"Without complaint?" Monsieur mused.

"Well, without too much complaint," Darcy confessed.

The man grinned. Shaking hands, the two stepped back inside the inn.

"Why, Mr. D., I just about didn't know ye all shaved and cleaned up. Ye look even better than when I first laid eyes on ye on the *Peregrine.*"

Darcy grinned at the lad, but his eyes searched for Elizabeth. She stood across from him in a dress she had worn in Hertfordshire, her hands meekly folded in front of her, her eyes downcast so her lashes rested against her cheek.

*Was she shy? What had happened to render her timid?*

"Elizabeth? Are you...?"

In slow motion, her eyes met his. When her chin lifted slightly and the corner of her mouth moved, Darcy spied the welcome he had dreamed of during the hours his valet took to make him presentable.

"Fitzwilliam." His name had no sooner left her lips than she moved towards him. Her arms wrapped tightly around his neck as her mouth met his. She was...*Oh God!* He simply...could not...think of...

Delicious! Yes, she was delicious. She was delectable. She was delightful, and she was smiling. Or was it him? He could not tell.

He whispered against her lips, "My darling, how can someone so heavenly tempt me beyond reason?"

She giggled. "Rhetorical, my love? Or do you expect an answer now?"

"Is it possible to love someone more each minute of each day?"

"I hope so, Fitzwilliam, because I do."

"Wow! That was sure some welcome, Mrs. D. Now, don't ye be

thinkin' ye ever want to try somethin' like that w' me 'cause...well...I don't mind it when ye kiss me forehead like Madame Vartan does when I tell her she be the best cooker in the world, but all that other stuff ain't fer me." Jonah stuck his thumbs in the waistband of the new trousers Stanton had purchased for him. "Look, Mr. D. I got shoes to fit me feet. They don't pinch." He stuck one foot out, turning it from side to side.

"I am pleased for you, Jonah." He vowed to himself to give Stanton a bonus in his next pay packet.

Having the two of them there at that moment in time, filled his heart with joy. Yes, he was a happy man.

Monsieur and Madame Vartan entered the sitting room where they broke their fast from a table laden with meats, breads, fruits, and jams. Jonah made so many trips to refill his plate that Darcy worried his trousers would no longer fit.

Later, Darcy asked Monsieur Vartan if he could have a private conversation with him. When the man readily agreed, they left the others and went to a separate room.

The conversation was lengthy. The negotiation was quickly settled. By the time the sun was high in the sky, Madame had stitched each one of the gold coins Darcy had presented to her husband inside her undergarments and the waistband of her skirt. Monsieur had done the same to a belt she had fashioned for him to wear about his waist. They would not suffer want during their travel to Canada or after. However, Darcy knew beyond a shadow of doubt that they would be as frugal as ever despite the fortune they carried.

THEY WERE LEAVING.

Elizabeth's chest hurt. Her heart still beat its regular rhythm, but her inner self was crumbling quickly. Torn between being happy for the life Jonah would have with his new guardians versus knowing how much she would miss him, she hugged him close.

She had stayed awake until late the night before writing a letter to the lad. Each stroke of the quill carried with it an attachment she never wanted to forget. This boy had been their friend when they needed it and a helper when they were desperate. He had brought so much joy to both her and Darcy that the sadness she felt at the upcoming separation was overwhelming.

That morning, the maid Darcy had hired for her quickly helped her to dress so Elizabeth could pen a letter to the Vartans. Elizabeth never wanted to forget the meaning of true hospitality as demonstrated by Madame. She never wanted to forget the priceless lessons she had discovered about the value of learning basic tasks for a household. One never knew when or how quickly circumstances in a life could change.

Elizabeth was pleased to see that in his hands Darcy carried neatly folded missives of his own. They were as thick as hers.

Her hand flew to her chest. Her heartbeat had quickened as soon as her eyes found his that morning. Yes, despite the sadness, her reason for joy stood close to Monsieur. Reasoning with herself that Jonah and the Vartans would have happy lives together, she was able to extend her goodbyes.

"Aw, Mrs. D. Don't ye cry. There's only a wee small ocean that'll be separatin' you an' me. I 'spect Madame will be just as hard on me to learn me letters and such, so you'll be hearin' from us perty soon. Mr. D. done gave us his direction. So, don't ye cry." The tears trailed down his cheeks, which were amazingly clean.

"Dear girl," Madame patted her cheek. "Be happy with your man."

"I will." Elizabeth did the unthinkable. She hugged the most unhuggable woman of her acquaintance. Madame squeezed her waist so tightly Elizabeth thought she might never need a corset again.

When Madame stepped back, she announced to the room. "We will go now. Do not follow us to the coach. We can see ourselves off on our journey. Once we settle, we will write, fully expecting a reply as soon as you are able."

She approached Darcy, taking one of his hands in hers. "Monsieur Darcy, you gave our Jonah something that money can never buy, an example of what it means to be an honorable man of worth. You gave me back my Alex when I was without him. You brought me a son to fuss over and to feed. You are my hero, Monsieur Darcy, on this day and for all of my tomorrows."

Standing on her toes, she kissed his cheek. Without looking back, she walked out of the room to the waiting coach. Monsieur Vartan shook Darcy's hand, bowed over hers, and followed his wife.

Jonah shook Darcy's hand like Monsieur had done. "I'm proud to call ye me friend, Mr. D. I'll not forget ye. Ye treat Mrs. D real nice-like, 'cause that would make me happy."

Darcy bowed to him.

The lad walked into Elizabeth's arms. When he leaned back to speak, she wiped the tears from his cheeks. "I'll never forget ye, Mrs. D. If Mr. D. hadn't already claimed ye and if ye knew how ta cook, I'd have married ye instead. But this way be best, I'm thinkin'."

"I love you, Jonah Hackett." Elizabeth smiled at the lad. "I always will."

He sniffed, kissed her on the cheek, whispered that he loved her too, then followed the Vartans out the door.

She had that combination feeling of sad and happy. Sappy? When Darcy held her tightly, she knew he felt it too.

"I believe, kind sir, that we will suffer greatly the day our sons leave for Eton or our daughters bring their young men home to introduce them to us."

He rested his forehead on hers. "Indeed." His sigh was heavy.

"I fear we will have the only thirty-year-olds entering school with their classmates aged thirteen because we simply cannot let them go. Do you not agree that thirty-six is the perfect age for a daughter to have her come out? Then, she might marry at forty so we might keep them with us longer."

Elizabeth chuckled at his silliness.

"I love you." She gave him a brief kiss, the perfect medicine for a melancholy heart.

"I love you too."

## 27

Plymouth Dock was surrounded by the dockyard to the west, by the barracks to the north and east, and by Mount Wise to the south.

Elizabeth sincerely appreciated that Darcy had arranged for a maid who had no difficulty keeping up with them as they strolled the narrow cobblestone streets of Plymouth and beyond. The days since the Vartans and Jonah departed had been filled with long conversations and discovery. As they walked around the city on that day, the air was cold and heavy with moisture. Snuggling into her new coat, she squeezed Darcy's arm to gain his attention.

"How long do you suspect until we see my father?"

He patted her hand. "Soon, I hope. Richard will push the horses, my driver, and the other passengers to the limit. However, he is not a cruel man. If he notes the strain of the long hours of travel on your father, he will adjust their schedule."

"I desperately want him to be well, Fitzwilliam. That the actions of the kidnappers and one Silas Bingley has caused my father to suffer at all is another reason for loathing the men responsible for our being here."

"We have many reasons to resent those men." Darcy agreed. "Elizabeth, by my not hiding who we are, I made our situation the subject for potential gossip."

"You have nothing to regret." She smiled up at him. "In my eyes and that of the Vartans and Jonah, everything you have done has been an act of bravery and love. My dearest man, I have learned over the past week that being respected by others is of critical importance to any male, including Jonah. For a female, we thrive on being loved and held in affection. By giving your name to the blacksmith in Fowey, you demonstrated that you held each one of us in esteem. If this means that others will speak poorly about our plight, then so be it. Both of us will scoff at their ignorance. And to be honest, I believe that having the final word on our value shows the world our devotion. When other gentlemen see how much your wife cherishes you and adores you and works alongside you, their hearts will fill with envy for what we have. In fact, it would not surprise me if they do not attempt their own grand feat to establish their importance in the eyes of others."

"Elizabeth Bennet, you are a wonder." He lifted her gloved fingers to his lips. "Indeed, I feel no shame for what I did. Like you, I was aware of the consequences but, if needs be, would I do it again for you? Absolutely!"

"Then you must congratulate yourself for having been kidnapped with me instead of a simpering female from the *ton*. Never let it be said that we are not the perfect match. We are partners in joy, my man." She stopped. "Oh my, I just thought of something that we probably should consider. When you left Hertfordshire, you were a reserved, taciturn man of fine reputation and honor. When I left, I was an impulsive, impertinent girl. Will anyone recognize us now, Fitzwilliam?"

For the first time in her twenty years, she appreciated her mother's nerves. How would her father respond to her? Of course, he would know her physical appearance, for it had hardly altered at all. Yet, her inner self had been through events that would forever change her outlook, her actions, and her opinions. Additionally, the circumstances of their kidnapping had put the whole Bennet family in a precarious situation. If Elizabeth's reputation could not be saved by her marriage, then all five Bennet daughters would be affected.

"While it is true that we are forever altered by our experiences, the simple fact is that we have no control over what others say or how they view us. Rather than fret over the gossip mongers and backbiters, we can retreat to Pemberley and remain there in perfect bliss until another scandal comes along that far outshines anything that happened to us. I will confess that Georgiana would be as happy as a lark to stay in Derbyshire. Should any of your sisters feel the need for escape, should any or all of your family decide that time away from Hertfordshire would improve their circumstances, we could have them all with us, if you would like."

"You would not mind? Truly?" Peering into his eyes, the depth of his sincerity was as evident as the nose on his face. He meant each and every word.

A large carriage pulled by a team of matching horses came into view as it rounded the corner at the end of the next street. Elizabeth stepped away from the road to allow the conveyance to pass. Darcy hesitated, then followed.

"Elizabeth, you were wondering how long it might be until your father appeared? Since that is my coach, I believe we might want to hurry back to the inn. By the time they disembark, we can welcome them to Plymouth."

Her heart pounding, they moved as quickly through the crowded thoroughfares as they were able. By cutting through several of the side streets, they arrived ahead of Darcy's carriage. Rushing up to her room, she refreshed herself as best as she could in a short period of time. Within minutes, she descended the stairs.

She heard him before she saw him. Her father had arrived.

"Lizzy!"

She walked into her father's opened arms once they were in a private room.

"My Lord, girl. You look..." One hand rested on her cheek, the other grasped her chaffed hand. "What has happened to you, Elizabeth? How did you end up in Plymouth? Your poor mother will never forgive you for not going to Gretna Green."

She heard his fear in every word. Closing her eyes, her senses filled with the familiarity of every day of her twenty years.

"Papa, I am pleased you are here." Stepping back, she surveyed his face. Were there more lines down his cheeks and at the corners of his eyes than there were before? Of course. How could there not be? Her father loved her. His pain at having her missing must have been devastating.

The colonel cleared his throat. "I beg your pardon, but we have ground to cover and plans to make. While I am not completely insensitive to your feelings, this discussion needs to happen now."

There were three large leather chairs and one sofa around the fireplace. Darcy was sitting at one end of the sofa. Instead of sitting next to her father in one of the chairs, Elizabeth moved next to her intended. At her father's raised brows, she smiled.

"Bingley," the colonel barked. "Perhaps you might want to discover the sights in the town or rest in your room?"

The words sounded more like an order than a suggestion.

Darcy stopped the younger man from leaving. "No, Bingley needs to remain since our story will begin and end with him."

To say that his comments surprised the room would have been an understatement.

"Explain yourself," the colonel demanded.

"The...ah, heated conversation Elizabeth and I had at your ball, Bingley, was not over when the music ended. I followed Elizabeth to the balcony where we were immediately set upon by kidnappers. They used that vile smelling oil of vitriol to render us both unconscious. We awoke the next morning aboard the *Peregrine*, a pirate ship headed to Charleston in the Carolinas where I would be turned over to Mr. Silas Bingley, for what purpose, I do not know."

"Uncle Bingley?" The younger man's mouth gaped open. "You know my uncle?"

"I do not." Darcy continued the tale. "Our ankles were bound, and our wrists were tied tightly behind us. We were placed in a dark room where we struggled for freedom. The captain and the crew believed us to be Mr. Charles Bingley and Miss Caroline Bingley. My question to you, Charles, is why would your uncle forcibly kidnap you? What did he want of you or what did you have that was valuable enough to him that he willingly and cunningly broke the law?"

"I do not know." Bingley ran his hand through his hair as he paced the room. "I mean, I started getting letters from him several months before I decided to lease Netherfield Park."

"That was six months ago, Bingley." Darcy stated.

"Yes, well, you know how poor I am at correspondence, Darcy."

"Did you read any of his letters?" the colonel asked, his stance over where Bingley had dropped into a chair threatening. "What did your uncle ask of you?"

"He only wanted me to come for a visit. Actually, he was pretty insistent that I come. Each letter became more and more demanding. I swear, that is all."

"Bingley?" Darcy insisted.

"Well, yes, he did happen to mention that I was old enough to wed his only child, a daughter named Priscilla." He threw his hands into the air. "Darcy, you cannot have expected me to drop everything for a trip across the ocean to marry a lady I had never seen. What if she was plain with a simple mind? What would I have done then?"

"Did you answer him? Did you write to him declining his offer?"

"I meant to." The timbre of Bingley's voice had changed to hesitating uncertainty. "I did mean to, Darcy, but I was busy learning all I could to be a proper landowner. Plus, there were so many balls and social events to attend that once I placed the letters on my desk, I never quite found the time to attend them properly."

"Yet you found time to criticize and tease me about writing letters while I was in your home. Bingley!" Darcy stood. Rubbing his jaw, he sat back down. Taking Elizabeth's hand in his, he addressed his friend. "Charles, I want you to think about what you would have done had it been you and your sister aboard the ship. There were seventy armed men and one young lad. You were the only one of value to the crew. What they would have done to your sister the first time she opened her mouth to insist on having her comforts, I can only begin to guess. Your being a landholder would have meant nothing to them. Your investments would have held no value in their eyes. What would you have done?"

"I...I do not know." Bingley stammered.

Darcy held the younger man's gaze.

"*Good Lord!* Lizzy, I could have lost you!" Mr. Bennet's hands and voice quivered. "How did you escape?"

Darcy replied. "You almost did lose her, sir. Our escape was made when the wind stirred the waves into a tumultuous sea. We went overboard, washing up on French shores."

"*My God!*" the colonel whispered.

"We were fortunate to land on the property of a woman with a heart as big as the whole continent and the fortitude of your

whole military battalion, Richard. Through her, we were able to
return to England on a smuggler's vessel."

"Incredible!" the colonel muttered.

Bingley looked like he was going to be sick.

Mr. Bennet's eyes glanced at Darcy then at Elizabeth. "What
happens now?"

Darcy cleared his throat. "What sort of talk has arisen from our
departure?"

"Before the ball was over, you were both found to be missing.
My dear wife fainted at the assumption of Elizabeth's eloping with
a wealthy man. Jane attempted to quiet her mother and her aunt,
but the speculation was already circling the ballroom."

The colonel added, "Although your valet shared the gossip
with me, I simply refused to believe it. However, as Stanton has
undoubtedly told you, we had nothing to go on."

Addressing his future father-in-law, Darcy said, "You have long
known how uniquely wonderful your second child is, sir. In my
arrogance, I failed to appreciate her value—at first. Oh, do not
judge me as completely ignorant for there was something about
her that captured and held my attention from the start. I am now
convinced that I could spend a lifetime with her and still find
more to learn and love about her. Your daughter holds my heart in
her capable hands, Mr. Bennet. I will forever cherish her, protect
her, and adore her, you have my word. Will you honor me with
your permission and blessing to marry Elizabeth?"

"My Lizzy?" Mr. Bennet asked, incredulous. "You *want* to
marry her? I apologize for questioning you, Mr. Darcy, but I did
not expect this reaction from you. Your attitude toward her, in fact,
all of us, was condescending in Meryton. This...this is quite unexpected." He paused, then continued, "I have learned since your
disappearance that you have a reputation for being an honorable
man. Thus, I fully expected you to offer marriage as any

respectable gentleman would do under the circumstances. But this proclamation of love...why, it is surprising."

He looked at his daughter. "Lizzy, I would not have you join yourself to a man whom you hold in little regard. If you cannot forgive his initial insult to your form and character, I will refuse my consent. I would rather take my family from Longbourn and resettle elsewhere than have you enter marriage unhappily."

She grinned at Darcy before turning back to her father. "Papa, I am madly and deeply in love with Fitzwilliam Darcy, gentleman, sailor, farmer, milkmaid, woodcutter, smuggler, and not-so-hardened criminal. Several times over the course of the past days he has protected me at the risk of his own health and life. I am safe when I am with him. I will marry none other."

The colonel lifted a glass to the couple. "My cousin, as a milkmaid and a woodcutter? These are stories I need to hear."

"In due time," Darcy replied. To Elizabeth, he said, "I am madly and deeply in love with Elizabeth Rose Bennet, gentleman's daughter, sailor, cook, smuggler, and the thief who stole my heart."

In front of her father, his cousin, and his friend, he kissed her soundly. Jonah would have been proud.

## 28

W ith her father to accompany her, Elizabeth's maid remained in Plymouth. Thus, it was five well-dressed travelers who set out for London.

They had not gone far when Colonel Fitzwilliam began his interrogation.

"Bingley, tell us all you know about your uncle."

"My Uncle Silas?" Bingley asked.

Both Darcy and the colonel rolled their eyes. Elizabeth's father snorted.

"Yes, Bingley."

"Well, in truth, my father did not like him very much. He was a spoiled younger brother who had dreams of grandeur. He resented how our background in trade separated us from the upper echelons of society. While I was still very young, my uncle took his portion of the business and left for America. I personally do not remember him."

Darcy asked, "What do you know of his financial situation?"

Bingley nodded. "I know quite a bit, actually. The first letter I received from him boasted of the size of his holdings, including slaves, and his income from his cotton and tobacco fields. I did not pay too much attention to those details as his descriptions of his daughter, his only child, were far more important due to the nature of the request he was making."

"Slavery is illegal, is it not?" Her father wondered.

Darcy replied, "I understand that the US Congress passed a law prohibiting the importation of slaves a mere three years ago. How that impacted existing plantation owners, I do not know."

"Vile practice," Mr. Bennet huffed.

"Agreed." The colonel continued by noting, "Interestingly, unless there was extremely poor management, your uncle should be a wealthy man. His cost to kidnap you would not come cheaply."

"Colonel, he requested nothing of me other than to become husband to his daughter. His wife died two years ago. He was in charge of making arrangements for Miss Bingley's future. He did mention that should something happen to him, I would inherit the sum of his properties and investments if, and only if, his daughter was my bride."

"You have no other Bingley cousins?" the colonel asked.

"None who are unmarried."

Elizabeth blurted. "I suspect that had we made it to Charleston, we would have been met by a man in ill health who is looking out for the future of his possessions. The sicker he became, the more desperate to have someone he could train during the time he had remaining to continue on his course after his demise."

"I agree with Elizabeth." Darcy smiled across at her. "The minute you said your vows, Bingley, you would have had the whole of his operations dropped on your shoulders."

"I believe you both to be correct as to the outcome," Bingley said. "Yet, there has to be an abundance of better qualified men in the area who would want the wealth that came with the property enough to marry my cousin, no matter her looks or personality."

Elizabeth's finger rested on her chin. "Did he happen to mention his daughter's age?"

"She was but sixteen, which is far too young to wed, in my humble opinion."

"I quite agree," Elizabeth paused. "While I think our conjecture as to his motives might be correct, that we would have met a man in ill health, I cannot believe Mr. Silas Bingley was as wealthy as we might suspect. Pray consider, what loving father would willingly marry off an only child to an unknown relative? Was he hiding something from local gentlemen or were they not interested because they knew his financial situation? I cannot believe that the desperation was due to poor health alone."

Bingley sank down into the squabs. "He cannot be sound in mind; that is all that I can add."

Darcy asked, "My question is, if he was so desperate to kidnap you, what will he do once he discovers you are not on the *Peregrine*? If you were his only hope, I cannot believe that he will give up until he draws his last breath."

"Which brings up the pirates," the colonel stated. "What tale will they tell when they arrive in Charleston with no Mr. Bingley? What might the consequences be since Silas Bingley paid for services that were not rendered? Might they seek revenge upon either or both of you when next they are in England?"

Darcy looked directly at her. "My dear, you knew Captain Lucien Bartholomew and crew as well as I. What is your opinion?"

These were matters that Elizabeth had considered during the hours when she was unable to sleep.

"I have no good feelings toward anyone of the crew on the *Peregrine* with the exception of Quartermaster Boone, who took exceptionally good care of Jonah. As to the captain, I believe that the niche he created catering to the wives of wealthy men in Charleston would have him far more concerned with getting the goods he had promised them into their greedy arms than one

Silas Bingley. It appeared to me that having a long-term business arrangement with the ladies was his motive, particularly since your offers of ransom fell upon deaf ears."

"I agree." Darcy's smile was solely for her. "He was offered double his income if we either turned back to London or traveled to New York or Boston. Captain Bartholomew never gave a moment's consideration to the gain he could receive from me either as Charles Bingley or Fitzwilliam Darcy. Of course, I do not discount that he would have thought up some means of gaining money from me and from Silas Bingley, such was his fiscal interest."

Her father added, "Perhaps this is a result of legislation from the American presidents. First Jefferson insisted on the *Embargo Act*, then Madison took up his cause with the *Non-Intercourse Act*. Little did they realize how much the people in their country would crave our British goods. Stopping the legal entry of these items served to irritate our Parliament and the Admiralty while increasing the demand and profit for pirates and smugglers willing to run through the blockades with our products."

The colonel nodded, then asked, "What about this Jonah or the French couple? Will they demand anything from you in the future?"

Elizabeth's reply was both immediate and firm. "Without a doubt, Colonel. Their claims on us will last a lifetime."

"Blackmail, you say?" The colonel harrumphed. "I have contacts in Canada who could set them straight. What do they have on you that we need to overcome?"

"Love, Colonel. Only love."

~

DURING THE FIVE days it took to reach London, his Elizabeth regained her strength, as did her father. It had been agreed that

Darcy would obtain a common license from the chapel he attended in town. The two of them would marry as soon as the license was issued.

The day was the 11th of December 1811—a Wednesday at eleven o'clock in the morning. A light snow had fallen the night before, coating London with an unparalleled beauty, welcoming Elizabeth Bennet as the future wife of Fitzwilliam Darcy.

Her aunt and uncle had delivered to Darcy House a gown Elizabeth had stored at their home for social occasions when she visited town. The vibrant blue trim was the color of royalty. She would be his queen.

Dressed in his finest day clothes, Darcy stood at the front of the church waiting for his bride. The colonel stood alongside him in dress uniform. Elizabeth's youngest sisters, who had been escorted to London by Darcy's man of business, giggled and waved at Richard, who ignored their antics. Bingley had managed a seat next to Mrs. Bennet, who concentrated more on him as a future husband to her eldest daughter than on the couple who would be wed that day. Apparently, the matron feared him being as negligent about proposals as he was with correspondence.

From each stop of their journey home, Darcy had sent instructions to his household. Bring the Bennets to London. Freshen the mistress's chambers. Clean the house from top to bottom. Prepare a small celebration for the wedding of their master to the woman of his dreams.

*There she was!* His breath caught in his throat. Her glorious hair was fashioned on top of her head with small white flowers in her curls that looked from a distance as if they were snowflakes. The light shining through the stained-glass windows glowed on her skin. When she stepped closer, he could see the twinkle in her eyes.

Mr. Bennet wisely did not hesitate in placing her hand in Darcy's.

"I love you, Fitzwilliam," she whispered. "I am happy to become your wife on this day."

"I thank you for the honor," was all that he could manage.

The clergyman had asked beforehand if there would be an exchange of rings, something rarely done. Darcy told him that the ring was waiting in his pocket.

After their vows, the bishop asked, "Do you have your ring, sir?"

Removing it from his pocket, Darcy slipped it on the second finger of Elizabeth's left hand. Her eyes never left his. The fit was perfect.

He loved that she cared more for him than what jewelry he could provide her. Lifting her finger to his lips, he kissed the stone as the bishop intoned, "Bless, O Lord, this ring to be a sign of the vows by which this man and this woman have bound themselves to each other; through Jesus Christ our Lord. Amen."

"Look at the ring, Elizabeth," Darcy whispered.

Hesitatingly, her eyes moved from his to her hand, whereupon they shot back to him.

The muted winter sunlight bounced off the rose-cut diamonds set in silver against a background of cobalt blue guilloché enamel. On the surface was a crown shaped from diamonds and filigree like that worn by Catherine the Great, Russia's ruler during the last century. Madame's ring.

"How? When?" she stammered.

Kissing the tear from her cheek, he inherently knew she would easily figure it out on her own.

To his surprise, she handed her flowers to her eldest sister standing next to her. Pulling something from the bouquet, she clasped Darcy's left hand in hers.

*What was she up to?*

Feeling a rough scratching against his finger, Darcy looked down. His heart almost exploded.

His Elizabeth must have had Jonah teach her about knots because around his second finger was an almost perfectly tied bowline.

He grinned. So *that* was the lesson she had missed the morning they were swept to sea.

*What a woman!*

With a final prayer, Mr. and Mrs. Fitzwilliam Darcy signed the registry and walked out of the church for the first time as man and wife.

Their first impressions of each other had long been replaced by admiration and tenderness. The trials and tribulations they had faced together had molded their characters until they were made for each other. They were forged together until nothing would ever separate them. Their knowledge of what was truly important aided them to sift through the chaff for what was most valuable. All of the rest was cast away.

# EPILOGUE

28 March 1812—Saturday
Without fail, Mr. Darcy searched through the stack of mail at his desk looking for a letter from Jonah or the Vartans. Without fail, he was a disappointed husband who had to inform his equally disappointed wife that there was nothing on that day.

Darcy was on his way back to his study when pounding on the front door startled him. This could not be good news. His butler took up a pistol in his gloved hand, then hid it behind his back before opening the door.

"Where be Fitzwilliam Darcy? Take me ta him now!"

The voice sent chills down Darcy's spine.

Of all of the people they had encountered on their journey, Boone was one of the last he ever expected to see again in his lifetime. Rather, Darcy assumed he would hide from society on both sides of the Atlantic since he was no longer a gentleman. He was a pirate.

When Darcy stepped into view, Boone ignored the butler and charged inside.

"Where is he? Where's the boy? I know ye got him, so hand him over."

"Come with me, Quartermaster Boone." Darcy turned his back to the man and entered his study. He signaled the door to be closed, then asked the sailor to be seated.

When the pirate began to speak, Darcy held up his hand.

"Pardon me, Boone, but if we wait just a few more...ah, yes, I hear her approaching now."

When the door opened, Elizabeth strolled in like she welcomed pirates during visiting hours on a regular basis.

"Good morning, Mr. Boone. Are you here for Jonah?" Elizabeth's polite boldness seemed to set the man at ease.

"I am."

"You cannot know how pleased we are to learn Jonah's respect and affection for you was deserved, Mr. Boone." She stood next to where Darcy sat behind his desk. "He spoke kindly of you."

"He is here then? I had hoped you would treat him well. Especially you, Miss B...?" The pirate slang was gone.

"Darcy. I am Mrs. Darcy, Fitzwilliam's wife."

The pirate chuckled. "I suspected that I was not the only one pretending to be someone else."

Revealing the events that transpired after they were washed overboard to the satisfaction of the quartermaster, Darcy asked what they most wanted to know.

The quartermaster had his own agenda. "Before I answer, I need to ask, will these Vartans treat the lad well?"

Darcy quickly replied, "They are solid gold. From the instant Madame Vartan set her eyes on Jonah, she treated him as if he was their long-lost son. He will be taught to be a good man. He will be loved without question."

"And he will be fed until he cannot eat a morsel more," Elizabeth added.

Boone chuckled. "That is good to hear. I can be at peace about him." He cleared his throat. "As to what happened after you went overboard, we were welcomed to New Providence Island by two ships which had partnered together like Gentleman Steve Bonnet and Bluebeard in an attempt to steal our booty. Captain Bartholomew was injured in the fray."

Elizabeth gasped.

"Oh, do not fret, Mrs. Darcy. It was a slight wound to his shoulder. Unfortunately, it was his sword arm, which would have weakened him in battle. The captain was taken in by a wealthy widow searching for a man to keep her company. Lucien decided his future was more secure in her arms than aboard ship. I've captained the *Peregrine* since."

He cleared his throat. "We saved our cargo from the...pirates...and made it to Charleston only to discover that our client, Mr. Silas Bingley had died before we left the London docks with you. His daughter, who hated slavery, impetuously ran off with an abolitionist from the north. Had you not gone overboard, you would have had a miserable welcome at your destination."

"I see." Darcy processed the information.

"Well," the man wiped his hands on his thighs and stood. "Now that I know Jonah's future is settled with the Vartans, I'd best get back to the ship. Perhaps someday I will sail into Nova Scotia and look him up. In the meantime, the ladies of Charleston are screaming for goods. I thank you for watching out for the boy. He was a good lad who deserved better than what he had."

Without a word of farewell, Boone departed for the docks.

Sliding his chair back, Elizabeth plopped herself onto Darcy's lap.

"There is a certain amount of valor to a man who cares that much for a child, is there not?"

"Elizabeth." Darcy was stern. "You have not romanticized our pirate adventure, have you?"

"Oh, I do not know." She flirted. "If you are wondering if I found Captain Lucien Bartholomew to be the man of my dreams with his white hair and striking blue eyes then you would be..." She kissed him on the cheek.

He waited, his impatience growing with each second. "Elizabeth?" he growled.

"Wrong, my husband. You would be absolutely, positively wrong. I could never admire another man more than the one I wed. I mean, could you begin to imagine the captain milking a cow or chopping firewood? No, dear man, I love only you. I always will."

LESS THAN A WEEK LATER, the first letter from Nova Scotia arrived. It was a sparsely written note saying they had made it safely to shore. At the bottom, Jonah drew a picture of stick figures they recognized as the Vartans and a boy, all with huge smiles on their faces. Madame had a pile of onions at her feet. Monsieur held a pitchfork. Jonah was the only one standing on a boat.

Over the years, they traded correspondence. Jonah's handwriting and artwork improved to the point that the Darcys learned more from the drawings than the words that they were all doing well.

Fifteen and a half years later, Madame Vartan and Jonah showed up unexpectedly at Pemberley. Accompanying them was a lovely young lady, Mrs. Sarah Hackett, and an infant baby girl they had named Rebekah Elizabeth.

Elizabeth took the time to study each of their visitors carefully. Madame was frail in form, though her personality was as powerful as it had been when they first met. Jonah had the look about him of the boy he had been, hair that refused to behave, a slender face, and large hands and feet. Yet, the deep timbre of his voice, his height, and the width of his shoulders announced without words that those childish years were long behind him. His wife was petite with vibrant red hair and the same green eyes as her husband. The baby was adorable.

~

Darcy knew that the joy on his wife's face mirrored his own. The grip of Jonah's hand was that of a man. Bowing to Jonah's wife, it was on Madame Vartan where Darcy's eyes landed and remained.

She walked into his outstretched arms without a word, squeezing his waist with the same vigor as she had done Elizabeth all of those years ago.

"I have missed you, Madame," he whispered for her ears. "I am pleased you are here. Very pleased."

She stepped back to pat him on the cheek. "You have a beautiful home, Monsieur Darcy. What is more beautiful is seeing you two smiling happily. Now, we have traveled a long way. We are tired. Jonah is hungry, as he always is."

They all laughed.

"Welcome to Pemberley!" Darcy's staff provided immediate attention to these valued visitors.

Darcy whispered to his wife once the visitors were settled into their rooms, "Do you recall how often Jonah teased us about kissing? He must have figured out that it is truly a marvelous way to pass the time when in company with the one you love."

"Fitzwilliam Darcy!" Elizabeth teased. "We hear the same from our sons, do we not? *There they go, kissing again.* I cannot imagine a day when our boys will feel any differently, but like Jonah, they will, I have no doubt."

Darcy nodded before pulling his wife into his arms. "Oh yes, one day they will meet the lady of their dreams. All of their disgust with the female sex will vanish like the wind." Kissing her soundly, the giggling of their youngest making smooching noises failed to interrupt Darcy with his most important task of the moment.

LATER, the Darcy's introduced their guests to their five sons, none of whom were named Jonah, Hercules, or Richard the Lionheart.

Elizabeth made certain they were all well turned out and that the three youngest had clean faces. Somehow, they routinely managed to get into mischief between the nursery and the drawing room.

The eldest two, Richard and Charles, politely mimicked their father by remaining silent.

"Are you pirates?" asked their middle son, Malcolm. Their youngest two, Simon and Caleb, who were precocious like their mother, both kept repeating their limited pirate jargon, "argh!"

Madame smiled at them all. "I am afraid that we did not meet your parents until after their escape from the dastardly pirates. Argh!!!"

After the laughter settled, the boys were sent outside to allow privacy.

"My Alex, he has been gone these past two years." Madame hastily brushed a tear from her cheek. "He worked hard, as did our Jonah. The land was good to us. I would think, even after seeing your Pemberley, that you would consider us to be prosperous."

"We are delighted to hear this," Darcy admitted. "Neither of us assumed anything less would happen to you, Madame. Your diligence could only be rewarded with good."

Jonah said, "Mr. D, soon after we arrived in Nova Scotia and the war of 1812 ended, massive numbers of Americans immigrated to Canada. While Father and I worked the farm, Mother cooked and fed these new ones. As we had helped many of them to get settled, they joined us in the fields alongside us until they could become established. This not only increased our income, it also allowed us to do greater good to others." He clasped Madame's hand. "My mother, she is not one to sit in her chair and allow others to aid her, despite the fact that she is not getting younger."

"I am as strong as I was when I met you, young man," Madame stubbornly insisted.

When Jonah smiled at her, then hesitated, Darcy asked, "What are you wanting to do?"

Elizabeth added, "How can we be of help?"

Jonah rubbed his chin in the same manner Darcy did when he was giving serious thought to a matter. "I have discovered about myself that my interest in growing things is greater than my love of the sea. Living on the Eastern Seaboard, I had the benefit of both. With Sarah's family returning to England last year, the three of us realized we had nothing other than the land and good memories tying us to Canada." He swallowed. "We have decided to move to England. We seek your guidance in where to settle."

Elizabeth could not contain her joy. "This is the best news. Where do Mrs. Hackett's family live?"

"In London." Jonah wiped his hands on his thighs. "We are not made for the city, Mrs. D. We need country life that is not too far from the sea. We wonder what you know of Kent?"

"As it happens, my aunt and cousin lived on an estate in Kent. Rosings Park was left to me for my second son when they died. My cousin and his wife are currently in residence. However, unlike you, they prefer the benefits of city life. It would be a relief to me should you choose to reside at Rosings until a permanent property can be found."

Jonah hesitated. "Is this estate similar in size to Pemberley? If so, I remind you that we are simple folk in comparison. I would not want to take on more than I am capable of doing."

"Not at all, Jonah. Even with Richard there, the estate is

managed by a capable steward under my authority. Please
consider yourself as guests for as long as you need. In fact, in less
than three weeks our whole family will be traveling to Rosings for
our annual visit. I ask that you rest here until then and join us in
our journey."

The young man looked at his wife and Madame before he
accepted.

THE GROUNDS of Rosings Park displayed the autumn colors at their
finest. The older Darcy boys were riding with their father and
Jonah on a narrow path leading southeast to the sea. The ladies
and younger children followed in open carriages. Ahead of them
had gone a plethora of servants to set up a picnic in a lovely glen
secluded behind a stand of trees bent from the wind.

Elizabeth had taken Sarah under her wing and the baby into
her arms. *Grand'Mere* Vartan made a game of having all of the boys
fetching the prettiest rocks for her inspection before sending the
youngest ones off for another specimen. She continued in this
until the lads fell at her feet, whereupon she fed them sweets she
had hidden in her reticule.

Once they were all sated and resting in the shade of the trees,
Darcy and Jonah walked to the overlook.

The sea looked like a solid sheet of glass, with barely a ripple.
A slight breeze rose from the water, bringing the smell of salt and
seaweed to where they stood.

"Do you miss it, Jonah?"

"At times." He picked up a pebble and tossed it to the water
below. "Sometimes, Mr. D., I remember the freedom and the
excitement of discovering new places and people. My heart yearns
to return—until I look at my wife, my daughter, and my parents."

"I have noticed you call her mother."

"Yes, she and Father were everything and more that I could have wanted in good parents. In fact, I had no clue until we were all together that I wanted a family more than anything. Now that I have Sarah and Rebekah, there is a contentment inside me I cannot explain. Do you understand?"

Darcy's chest filled with emotions that threatened to undo him. "I do understand. You see, had Elizabeth and I not been kidnapped, we might not have seen each other clearly enough to marry. We would not have had the happiness we now enjoy. She tells me quite regularly how grateful she is for our marriage, and I am glad. In addition to having our own family, we have been able to see all of her sisters married. We continue to care for both of her parents. Her father, who had been ill, was able to recover once the pressures of estate management were shared. My sister is also well-settled. All of this makes Elizabeth exceedingly happy. Therefore, I am happy too."

"Then you do not resent me for my share in what happened to you?" Jonah was crumpling the rim of the hat he held in his hands, threatening to damage it beyond repair.

"Not at all." Darcy rested a hand on Jonah's shoulder. "Jonah, I have always hoped that Elizabeth and I would have made peace and fallen in love with each other without being taken aboard the *Peregrine*. Nevertheless, we were two stubborn individuals who had not treated each other well. Both of us were filled with pride and were prejudiced against the other—wrongly so, I am afraid. The journey that began that night defined our characters until all of the façade was stripped away. We could see each other clearly. Fortunately, we loved what we discovered. With Elizabeth, I found comfort, security, and love. This is my treasure."

Jonah inhaled slowly. Closing his eyes, he nodded. With one final glance at the sea, Jonah looked directly at Darcy. "I have sailed a million miles. I, too, have found love. It all began with you and Mrs. D. I thank you."

ELIZABETH WOKE TO UTTER DARKNESS. The sights and sounds told her more than words that she was not at Pemberley. Listening for the deep breathing of her husband, she reached her hand to the other side of the bed—he was not there.

"Fitzwilliam," she whispered, hoping not to wake anyone else.

"I am here, my love." Flicking back the corner of one of the curtains to allow the moonlight inside, Darcy held out his hand to her.

Without hesitation, she joined him at the window.

"What has happened, Fitzwilliam?" Quickly, she ran her hand over him, looking for possible injury. "Is something wrong?"

"I am well." Taking one of her hands in his, he kissed the tips of each finger. "Elizabeth, something Jonah said today has weighed upon my mind. I do not believe that I will be able to put it to rest until I ask you, do you believe we would have fallen in love and married had we not been kidnapped?"

She leaned back to look at his face, hoping to see a fraction of humor. He was entirely serious. As with all married couples, they had experienced both ups and downs in their marriage. Each trial served to bind them closer together. Thus, it was rare for her husband to seek reassurance.

"My dear man, had we remained in Hertfordshire we would have been constantly thrown together by Bingley courting Jane. Eventually, even two hard-headed individuals such as we are could not have helped but reveal our true selves to each other. Thus, yes, I am convinced we would have married...eventually. Do you not feel the same?"

"I do." He paused. "I told Jonah that in you I found comfort, security, and love. I spoke the truth. But, Elizabeth, there is more that I cannot seem to accurately describe. I feel...so much more."

She embraced him tightly. "Fitzwilliam, I love you with my

whole body and soul. I always will. What I discovered on that journey was that it did not matter whether we were on a ship in the middle of the Channel, on foreign soil, in a rundown inn, or at Pemberley. You are my heart, my security, my future, and my home."

His lips brushed her hair. "Home," he repeated to himself. "Yes, I am home."

The End (*La Fin*)

# ABOUT THE AUTHOR

Joy Dawn King fell in love with Jane Austen's writings in 2012 and discovered the world of fan fiction shortly after. Intrigued with the many possibilities, she began developing her own story for Fitzwilliam Darcy and Elizabeth Bennet.

In 2017, she experimented with shorter Pride & Prejudice variations using the pen name, Christie Capps.

The author is currently working on another tale of adventure and romance for Mr. Darcy and his Elizabeth.

## ALREADY AVAILABLE

FROM CHRISTIE CAPPS:

*Mr. Darcy's Bad Day*
*For Pemberley*
*The Perfect Gift*
*Forever Love*
*Boxed Set: Something Old, New, Later, True*
*Elizabeth*
*Lost & Found*
*His Frozen Heart*
*Henry*
*Boxed Set: Something Regency, Romantic, Rollicking, & Reflective*
*A Reason to Hope*
*One Bride & Two Grooms*
*Mischief & Mayhem*

# ALREADY AVAILABLE

FROM J DAWN KING:

*A Father's Sins*
*One Love, Two Hearts, Three Stories*
*Compromised!*
*The Abominable Mr. Darcy*
*Yes, Mr. Darcy*
*Love Letters from Mr. Darcy*
*Friends and Enemies*
*Mr. Darcy's Mail-Order Bride*
*The Letter of the Law*
*A Baby for Mr. Darcy*
*The Long Journey Home*

# MY SINCEREST THANKS!

Thank you very much for investing your time and money with this story. A gift for any author is to receive an honest review from readers. I hope you will use this opportunity to let others know your opinion of this tale. Happy reading!

Printed in Great Britain
by Amazon